# THE SOLDIER'S SCOUNDREL

# THE SOLDIER'S SCOUNDREL

## CAT SEBASTIAN

AVONIMPULSE

*An Imprint of HarperCollinsPublishers*

Excerpt from *This Earl is on Fire* copyright © 2016 by Vivienne Lorret.
Excerpt from *Torch* copyright © 2016 by Karen Erickson.
Excerpt from *Hero of Mine* copyright © 2016 by Codi Gary.

EPub Edition SEPTEMBER 2016 ISBN: 9780062642486

Print Edition ISBN: 9780062642493

Avon, Avon Impulse, and the Avon Impulse logo are trademarks of HarperCollins Publishers.

10 9 8 7 6 5 4

## ACKNOWLEDGMENTS

Many, many thank yous to the AFL writers for being the most tireless of cheerleaders and without whom I'd never have had the confidence to write anything. A special thank you to Margrethe Martin, for valuable critiques and also dog pictures.

# CHAPTER ONE

Jack absently skimmed his finger along the surface of his desk, tracing a swirl through the sand he had used to blot his notes. Another case was solved and done with, another gentleman too drunk on his own power and consequence to remember to pay servants and tradesmen, too dissipated to bother being faithful to his wife. Nearly every client's problems were variations on that theme. Jack might have been bored if he weren't so angry.

A knock sounded at the door, a welcome distraction. His sister always knocked, as if she didn't want to interrupt whatever depravities Jack was conducting on the other side of the door. She did it out of an excess of consideration, but Jack still felt as if she were waiting for him to do something unspeakable at any moment.

She was right, of course, but still it grated.

"Come in, Sarah."

"There's a gentleman here to see you," she said, packing a world of both disapproval and deference into those few words.

Really, it was a pity she hadn't been born a man, because

the world had lost a first-rate butler there. The butlers Jack had served under would have been put fairly to shame.

"Tell him to bugger off." Sarah knew perfectly well he didn't take gentlemen as clients. He tried to keep any trace of impatience out of his voice, but didn't think he quite managed it.

"I have customers downstairs and I don't want a scene." She had pins jammed into the sleeve of her gown, a sign that she had been interrupted in the middle of a fitting. No wonder her lips were pursed.

"And I don't want any gentlemen." Too late, he realized he had set her up for a smart-mouthed response. Now she was going to press her advantage, because that's what older sisters did. But Sarah must have been developing some restraint, or maybe she was only in a hurry, because all she did was raise a single eyebrow as if to say, *Like hell you don't.*

"I'm not your gatekeeper," she said a moment later, her tone deceptively mild. But on her last word Jack could hear a trace of that old accent they had both worked so hard to shed. Sarah had to be driven to distraction if she was letting her accent slip.

"Send him up, then," he conceded. This arrangement of theirs depended on a certain amount of compromise on both sides.

She vanished, her shoes scarcely making any sound on the stairs. A moment later he heard the heavier tread of a man not at all concerned about disturbing the clients below.

This man didn't bother knocking. He simply sailed through the door Sarah had left ajar as if he had every right in the world to enter whatever place he pleased, at whatever time he wanted.

To hell with that. Jack took his time stacking his cards, pausing a moment to examine one with feigned and hopefully infuriating interest. The gentleman coughed impatiently; Jack mentally awarded himself the first point.

"Yes?" Jack looked up for the first time, as if only now noticing the stranger's presence. He could see why Sarah had pegged him straightaway as a gentleman. Everything about him, from his mahogany walking stick to his snowy white linen, proclaimed his status.

"You're Jack Turner?"

There was something about his voice—the absurd level of polish, perhaps—that made Jack look more carefully at his visitor's face.

Could it—? It couldn't be.

But it was.

"Captain Rivington," Jack said with all the nonchalance he could muster. "What brings you here?"

Jack saw Rivington's eyes go wide for one astonished instant before he gathered his wits. That was faster than most people, and Jack had to give him credit.

"Have we met?" the other man asked, his voice indicating exactly how unlikely it was that he would ever have met the likes of Jack Turner.

"Not exactly," Jack said, holding back the details as a matter of principle.

The truth was that a man would make a poor go of it in this line of work if he couldn't remember a face like Rivington's. Though the last time Jack had encountered this pretty specimen of the English upper classes, the man had been a few years younger and didn't have that limp.

Nor that murderous look in his eye, for that matter.

What he'd had was his cock in the mouth of some other lazy young fool at his father's house party. That had made Rivington of particular interest to Jack. There were few enough men who shared Jack's preferences—let alone sons of earls—that he certainly wasn't likely to forget a single one. Jack had added that fact to the stockpile of secrets he kept, never knowing when he might need to avail himself of some especially unsavory truth.

Jack kept his gaze fixed expectantly on the other man's face. The fellow was handsome, Jack would hand him that. Fair hair, bright blue eyes, very tall, very thin. Not Jack's type, but nothing to sneeze at either. A pity about that limp.

"May I ask what type of business you run in this establishment?" The brusqueness of Rivington's tone suggested that he expected an answer.

And just for that, Jack decided he wasn't going to give him one. "I'm not taking gentlemen as clients at the moment." It was always an unexpected pleasure when the truth aligned with what he wanted to say.

"What the devil does that mean?" Rivington's hands were clenched into fists.

"My clients are ladies and other sorts of people who need help solving problems. Wealthy gentlemen seldom need the kinds of services I offer." That, and Jack would sooner have gouged out his eyeballs than work for an aristocratic man ever again.

Not to be trusted, that lot.

"Well, I certainly have a problem and you would seem to be the man to fix it," Rivington all but spat. "My sister paid two hundred pounds to someone of your name at this address."

Lady Montbray. Of course. The usual arrangement was for ladies to pay through Sarah's dress shop, so the expense would pass unnoticed by suspicious husbands or fathers. But Lady Montbray had quite a bit of her own money and had been moved to displays of extreme gratitude by the services Jack had rendered. She'd paid Jack directly, not to mention generously.

Not that Jack was going to tell this amusingly irate toff any of that. "Did she now?" he murmured. God, he wished he had someone here to admire how well he was getting this fellow's dander up. The poor sod's pretty face had practically turned red.

"You very well know that she did," Rivington said in tones that were clipped with barely restrained fury. "I'd like to know precisely what services you render, for such a fee."

Jack bet he would. Really, he ought to leave the matter there and refuse to say anything else. He half wanted to see what this fine gentleman would do if he got any angrier. But he also didn't want Rivington talking to magistrates or Bow Street Runners about him. The success of this operation depended on Jack's relative invisibility. He would have no clients at all if his business were exposed in the newspapers.

"As I said, I help people with problems. If a lady is wondering whether her servants are robbing her or whether her husband is playing her false, I find out. And I fix it." There were other situations he helped with, but he certainly wasn't discussing those predicaments today.

Not ever. Not with this man.

"You're saying that Charlotte—Lady Montbray—called upon you to solve some sort of domestic dispute?" Rivington shook his head, plainly incredulous. "I don't believe it. It's a ruse. Two hundred pounds! My God." His face was dark with a degree of anger that Jack guessed did not come readily to him. "I think you're a crook, Turner."

Jack gave the man his due for knowing a crook when he saw one, even though he had been more or less on the right side of the law as of late. "If any of my clients think I've defrauded them or failed to uphold our bargain, they can bring an action against me. But your opinion doesn't enter into it."

That was the whole point. This prig's opinion *didn't* matter. Two years earlier, Jack had set up this business to make himself independent of men like Rivington, and to do something to get other people out from under the thumbs of wealthy, highborn men. And there Rivington stood, carrying a beaver hat that a younger Jack would have pinched just on the principle of the thing. With a curl to his lip, Rivington surveyed Jack's shabby little study like he owned the place. Like he owned Jack.

But then the man helplessly scrubbed a hand through his pale hair. At the same time he shifted his weight onto his walking stick.

Jack stilled. It would never do to feel anything like compassion for this man, but then Jack was a practiced hand at overcoming any stray decent impulses. More worrisome were the decidedly indecent impulses he was feeling towards Captain Rivington. Even after four years, Jack had never quite been able to rid himself of the image of the young gentleman in the throes of passion, all that restraint and hauteur gone up in smoke.

Mercifully, there was a brisk rap on the door. "Come in, Sarah," Jack called.

"And now there's a lady here to see you. I'm sending her up. I have two ladies downstairs for fittings and heaven only knows where Betsy has gotten to," she said, already heading back down to her shop.

"If you'll excuse me, Captain Rivington, I need to meet with a client. I'm sure you'll understand the need for privacy." He could hear the lady's steps coming up the stairs.

Rivington made for the door before hesitating, then turning back to Jack. "No, I think I'll stay," he said, his voice thoughtful, his feet planted firmly on the floor.

"Not possible." There was no time for this nonsense. But Rivington didn't budge. "Good day, sir."

Rivington, blast him, raised a single eyebrow. Worse, his mouth quirked up in the beginnings of a smile. Oh, he knew perfectly well that he had the whip hand in this situation, did he? There was nothing Jack could do to get rid of him without risking a scene that would frighten off Sarah's customers or his own client. He certainly didn't want to turn their landlord's eye more closely to what was occurring on these premises.

Jack sighed, resigned. "Then stay, on the condition that you swear not to breathe a word of anything you see or hear in this room." Besides, if Rivington ever tried to breach a client's confidence it wouldn't take much for Jack to ruin him.

A comforting thought, as always.

Rivington regarded him for a moment. "I swear it."

The earnestness in his face was almost laughable. Ever so honorable, these gentlemen. Always so eager to uphold their oaths, to value their word. It was one of the few things they actually managed to get right, and maybe they ought to be encouraged, but it wouldn't be by Jack.

"Then sit over there." He gestured to an empty chair in a shadowy corner of the room. "And don't speak."

As Rivington sat, a spasm of pain crossed his face. It was brief, just as soon replaced with more bland aristocratic chilliness.

"Are you all right?" Jack asked, before he could remember that his official stance was not to give a damn about Rivington. But how the hell badly was the man's leg injured? Small wonder he had turned up ready for bloodshed after climbing that steep flight of stairs.

Jack wasn't ready for the smile Rivington shot him. *Fuck.* A startled flash of perfect teeth, accompanied by a choked laugh. Was that all it took to dismantle Jack's composure these days?

"Christ," Rivington said, "I must be in bad shape if I have career criminals asking after my welfare."

"Don't get too excited." Jack tried to sound bored. "It's just that it would be a bloody inconvenience for the Earl of Rutland's son to die in my office."

Those blue eyes were now plainly shining with amusement. "I'll endeavor to keep body and soul together until I reach the street."

Jack bent in a slight, ironic bow. God's balls, was Rivington flirting with him? Was he flirting with Rivington? Before Jack could decide, his client appeared in the doorway.

She was dark, pretty enough, and expensively dressed. Neither plump nor thin, neither tall nor short. There were probably five hundred women like her within two miles of where they stood. About five-and-twenty years old, maybe a bit less. She had circles under her eyes that suggested weeks of insufficient sleep.

She handed Jack a card—ladies always did, as if they had come to take tea. He nearly felt bad for them, so at sea were they in these circumstances. The women of a lower station got right to business, but ladies were at a loss. He gave the card a cursory glance.

"Mrs. Wraxhall, please take a seat," he said with exaggerated courtliness, entirely for the purpose of letting Rivington know that he hadn't merited Jack's best manners. He drew his own chair closer to hers to preserve the illusion of this being a social visit. "I have an associate with me today," he said, gesturing dismissively to Rivington, "but you can pretend he isn't here." Out of the corner of his eye he watched for Rivington's reaction—a fraction of a smile. Not that Jack cared in the slightest. "How may I help you?"

"I . . . well." Her gaze flickered between Jack and her own lap, where she fiddled with the edge of a glove. "Mary said you see all manner of things and nothing I could possibly say would surprise you."

"She was right." He'd ask who this Mary was in due course. "It's best if you just come out with it."

"I lost some letters." She hesitated before continuing, her gaze darting around the room. "They were stolen, rather." Another pause, this one longer. "And in their place I found a note threatening to expose the letters to my husband unless I followed instructions."

Ah, blackmail. That was Jack's favorite. It warmed the very cockles of his heart.

To be fair, he liked any reminder that he was entirely middling when it came to sin and nastiness. He was a veritable baby in a cradle compared to blackmailers. The best part was that very often all it took was a bit of sniffing around and you could turn the situation on its head, blackmailing the would-be blackmailer into silence. And you needn't feel the slightest bit ashamed of it either.

Jack felt like a regular Robin Hood when he could manage that kind of trick.

"Mrs. Wraxhall," he said. "You've come to the right man. Now tell me everything."

Oliver hadn't known what to expect when he arrived at this address, but it certainly wasn't an utterly ordinary man posing questions in the manner of a family solicitor or a country doctor, as if blackmail were no more distressing than a case of chilblains.

He had feared that the mysterious Mr. Turner would turn out to be a money lender of some sort. That would almost have made sense—one did hear stories of ladies with gaming debts, although he would have thought Charlotte had too much money for her ship to run aground in precisely that way.

If Charlotte was in some kind of distress, why had she not turned to their father or elder brother? Ideally she would have gone to her husband, but Montbray had been overseas in recent years. As had Oliver himself, for that matter, which he had to assume was why his sister had not come to him for aid. For Charlotte to find herself in a predicament that drove her to give two hundred pounds to a man who conducted business out of a room above a dressmaker's shop, and then never breathe a word of it to anyone? That was beyond astonishing.

This Turner fellow looked vaguely familiar, but Oliver couldn't quite put his finger on why. Had he been a soldier? He didn't look like it. Could they have gone to school together? Certainly not. Oliver couldn't have said why, but he would have bet good money that Turner had not been to Eton. But why was he so sure of that, now? There was nothing about Turner's demeanor that seemed common, precisely. His accent was unremarkable, which likely meant that it was close to Oliver's own. But why on earth would a man with a good accent have an office with mismatched furniture and threadbare carpets? Why would he have any office at all, for that matter? It didn't add up.

He was absolutely ordinary looking. There was nothing remarkable whatsoever in his appearance. His hair was dark, his eyes could have been any color at all in this badly lit room. Not handsome in any traditional sense of the word—his nose was rather too much of a good thing, to be honest. He was broad in the shoulders and chest. His clothes, Oliver noticed, were scrupulously clean, but there was something about the way Turner wore them that suggested insolence. His cravat was tied in a haphazard knot. His coat was of a cut that could easily be shrugged off; it was unbuttoned, giving Oliver an impression of muscles working beneath the linen shirt.

At the thought of what else might lie beneath those not-quite-gentlemanly clothes, Oliver felt a familiar ripple of awareness course through his body. He crushed it, as usual. This was hardly the place for that, for God's sake.

There *was* no place for that. Not anymore. He was finally

home, and he was so damned grateful to be in a place with rules and laws that he was going to follow them, come hell or high water. He had come here to get to the bottom of whatever hold, if any, this fellow had over Charlotte, not to mentally undress criminals.

He forced himself to attend to Mrs. Wraxhall—and why did that name sound so familiar? There was certainly a Wraxhall at his club. Could there be a connection? The lady was now giving Turner the story of her life, it would seem, with Turner occasionally pausing to scribble something on a sheet of paper.

Before her marriage, Mrs. Wraxhall had evidently indulged in a youthful escapade with a man from the Yorkshire village where they'd both grown up. They had, stupidly, exchanged letters. At the conclusion of the affair she had requested that her paramour return her missives, and he had complied. Of that, Oliver approved. He would like to think that if he ever had an affair with a lady—and he had to concede that the likelihood of that ever coming to pass was precisely zero, thank God—he would promptly return any letters she had been foolish enough to send him.

But why had she not burned them? Oliver found that troubling.

In any event, she had kept both sets—those she had written and those she had received—in her jewel box until, about a month ago, she noticed that they had disappeared.

"Tell me more about the blackmail letter you found. Did you bring it with you today?" Turner asked.

"No." The lady twisted her handkerchief into knots. "I threw it immediately into the fire."

Oh, she managed to burn *that*, did she? Oliver was beyond exasperated. Perhaps Turner was too, because he let out a long breath before speaking again. "Do you recall what it said? What were the demands?"

"The letter said that further instructions would be forthcoming." That handkerchief would not be long for the world if the lady kept on abusing it.

"But this was a month ago, and you have received no further word?" Turner's voice had the same too-patient tone Oliver had heard from the dozen surgeons who explained that there was nothing left to be done for his leg.

The lady nodded her assent. Oliver gave it five minutes before she worried a hole into the cambric of her handkerchief.

Another pause from Turner. "Did anyone other than you and the gentleman in question know about these letters?" Turner asked. "Your maid?"

"No. I always get my own jewels out of the case and I keep the key to myself." The lady mercifully put her handkerchief aside and began to pick apart the string of her reticule.

"And you never told anyone of the liaison at the time? Your mother or a sister, perhaps?"

"I have no sister." She hesitated before continuing. "My mother knew to expect an engagement between myself and Mr. Lewis, but did not know about the letters."

"How did you receive these letters without your parents or servants knowing about them?"

"We had a secret location. It was the place where we . . . met." Color rose into Mrs. Wraxhall's pale cheeks, and Oliver felt his own cheeks flush in sympathy and mortification. He was no stranger to illicit rendezvous and it was only by the grace of God that he had never been caught out. Now he felt even worse that this lady was desperate enough to go to a scoundrel like Turner. "We left letters and presents there as well," she said faintly.

Turner drummed his fingers on the desk. "May I ask who sent you to me?"

"It was my lady's maid, Mary Wilkins. She doesn't know the details of my problem, only that I've been distressed, and she told me that you had handled a situation for her former employer."

Turner nodded. "Tell me about your house."

"My house?" She looked curiously at Turner. "All right. It's on the south side of Grosvenor Square. We've lived there since we married, at the beginning of last year. We have a place in Kent as well, but we haven't been there since the Season started."

Grosvenor Square? That was quite an address, right around the corner from Charlotte and half the *ton*. Oliver leaned forward in his chair, ignoring the throbbing in his leg. As if it wasn't bad enough that Charlotte had some sinister goings-on with Turner, now it seemed ladies all over Mayfair turned to him for help? Oliver hardly knew what to think. For a moment, he wasn't in the heart of civilized London, but rather in a stinking battlefield in Spain, where decent people were revealed to be monsters.

And what Turner said next only made it worse.

"I'm sure Miss Wilkins explained my terms to you, but it bears repeating. I am not a Bow Street Runner, nor am I a magistrate." He spoke with the air of one who had delivered the same speech too many times to remember. "I solve my clients' problems in the way I deem best. I won't ask for your approval before acting and I won't keep you apprised of my progress. It may come to pass that I won't tell you who took your letters or why. You pay me, I make the problem disappear, and that's the end of our arrangement. If you have any misgivings, I'll throw my notes on the fire and we'll pretend this never happened."

Oliver felt the blood drain from his face. This scoundrel was taking money from ladies and acting with blatant disregard for law and order? Oliver clenched his teeth to keep from speaking. This was anarchy. He had witnessed firsthand what happened when people felt entitled to deliver their own justice, and he absolutely wouldn't stand for it happening in his own country, within a stone's throw of his house.

But Mrs. Wraxhall was evidently not a student of recent history, because after sitting silently for a moment, she spoke in a calm, clear voice. "Yes, that's fine." She smoothed her mangled handkerchief across her lap.

He wondered if the French Revolution or Bonaparte's rise to power had been planned in places like this, little rooms with worn furnishings and sparse light. A single window let in whatever daylight managed to make its way through the clouds that had blanketed London since Oliver's return earlier that spring. There were few objects beyond a shelf of books, some unlit candles, and the supplies necessary for writing.

It didn't take much more than that to sow disorder, though.

Christ, the hellish aftermath of Badajoz had been accomplished with even less. Piles of bodies, his own soldiers doing unspeakable—

But no. He had to stop that line of thought. He was not at war any longer. The war was over and he was home.

What he was witnessing was at worst petty crime, nothing involving bloodshed or mayhem. He took a deep breath, willing his heart to stop pounding in his chest.

"Have you had any house guests? Any dinner parties?" Turner's voice cut through his thoughts and Oliver dragged his attention back to the present.

Mrs. Wraxhall shook her head. "We hardly entertain."

Now, that didn't make any sense. Why live in Grosvenor Square if you weren't going to entertain? What was the point of such a lofty address, then?

Some of his consternation must have shown on his face, because when he raised his head Turner was looking in his direction. One corner of his mouth had lifted in a half smile, as if they were in on the same joke. Oliver shot back a smirk before he could remember that it was unwise to fraternize with this sort of unsavory fellow.

Turner had noticed that the lady's story didn't make sense, had he? Well, by all rights he ought to, if he was charging these ladies a princely sum to solve their problems. For two hundred pounds he ought to do all but read their minds.

Oliver held on to that thought as Turner rose to escort Mrs. Wraxhall downstairs. When he came back, he shut the door with a flick of his wrist, not even breaking stride as he strolled over to where Oliver still sat. He came to a stop altogether too close to Oliver's legs.

"I trust that you're satisfied I truly do what I said I do, and that I haven't defrauded your sister." He sounded offended, which was rich coming from a man who had all but admitted to playing fast and loose with the law. "And now you may leave."

Turner was looming over him, blast the man. If Oliver were to stand, his shirt front would nearly brush Turner's, and it wouldn't do at all to dwell on how *that* prospect appealed to him.

Turner's posturing was a primitive display of aggression and Oliver knew it. The right response was to get to his feet, shouldering the man aside if need be.

Instead, he felt transfixed by the darkness of Turner's glare. They had been almost cordial in that moment before Mrs. Wraxhall entered. Perhaps even more than cordial, although he would do best to put that notion clear out of his head. He hadn't come here to provoke the man, only to get to the bottom of why Charlotte had paid him such an obscene sum. And if he left now, he'd never find out. Nor would he be able to help poor Mrs. Wraxhall—for surely there had to be a way for that lady to get her letters back without resorting to Turner's methods. Oliver had to believe that there was a lawful solution to that lady's distress.

Besides which, he had now been sitting for half an hour and there was no saying how long it would take to get his leg into a state fit to descend the stairs. He certainly wasn't going to let Turner see him at such a disadvantage. It was one thing to have a bad leg, quite another to be embarrassed about it in front of thieves or confidence artists or whatever variety of criminal this man actually was.

"No," Oliver said, dragging the word out. "I'm not done here, Mr. Turner." He looked up to see Turner's face scowling darkly in the half light. "I've hardly even started."

# CHAPTER TWO

Jack could almost feel the heat coming off Rivington's body, almost pick up the scent of whatever eau de cologne the man undoubtedly wore. If he moved half a step closer he'd be standing between Rivington's legs. He knew that would be a bad idea, but at the moment could not seem to recall why.

"What I don't understand"—Rivington tipped his head against the back of Jack's worst chair as if he hadn't just been told to leave—"is why she didn't destroy the letters. If she knew the contents would harm her, why not throw them on the fire?"

Ah, but the ladies never did. Not in Jack's experience, at least. Mothers and governesses ought to spend more time instructing young ladies in the importance of destroying incriminating evidence and less time bothering with good posture and harp lessons and so forth.

Besides, that wasn't the right question to ask. The real wonder was that Mrs. Wraxhall hadn't kept the blackmail letter, the one clue that might lead them to her stolen letters.

Of course, people did all manner of foolish things when

they were distressed, but Jack would have thought a woman who had the presence of mind to stay so tidy on such a muddy day wouldn't do something as muddle-headed as flinging a blackmail letter onto the fire.

Jack looked down at Rivington, who still hadn't moved. The man was apparently under the impression that they were going to sit here and discuss the Wraxhall matter, and really Jack ought to waste no time in disabusing him of that notion.

But instead Jack kept looking. A man this handsome was a rare pleasure to admire up close. He was younger than Jack had first thought—somewhere between five-and-twenty and thirty. Perhaps five years younger than Jack himself.

Yet he looked tired. Worn out. For God's sake, his coat was all but falling off him, despite obviously having been well-tailored at one point. "Shouldn't you be home, resting your leg?" Such a question might just be rude enough to send Rivington packing, and besides, Jack couldn't remember the last time he had seen a gentleman in such clear need of sleep and a decent meal.

Rivington opened his mouth as if to say something cutting but then gave a short, unamused huff of laughter. "If only rest worked." He didn't seem offended by Jack's rudeness. He was, Jack realized, likely a good-natured fellow. He had arrived here in a pique of anger—and likely pain—that had since worn off. Now he had the wrung-out look of someone exhausted by an unaccustomed emotion. Jack would guess that Rivington was not a hot-tempered man. And now he was contemplating his walking stick with something that looked like resignation bordering on dread.

"They always keep the letters," Jack said quickly, before he could remind himself that he ought to be ordering this man to go home, not engaging him in conversation.

When Rivington looked up, something flashed across his face that could have passed for relief. "Sentiment, I suppose."

Jack stepped backwards and sat on the edge of his desk to preserve the advantage of height. "I tend to think people hang on to love letters in the event they might choose to blackmail the sender." But then again, he never did quite expect the best from people. Maybe the lady was simply being sentimental, but in Jack's experience of human nature, people were more likely to plot and connive than they were to indulge in sentiment. Jack's experience with humanity was admittedly a trifle skewed, however.

Rivington's eyes opened wide with disbelief. "I knew a man who couldn't bring himself to sell his father's watch, even though he had creditors banging on his door at all hours. But he kept the watch because he couldn't bear to part with it. It may be the same with your Mrs. Wraxhall."

Jack shrugged. "Could be." Never having had a parent who inspired any feelings of tenderness or loyalty, or indeed any sentiment at all beyond a resentment that lingered years after their deaths, Jack mentally substituted his sister for Rivington's example. What if Sarah had a brooch or some other trinket—would Jack hesitate to sell it in the event of a financial emergency? He doubted it. Sarah would be the first person to tell him to sell all her brooches if need be. If she had any, which she did not.

"What will you do to recover the letters?" Rivington stretched one leg before him and started rubbing the outside of his knee.

Jack knew he ought to send the man on his way, but found that he didn't want to. Not quite yet. Maybe it was the dreariness of the day. Maybe it was the fact that this man clearly needed to rest his injured leg. Maybe it was simply that it had been a long time since Jack had been able to discuss his work with anyone. Sarah thought—correctly—that Jack's work was too sordid to be discussed. Georgie never sat still long enough to have an entire conversation. And nobody else in all of London was to be trusted.

Or, hell, maybe he just wanted to spend fifteen bloody minutes enjoying the sight of this man, appreciating the way the slope of his nose achieved the perfect angle, the way his eyes shone a blue so bright they likely made the sky itself look cheap by comparison. How often did Jack get an opportunity to admire anyone half so fine?

He pulled open the top drawer of his desk. "Care for a drink, Captain Rivington?" He poured them each a glass of brandy without waiting for an answer.

"I sold my commission earlier this spring." A sharp edge crept into his tone again. "It's plain Rivington now."

Jack leaned forward to hand the man his drink, catching a scent of damp wool and pricey soap. He had been wrong about the eau de cologne. "To answer your question, I'll likely search the Wraxhalls' house."

"You didn't mention that to her."

"No, the 'not mentioning' is part of the service I render. They never want to know about the dirty work, so they never find out." He took a long sip of his brandy, regarding the gentleman over the rim of the glass. "Also, she would have insisted that the letters weren't in the house because her servants and husband are above reproach, and I really didn't feel like arguing the point."

"How will you get in?"

Jack only raised his eyebrows. He would share a drink with this man but he wasn't going to pretend to be anything other than what he truly was.

"Ah." Rivington seemed to need a moment to accept the fact that he was drinking the brandy of a housebreaker. "Do you think the letters are indeed at her house?"

"I'd give even odds that a servant or the husband has them. Even if they don't, I'll find something in the house to point me in the right direction. Moreover," he added, "I'd like to dig up some dirt on the husband to use as a bargaining chip to broker a peace with his wife in the event her letters do get exposed."

Rivington paused, glass halfway to his mouth. "Are you saying that you'd blackmail Mr. Wraxhall?" Now he was regarding his glass as if he expected to discover that it was filthy, unfit to drink.

"If he's the sort of man to mistreat his wife for having had an affair before marriage, when his own behavior hasn't been perfect? Then most definitely."

Jack watched as Rivington's mouth set into a grim line. Well, that had done the trick. Jack had wanted to get rid of the man and it turned out all he had to do was tell the truth.

Rivington hauled himself to his feet and placed his mostly full glass on the edge of the desk farthest from where Jack sat. "Good day, Mr. Turner," he said, limping to the door.

Jack heard the door close with a snick before he could think of any sufficiently cutting way to get in the last word.

Oliver did not like this one bit. It was simply wrong for shadowy figures to break into the homes of respectable people, rifle through their belongings, blackmail unsuspecting gentlemen, and perform God-only-knew what other illegal acts. Outrageous. He would not—could not—let a thing like that stand. If he had wanted chaos and disorder he would have stayed in the army, however improbable that might have been with his leg steadily worsening. He had returned to England in search of civilization, and civilization he would have, Jack Turner be damned.

He would go to his club and sit in his usual chair and think about what to do. To be fair, he had not been in London long enough to have a usual chair, but in time he would. He would make sure of it, by God.

But first he would visit his sister and get her side of this sorry story. Charlotte lived not terribly far from Turner's Sackville Street premises. It was only perhaps a ten-minute walk, but that was about nine minutes more than Oliver's leg could comfortably endure on such a damp day. London in late spring was always rainy, this year exceptionally so. Oliver had only seen the sun a handful of times in the past few weeks, which would be dismal enough even without a limb whose health apparently depended on decent weather. After being shot in the back of the knee, his leg was a veritable barometer.

Deep in thought, he nearly lost his footing on a slick cobblestone. Christ. Another injury was all he needed.

He was on the verge of collapse by the time he entered Charlotte's drawing room. She had half a dozen ladies and gentlemen gathered around her, drinking tea and eating tiny cakes, as per usual. But somebody vacated a chair in time for him to drop into it, and then all he had to do was wait for Charlotte's guests to depart before he could lay into her about this Turner business.

Small talk was not an option in this state, so he pretended to be fascinated by Charlotte's drawing room. It was all done in shades of cream and gold that matched his sister's coloring. His too, although that sounded an asinine thing for a man to think. But, at any rate, she had put this room together to flatter herself, and she had been successful—she looked every inch the fashionable hostess. When he had joined the army, Charlotte had been a child of twelve, her flaxen curls arranged in tidy plaits. It still came as a shock that she was now a grown woman with a house and family of her own.

"Do you have anything stronger than tea, Charlotte?" he asked when the last of the visitors had left.

"You look terrible," she said, not mincing words. But she rang the bell and a servant materialized with brandy.

"I paid a visit on your friend Mr. Turner."

She whipped her head around to face him, golden curls bouncing. "Oliver, I have a mind to—"

"What did you hire him to do?" he demanded.

"I had forgotten how much you like to stick your nose where it doesn't belong," she said with a little sniff. "I've done my own accounts since Montbray left and I was managing perfectly well. I only asked you to look them over because you seemed so bored."

Humiliated, Oliver fought the blush he felt rise to his cheeks.

"If you must know," she continued, her voice quiet enough

not to be heard from behind the closed door, "Mr. Turner is responsible for Montbray spending his time overseas."

It didn't take much imagination to figure out what that meant, unfortunately. Montbray and Charlotte were estranged. And his sister, the same woman who sat before him in her impeccable drawing room, had paid Jack Turner to achieve that result. "Good God."

"Language, Oliver," she chided.

But at that moment Charlotte's companion entered the room. Miss Sutherland, he recalled. She looked like a little gray mouse in the midst of the golden splendor of this drawing room. A cousin of Charlotte's husband, she was nominally present in the house as a guest, but seemed to function as housekeeper as well as child minder. She and Charlotte were thick as thieves, that much was clear.

After a few moments Oliver could tell that his presence was extraneous. He took his leave and let a footman call a hackney to carry him the short distance to his club.

At White's he flipped idly through the pages of the evening newspaper, but his mind kept returning to Turner's office. The next time a waiter refilled his glass, Oliver couldn't resist asking, "Is Wraxhall here tonight?"

"Mr. Wraxhall, sir? Yes, you'll find him sitting near the window." The waiter gestured discreetly.

Oliver craned around, wanting to get a look at the man whose fate was now in Turner's hands, but the high back of the fellow's chair was in his way. "Is he the same Wraxhall who lives in Grosvenor Square?"

"I believe so." The waiter was too well-trained to indicate whether he considered that an odd question. "He's

Lord Hampton's youngest son." Hampton was a famously poor viscount. There was scarcely any money in that family, hadn't been for generations. For Wraxhall to have a house in Mayfair and a wife as fashionably dressed as the woman who sought Turner's help today could only mean that the money came from the lady's side. In the ordinary course of things a man of Wraxhall's fortune would consider himself lucky to be a vicar in Northumberland, but here was Wraxhall, sitting in a fashionable and expensive club.

It was more than simple curiosity that made Oliver haul himself to his feet, ignoring the scream of pain from his sore knee. This dread was how it felt to see a soldier in the clear path of an enemy sniper. But in this case, Oliver felt that he could do something to save the man. What, he did not know, but he had to try. He limped across the room to Wraxhall's chair and cleared his throat. Wraxhall lowered his newspaper, revealing a pale countenance spotted with freckles.

"I say, but did we go to Eton together?" It was a trick Oliver had picked up in the army. Friendships had to be made quickly during wartime. But half the British gentry knew one another, so it was easy enough to find the requisite common ground.

"No, Harrow," Wraxhall replied, looking vaguely apologetic.

"Oh, then you'll know my cousin, Sir Lionel Derry." It was as simple as that, rifling through the names in his mind until he found a man of the right age and experience. When Wraxhall nodded, Oliver stuck out his hand. "I'm Rivington."

"Wraxhall." The other man grasped the hand Oliver offered.

"Mind if I sit?" He gestured to his leg.

"Oh, bad luck. Army?"

"Yes, a musket ball in the back of the knee. You?" Oliver suddenly realized that he didn't know whether this man had been a soldier. He was still getting used to the idea that the men he had fought alongside were to be found at tea parties and coffee houses and other places that didn't have death and destruction as their primary goal.

"No," the fellow said, a trace of embarrassment flickering across his face. If they had been on the battlefield, Oliver would have instantly pegged him as the sort of nervous fellow who needed constant reassurance. A decent enough chap, most likely, if a bit soft around the edges. He was a younger son, like Oliver himself, but unlike Oliver he had not been required to enter into a career. Instead, he had apparently married money. Oliver had heard people describe the army as the making of a man. As if it were a bad thing to go through life not knowing what a pile of bodies looked like, not knowing what it felt like to watch the life slip out of a fellow who had been sharing one's brandy a few hours earlier.

He felt a surge of protectiveness toward Wraxhall. The man was innocent in a way that Oliver never again would be, and it seemed all the more galling that this was a life that Turner could upend at any moment.

Jack had taken his notes from the interview with Mrs. Wraxhall and copied them onto the little cards he used to organize his thoughts. Obviously he didn't have nearly enough information yet, but it was never too soon to start looking for answers.

There was a knock at the door. "Come in, if that's you, Sarah."

She entered and looked disapprovingly down at his notes. He hastily swept them into a tidy stack to spare her the sight. He had never asked if her distaste for this process was due to the distaste she had for all aspects of his work, or if it was because seeing him pore over his cards reminded her too much of their mother. And it was hardly the sort of thing he could ask her.

"Betsy's made soup and I have a loaf of bread if you want to come upstairs," she offered. She issued this invitation every evening Jack was home, as if they hadn't been taking their supper together for the past couple of years. But they spent a good deal of time walking on eggshells around each other. She had worked so hard to become respectable. Jack's presence had to be an unwanted reminder of their unsavory beginnings.

"I'd love to," Jack said, as he always did. He snuffed his candle and followed Sarah upstairs to her own set of rooms.

"What did you think of this afternoon's client?" Jack asked after they had both sat down with bowls of soup and thick slices of bread. He had come to his own conclusions but wanted to hear if Sarah had reached the same ones.

"Her dress was costly," she said without hesitation. She must have known this question was coming—Jack wasn't fool enough to have a fashionable dressmaker as a sister without taking advantage of her knowledge whenever it could be useful. "And not versatile. Her pelisse and gown were trimmed with the same shade of Pomona green as her hat, gloves and boots. Each of those articles could only be worn as part of the ensemble, or not at all."

"You'd say she has a fair bit of money, then?"

"Whoever pays her dressmaker's bills certainly does. Any woman who saw the lady would know she was well off, but there was nothing too vulgar or showy about what she was wearing."

Jack nodded. Sarah's observations verified his own thoughts.

"But it wasn't flattering, no matter what she spent on it," Sarah went on, gesturing with a piece of bread. "She didn't look well. The color was all wrong and the skirt was too narrow. A girl with that complexion has no business going anywhere near Pomona green. Emerald green, perhaps, but Pomona green? Certainly not," she sniffed. "I'm surprised Madame Thomas—because I'm certain she's the modiste who was responsible for that getup—didn't steer her towards something more becoming. But some ladies will dress in whatever the fashion plates show them." She took a sip of soup before continuing. "Sometimes I think fashion magazines are run by revolutionaries just to make the aristocracy look stupid."

He suppressed a grin. From Sarah's mouth this comment was not praise. She was a staunch monarchist and a firm believer in the social hierarchy. Jack, however, had no such faith in social order; the idea of *La Belle Assemblée* being run by a cabal of anarchists gave him fond feelings for that periodical.

"Pomona green, indeed," Sarah went on, obviously impassioned about the topic. "But there's no pulling certain ladies away from fashion. Her maid ought to have made an effort, though."

"Did you see the maid?"

"No, the lady came on her own." Another moue of disapproval from Sarah.

"She said her maid is Molly Wilkins."

"No!" Sarah dropped her bread and reared back in astonishment.

"Calling herself Mary now."

"Well, that explains the Pomona green, I suppose. The lady is lucky to have clean clothes at all if Molly Wilkins is attending her. Lord. I'd think a lady with that kind of money would pay for a proper lady's maid, not a jumped-up urchin like Molly Wilkins."

"Perhaps she doesn't know any better. Or doesn't have anyone to tell her who she ought to be employing."

Sarah looked at him sharply. "Spit it out, then."

"Just wondering where she got her money from. Wasn't born to it, if she's hiring the likes of Molly Wilkins."

"I don't know," Sarah said slowly. "She could be a merchant's daughter."

"Still," Jack said. "That's not the same thing as a gentleman's daughter, is it?" It was a question that didn't need answering—they both knew the gradations of gentility, just as they both knew they would perpetually be beneath even the lowest rung.

After they finished their soup, Jack rose. "I'm going to take a walk."

"It's late." It wasn't even nine o'clock, but this too was part of their evening ritual: Sarah admonished Jack for his habit of taking a walk after supper, as if the two of them hadn't been raised on the streets of St. Giles, every night encountering dangers far worse than anything Jack could turn up in

Mayfair. But Sarah was one of the few people who had ever displayed more than a passing interest in whether he lived or died, so Jack tolerated her fussing. Rampant disapproval seemed to be the only way his siblings knew how to express their affection these days.

"I'll bring a pistol if it'll make you rest easy, Sarah," he offered.

"It won't." She stacked the dishes. "Send Betsy up if you see her, will you?"

He bent down to kiss her cheek before taking his leave.

It was dark but the streetlights were lit, and when he reached Piccadilly, it was crowded with carriages. Young ladies and lordlings headed to their evening's entertainment, he gathered. If he got a peek into one of the carriages he could have instantly told where the occupants were headed—the theater, the opera, a ball, a dinner. Before beginning in his present line of work he had served as a valet, first for a barrister, then for a gentleman who had since gone to India, and finally for Mr. Rivington's brother-in-law, Lord Montbray. He had spent more evenings than he wanted to remember selecting precisely the right waistcoat and ensuring that his gentleman's cravat was exactly as it needed to be. The fact that he had also spent some of that time pocketing silverware and whatever trinkets he could fence was not something he liked to dwell on overmuch.

That was how he had first seen Rivington. Lord and Lady Montbray were spending a few weeks at the lady's father's estate as part of a hunting party. Rivington had been home on leave. One evening Montbray hadn't turned up in his bedchamber after dinner, so Jack went to see whether he had fallen drunkenly into the well or whether he was imposing himself on one of the housemaids, the latter being a situation he had to actively work against in their London household. He had heard some rustling in the orangery and slipped inside, intending to defend the virtue of whichever servant his master was accosting. Instead he found Rivington getting serviced by another young gentleman. Jack had left as quietly as he came, but he hadn't forgotten.

And who could blame him for keeping that memory locked away in a dark corner of his soul? From time to time Jack would take it out and turn it over, as one might admire a bauble. Rivington had been—oh, hell, it was mortifying to even think it, but Rivington had been *beautiful*. Jack still remembered the way his head had been thrown back in pleasure, the way he had twined his long fingers in his lover's hair. He even remembered the single helpless sigh that had escaped the man's lips.

Rivington was likely in one of these carriages tonight, heading out to dine or gamble or get up to more of the same business Jack had witnessed in the orangery all those years ago. Not that it mattered. With any luck Jack had seen the last of him.

He walked clear out of the genteel part of London, listening as the sounds of carriage wheels on well-maintained cobblestones gave way to the sounds of discord and drunkenness that permeated the rookeries to the north—the same rookeries where Jack and his siblings had been born. Bloody hell, it stank. He was sure he had never noticed the smell as a child, but now the stink of piss and sick and filth and worse assaulted him as soon as he approached.

Jack stopped at one of the neighborhood's less squalid looking public houses. He scanned the room, looking for a familiar face and not finding any. There was no sign of Georgie.

He waved over the barmaid. "Gin, please." There was no sense in attempting to order anything other than gin in a place like this.

"Yes, gov'nor," she said with an awkward attempt at a curtsy.

"Has Georgie Turner been here lately?"

She eyed him suspiciously. "Who's asking?"

"I'm Jack, Georgie's brother." He produced a shilling from his pocket and slid it toward the end of the table. The girl's eyes went wide.

"Haven't seen him in weeks," she said, and Jack thought she was telling the truth. "They say he has fancier haunts these days." She snatched up the coin and darted off, and it was a different girl who brought Jack his gin a few minutes later.

When he spoke with the barmaid, he had attempted to drop the bland, public-school accent he had adopted so many years ago. But no matter what he did he could hear lingering traces of Mayfair in his tone. What had once been a sham now sometimes seemed more real than these rookery voices around him.

There was a burst of laughter and he turned his head to see the barmaid engaging one of the locals in some ribald patter. He remembered that she had called him "governor." He didn't belong here anymore. And if he didn't belong here, then where the hell did he belong? Certainly not the fashionable quarter where he and Sarah now lived and did business.

All at once it dawned on him that Mrs. Wraxhall was as much of an impostor as he was. Well, perhaps not quite so much—that would be no mean feat. But her accent was as fraudulent as his own. Jack knew, knew as an absolute certainty, that Mrs. Wraxhall had practiced speaking in front of the looking glass as surely as he and Sarah had done. Her words had been too exact, each vowel precisely calibrated to correctness.

He finished his gin—it was predictably terrible, but that was almost the point of gin—and glanced around the room, still not seeing anyone he knew. With a sigh, he pushed away from the table and returned to the noisy, malodorous street.

He took a circuitous route back home, not wanting to go back to his empty rooms. He kept his eyes on the pavement before him lest he catch a glimpse of any courting couples walking arm-in-arm, any happy families sitting down to dinner inside the ramshackle buildings lining the street. Ordinarily he could train his mind not to dwell on all the things he wanted but would never have, but tonight he didn't trust himself.

## CHAPTER THREE

It was too early for anyone to be about, aside from servants returning from the market and nursery maids wheeling babies through the park. An old man was letting a couple of spaniels off their leads to run, but Jack couldn't see any other gentry.

He spotted Molly Wilkins before she saw him. Well, well. The maid had certainly come up in the world. She was wearing a sober gray day dress and a tidy-looking bonnet that only a few years ago she would have stolen as soon as look at. A pair of kid gloves covered hands that were likely still red from all the time they had spent scrubbing floors and hauling coal scuttles. She had been a scullery maid at a house Jack had worked at several years ago, and now she had achieved the pinnacle of a servant girl's career.

"How did you sweet talk Mrs. Wraxhall into hiring you as lady's maid?" he asked before she had turned to notice him.

She visibly started. "A fine greeting, Jack. Have you forgotten all your manners now that you're a constable or whatever it is you are these days?"

Jack ignored this because Molly knew perfectly well he was no constable. "Did you have something on her? Or did you simply forge your references?"

"I have impeccable references, if you must know." Her chin was in the air and her pert little nose was turned up.

He regarded her for a moment. "You were up to no good with the dowager's son, so she got rid of you by offering you references that stated you had been her lady's maid."

She made a sound of pure frustration. "Ooh, Jack Turner, I don't know how you do that!"

"It's sorcery," he said lightly. "I've been telling you that since you were a girl." That had always kept the younger servants on their toes around him. "I hope the old lady gave you more than a reference."

She scuffed the toe of her boot along the path. "Some money may have changed hands."

"Good girl," he said with a nod of approval.

"Now tell me what you want. It was murder to get away from the house without anyone seeing me, so make it fast."

"Your mistress came to see me the other day. What do you know about this problem of hers?"

"Only that she's torn the house apart looking for something, which is never a good sign. And she hasn't slept right in weeks. Her skin is all over flaky and her hair is falling out in clumps. Makes my job right awful to do, it does. I can't make her presentable when she's such a mess."

"Anything odd in the house?"

"No, everything is what you'd expect. Butler's a git but they always are."

"How's the husband? Any of the usual trouble?" If Wraxhall were at all the type to attempt bedding his servants, pretty Molly would be the first to find out.

"God, no. He's not that sort at all. He's almost as safe as a man of your own habits." She said this with a knowing air and a sidelong glance.

Jack shot her a quelling glare.

"Anyway," she said, "I remembered how last year the dowager called you in to find those lost jewels, and I figured maybe you could do something to help this lady."

Jack had found the jewels, all right. They had, it turned out, been brought to a pawn shop by the same wayward son with whom Molly had been making mischief.

"How about Mrs. Wraxhall? Any indiscretions or secret correspondence or anything else out of the ordinary?"

"No. She's bored, but who wouldn't be, sitting in that house with nothing to do all day? She hardly ever goes out, she almost never has any visitors. She might as well be on the moon for all the life she has."

He looked carefully at her, taking in the glossiness of the hair that peeked out from beneath her bonnet, the curves beneath her discreetly tailored dress. Not only was she well dressed, but she looked well fed and clean. He had wondered whether Molly herself might be the blackmailer. She was in the best position to slip the key to the jewel box, and he knew she had no reservations about a little thievery. But would she stoop to blackmail, such an ugly and desperate act, when she had landed a job that obviously agreed with her and paid her well?

He sent Molly on her way and returned to his office. When he got back, Betsy was waiting for him at the foot of the stairs.

"A gentleman came to see you. I put him inside your office," she blurted out.

Bloody gentlemen. You'd have thought having an office above a dressmaker's shop would be enough to deter them, but they were a dense lot.

The door at the top of the stairs was ajar, and through it Jack could see the tip of a mahogany walking stick before he reached the top step. He felt his body tense, and not only from irritation.

"Mr. Rivington," he called up the steps. "To what do I owe the pleasure?"

If Jack had hoped to put Rivington at a disadvantage by surprising him like that, it didn't work. The man was sitting once again in Jack's least comfortable chair, his face betraying nothing at all beyond a faint trace of boredom.

"I've come to reimburse you for any expenses you incurred on behalf of my sister's family." Rivington's voice was crisp and cool and devoid of any interest. "After speaking with her, I realize that two hundred pounds was hardly adequate."

Oh for God's sake. What a pile of shite. If Rivington wanted to fish for information, he would have to come up with a more plausible story. Jack stayed by the doorway, intending to make fast work of this situation before going back downstairs to be very stern with Betsy on the topic of uninvited visitors.

"Two hundred pounds more than covered Montbray's passage on the ship." Jack crossed his arms in front of his chest.

"True, but whatever was left over wouldn't have been enough of an inducement to keep my brother-in-law away for two years."

What was left over, however, was more than enough to induce a man of Jack's acquaintance to cosh Montbray on the head, haul his unconscious body onto the ship, and keep his lordship there until the ship had sailed sufficiently far from his wife and child. But Jack wasn't going to mention any of that.

"Also," Rivington added, brushing imaginary lint from his sleeve, "I have reason to believe that you used your own funds to satisfy some of Montbray's less-savory creditors, without letting my sister know of their existence."

Gaming debts and whorehouses, he meant. Jack sighed with disappointment at the euphemism. "His lordship settled those bills himself. I only eased the process along."

"Which means precisely what?" One side of Rivington's mouth curled up in the beginnings of a sneer. But he didn't look away from Jack, even though from his seated position he had to crane his neck back.

"I took the liberty of selling some of Montbray's trinkets and using the proceeds to settle his accounts."

"Are you saying that you stole from my sister's household?" He sounded incredulous, as if he hadn't insisted only two days earlier that Jack was a crook. What in hell did he expect crooks to do, if not steal?

Jack knew he ought to keep his mouth shut, but watching Rivington's coolness and reserve go up in flames like this was too good a spectacle to be missed, too tantalizingly close to other forms of passion that Jack shouldn't be thinking of right now. "Well, I suppose if you want to be technical about it, then yes, I did." And from a good number of other households besides. "You could call it one of the key services

I render my clients." He waved his hand airily. It was true, though. The Montbray predicament had been the first time Jack had stolen for anyone's advantage but his own, but since then he had sort of gotten into the habit.

"Do explain." The muscles of Rivington's jaw clenched. How much longer before his cheeks reddened?

"Well, I sell some candlesticks or cuff links or what have you, and use the proceeds to pay people who are owed money—servants or tradesmen, usually. That way, those who are owed get what's theirs, and the gentleman gets to stop being a thief."

"Gets to stop being—" He stopped and fixed Jack with a hard stare. "You're having me on."

Jack opened his eyes wide and put his hand over his heart. "Me?" He let his voice drip with facetiousness. But he had told the truth. He always warned his clients that he would solve their problems the way he thought best, and if that included making them—or, more likely, their husbands—honest, however briefly, he considered it an excellent day's work. If that wasn't justice, he didn't know what was.

He decided his highborn visitor was overdue for an education. "Do you know that your brother-in-law owed money to his tailor and most of his servants?" That wasn't even mentioning the bills his mistress had run up. "But instead of giving them what they were due, he paid a gaming debt to the Marquess of Rotherham and then bought a racehorse."

Rivington was silent for a moment. "Did you break into my sister's house? To steal the items, I mean."

Jack realized then that Rivington still had no idea that Jack had been Montbray's valet at the time. Nicking a couple of snuff boxes and cravat pins had been no trouble at all. That had been before he opened this business—right before, in fact. "Oh, I have my ways," he said.

"Is that supposed to pique my curiosity?" Rivington's demeanor was once again cold and bored. Jack hated that distant refinement, that cool bloodlessness that spoke of generations of breeding and piles of money. He wanted to replace that chilliness with anything else.

"No, it's supposed to make you bugger off," Jack said, hoping to provoke him.

But Rivington didn't take the bait. Instead he sighed and rose to his feet, apparently with some effort. He reached inside his coat and pulled out a sheaf of banknotes.

Somehow, Jack hadn't realized that Rivington was so tall. He wasn't used to the sensation of having to look up to meet someone's eye. With one arm he reached out and swung the door shut, never taking his eyes off Rivington. He heard the gentleman's quick intake of breath,

"No." Jack gripped the other man's forearm to stop him from offering the money.

Rivington froze the moment Jack's hand touched his sleeve. Oh, that bored look was quite gone now. In its place was something dark and intent. Jack liked it very, very much. He took a fraction of a step closer and watched the other man's eyes go wide, his lips parted.

"Giving me money doesn't change the fact that your sister did business with me." Jack slid his fingers up Rivington's sleeve, enjoying the feel of sinewy muscle under expensive wool, enjoying even more the hungry look in the other man's eyes. "It only means that you're doing business with me as well." Rivington's cheeks went a satisfying shade of pink, and this time Jack suspected the flush was not from anger. "The question is, though, what kind of business you want to do with me." He had let his voice drop to a murmur. "There are so many possibilities." Jack slid his voice even lower, Rivington's eyes going darker by precisely the same measure, as if one man's voice and the other's eyes were connected.

Still Rivington remained motionless, rooted to the ground, his gaze fixed on Jack's face. Under ordinary circumstances, Jack would not have considered torturing a man by pretending to offer his body for sale. That sort of transaction was—not to put too fine a point on it—rather too close to what had once been the case. But he felt like he would say anything, no matter how ill-advised, to watch Rivington's cool facade crumble completely away, and stark, honest desire take its place.

Seized by the rash urge to make that happen, he reached up and traced Rivington's perfect mouth with his coarse thumb. Oh, he took his time with it, sliding his thumb slowly along that soft lower lip, letting himself imagine what the man's mouth would feel like—

Rivington made a barely audible sound, the merest hiss. Jack felt it on his hand more than he actually heard it. For a moment Jack thought he was going to get punched, or arrested, or who knew what. But then Rivington darted out his tongue and licked Jack's thumb.

Jack pulled his hand back as if he had been scalded. *Fuck.* His breaths were coming fast and heavy. When the hell had he started to pant, for God's sake?

They simply stared at one another. After a moment of

thick silence, Rivington eased his arm away from Jack's touch, as coolly as if he had accidentally bumped into a piece of furniture, and silently took his leave.

"Please tell me you're going home to change before dinner, Oliver."

Oliver suppressed a groan. He had barely managed to haul his body up the steps to Charlotte's drawing room and cast himself into this profoundly uncomfortable chair. Going back home, changing, getting into a carriage and then climbing these godforsaken stairs once again would be the end of him, he was sure of it. He was staying in this awful chair until he died or the butler announced dinner, whichever came first.

"Do I look that bad?"

Charlotte's gaze swept over him. "You absolutely must get new clothing. What you are wearing simply does not fit. It's very fashionable and Byronic to be thin, but you cannot go about in clothing that hangs off you. Besides"—she eyed him with distaste—"Are you sweaty?"

"I was fencing." *And licking the thumbs of confidence artists.*

"Are you certain that's wise? Doesn't fencing bother your leg?"

Oh, wisdom hadn't entered into this day's events. Besides, everything bothered his leg. Sitting still bothered his mind, though. So he took the pain.

Miss Sutherland intervened, looking up from her embroidery. "Mr. Rivington will avoid this house entirely if he is chastised about his clothing and his modes of exercise every time he enters it."

"Frankly, I don't think Oliver has anyone else to chastise him, so if I hold back, and consequently he's mistaken for a dockworker or stable boy, think of how upsetting that will be for him." Charlotte turned sideways on the settee to address this to her companion, as if Oliver were not present.

"Do you ladies know a Mrs. Wraxhall?" Oliver asked, taking advantage of Miss Sutherland's stunned silence.

"Mrs. Wraxhall?" Charlotte bit her lip, apparently going through a list of names in her head. "Wraxhall. Anne, can you think of anyone?" But before her companion could answer she cried, "Wait! You cannot mean Lydia Wraxhall. Good heavens, Oliver. What can you possibly want to know about *her?*" She leaned forward and lowered her voice to a conspiratorial whisper, her eyes dancing with mischief. "Are you looking for a mistress? You can't really expect Anne and me to screen your lady loves."

"No, I am not looking for a mistress, Charlotte," he ground out. Out of the corner of his eye he saw Miss Sutherland pursing her lips. He was glad at least one person in this room had a sense of delicacy. "I met Mr. Wraxhall earlier this week and realized I knew nothing of his wife. That is all."

Charlotte regarded him, her eyes wide with disbelief. "There was something dubious about her marriage, was there not, Anne? She was found with Wraxhall out on a balcony or behind a shrubbery and he had to marry her. Or maybe that was some other poor gentleman and some other enterprising heiress."

"Her father was not quite a gentleman, I believe," Miss Sutherland supplied. "He earned his money in some way or another. A good deal of money, but the family has no background at all."

"You don't recall what type of trade?" Oliver asked.

"How on earth would we know?" Charlotte was plainly bemused that her brother thought she would know the details of how some nobody made his money.

"There's a difference between being a grocer and a mill owner," he argued, which only caused Charlotte to open her eyes even wider. That difference did not matter at all to Lady Montbray, it would seem.

"If you say so, Oliver. Whatever the case, her manners are good. You can forget for minutes at a stretch that she has no breeding."

Oliver was speechless.

"She's from Yorkshire." Miss Sutherland once again came to his rescue. "I met her at Lady Davenport's ball last year. We talked for quite a while." This likely meant that neither lady had anyone to dance with. "I introduced her to a few similarly situated ladies." Other wallflowers, spinsters, and less fashionable matrons, that meant. "I had the impression that she knew hardly anyone in London."

"Since when do you care at all about your acquaintances' wives?" Charlotte asked.

He could not very well tell her the truth—that he was lusting after a criminal and also afraid that this same criminal would misguidedly plunge the Wraxhalls into lawlessness. Belatedly, he realized that it would have been cleverer to let Charlotte think he was indeed cultivating Mrs. Wraxhall as a mistress. That would have provided an excuse for his questions. His sister, after all, had no reason to suspect that Oliver didn't have and never would have any interest in a mistress.

"What do you suppose they do all day?" he mused. "She has few acquaintances and no children. He has no career in politics or the church. What do they do? They wake up, they have their toast and eggs, and then what?"

Now both Charlotte and Miss Sutherland were staring at him speechlessly.

Oliver shifted uncomfortably. "In the country I suppose there's always some boundary dispute to settle between tenants, or a horse that's foaling or something to that effect. But in London, what does such a couple do all day?"

The ladies exchanged a meaningful glance.

"Oliver," his sister said patiently. "What do *you* do all day?"

He turned that question over in his head throughout dinner and long after he had gotten into bed. What *did* he do? Why, in the day he fenced and boxed and took ill-advised walks. In the evening, he dined with Charlotte or other acquaintances and he went to his club.

Was that what his life would look like for the next forty or fifty years, until he died? Burning the daylight hours without any purpose, without any close friendships, certainly without anything closer than friendship. But what else was there? Returning to the army was quite out of the question. His leg couldn't take any more of it and neither could his mind.

He thought of Turner. Now, that was a man with a purpose. Oliver felt almost sick thinking of Mrs. Wraxhall's predicament. He knew what it meant to have a secret that could undo one's entire life. But who was Turner to decide what laws were worth following and which were best ignored? There had to be a better way to go about helping the lady.

He thought of those last few moments in Turner's study. He had a purpose there, too, but Oliver couldn't tell whether the man had been bent on seduction or rather luring Oliver to commit an act that would be fodder for blackmail all its own. But how had Turner known that Oliver would be tempted by another man? Because Oliver most certainly had been tempted. He wouldn't soon forget the feel of Turner's calloused finger on his lips. God, even the recollection was making his heart beat too fast. How would that strong, sure touch feel on other parts of his body? But then he remembered how Turner nearly flinched when Oliver had been mad enough to touch his tongue to the other man's thumb.

He sighed, his desire evaporating like the dream it likely was. Probably Turner had only touched him as part of some blackmail scheme, and then had been too repulsed to go through with the act. After all, London probably had far more blackmailers than it did men who wanted to look at him like they could see straight through his clothing, right into his most secret longings.

Christ almighty, the places Jack had to go to find Georgie these days. If it weren't for the fact that Georgie had a knack for picking up all manner of useful information, Jack wouldn't even consider going near such a place. The rookery gin palace had been bad enough, but this?

Jack stood outside White's, unable to fathom how on earth Georgie had come to spend an evening at a conservative gentlemen's club. Was this part of a joke Jack wasn't in on? Could Georgie possibly be a member? Surely not, unless . . .

And suddenly, there was Georgie, dressed in a preposterously rich dinner coat and absurd pantaloons, a waistcoat embroidered with silver thread, and with hair slicked back very à la mode. First Molly, now Georgie. It would seem all Jack's old St. Giles comrades were flush in the pocket. Jack had half a mind to nick that cravat pin just for old times' sake.

Georgie went on tiptoes and kissed Jack on the cheek. Silly old habit, one that needed to end, but affection was in short supply these days.

"How can I help you, Jack?" And that was the type of upper-class accent that Jack and Sarah never even dreamt of attempting, the kind that sounded like whiskey and smoke and expensive dissipation. Georgie had always been better at these things.

"I need to know about the Wraxhalls. Any debts, scandals, whispers of anything interesting. I'm not turning much up."

"I'll take a look and send you word—" Georgie abruptly pulled Jack into the shadows as a couple of gentlemen descended the stairs from the club. The gaslight shone full on their faces and Jack saw that one of them was Wraxhall himself. And the other was none other than Oliver Rivington. Very interesting. Rivington had failed to mention that he was friendly with Wraxhall. Jack flattened himself against the building to remain unnoticed. "Speak of the devil," Georgie whispered. Jack watched as they shook hands and exchanged a few words, Wraxhall then climbing into a waiting hackney and Rivington limping down the street. Jack didn't take his gaze off Rivington until the man had turned a corner and was out of sight.

Well, well. If Georgie couldn't turn anything up on the Wraxhalls, maybe Rivington was on the scent. Jack would just have to find out. And if that meant keeping his eye on the pretty young gentleman, then that was no hardship.

Georgie had been fiddling with a glove button but abruptly stopped when he noticed the trajectory of Jack's gaze. "Oh, no. No, no, no, no. Not one of them, dear fellow."

"Don't try to dear fellow me." Jack crossed his arms, annoyed that Georgie had noticed Jack's interest in Rivington, even more annoyed that there was anything to notice.

"Don't try to distract me." Georgie pulled out a silver snuff box that glinted even in the shadows. Jack rolled his eyes at the habit. "I'll grant that Rivington's pretty enough, but your former employer's brother-in-law? Certainly not."

"You sound just like Sarah when you talk like that."

Georgie looked up from the snuff box long enough for Jack to see one elegantly shaped eyebrow shoot upwards. "So Sarah knows about this too?"

"No. There's nothing to know, I mean," Jack grumbled, and knew he sounded like a petulant toddler.

"Take it from me, Jack, you do not want to get in bed with these fellows. Literally or figuratively."

"I'd really like to know who you and Sarah think I properly ought to sodomize," Jack said, in a vain attempt to regain the upper hand through shock. "There wasn't a chapter on that in the etiquette book Pa made us memorize."

Georgie snapped the snuff box closed and pushed off the wall they had been leaning against. "I'm more concerned about you letting yourself get bought and paid for."

Jack bristled, but knew Georgie was right. As a young

man—little more than a boy, really—Jack's father would send him into a dark alley with a man like Rivington. Jack would emerge a few shillings richer and sometimes even satisfied. He wasn't ashamed of that time, but he didn't want to repeat it. Especially not with Rivington. What if the other day in his office, he had gone to his knees before the man? Rivington wouldn't have stopped him, he was almost sure of it. But afterwards, would Rivington have tried to slip him a coin? Jack felt the anger boil up inside him even at the thought.

A cloud must have blown away from the moon, because suddenly Georgie's face was illuminated. There were new lines, traces of weariness. "What swindle are you running now?" Jack asked. "I haven't seen you in daylight for weeks."

"We're done here, Jack. Don't try your tricks on me." And with that Georgie was gone, and Jack was once more alone, in a too-fashionable part of London, with more questions than answers.

## Chapter Four

"But have you tried thin gruel?" demanded the lady seated to Oliver's right, using the tone of voice he associated with the least tolerable kind of schoolmaster. "My uncle always said it helped his gout."

Oliver wanted to know how gruel of any consistency could magically unfire the French musket that had damaged his leg, and how gout had anything to do with gunshot wounds. Oliver hadn't been prepared for this aspect of his injury—always having to talk about it, always having to act faintly apologetic when other people's proposed cures failed to work.

"No, ma'am," he said. "I'll be certain to tell the cook." The lady wore a turban that listed dangerously to one side, and it was all Oliver could do not to reach over and set it right.

Oliver resolved to escape from this dinner party as soon as he decently could. Perhaps Charlotte had been right, and this invitation had been the last in the world that he ought to accept. But the Wraxhalls would be here, and he wanted, somehow, to get them away from Jack Turner's influence. Oliver still had nightmares about what happened when men made their own justice, and he wanted to prove to Turner that even someone in as pitiable a circumstance as Mrs. Wraxhall could be helped without such a dangerous recourse. If that meant spending an evening in company just this side of shabbiness, then so be it.

Oliver nearly felt guilty at how easily he'd finagled this invitation and a good many other ones besides. He had paid a visit to that tailor Charlotte had recommended, left a couple of calling cards here and there, and made a few appearances at the theater and Almack's to remind the *ton* that he was still alive, and now he was positively inundated with invitations. Of course that success owed more to who his father was than it did to any of his own charms.

He could have vanished and been replaced with the page in Debrett's that listed his birth, and it would likely not have made much of a difference. This was all a bit lowering after having spent his entire adult life making himself useful in the service of king and country.

Still, he had put his pedigree to good use tonight, because now he knew a little bit more about the Wraxhalls. For instance, they were the sort of couple that scarcely looked at one another when in company. They were terribly cordial—devastatingly polite—when forced to speak to one another. He didn't notice any coolness or animosity, only a total bland indifference. Wraxhall drank too much, though. Oliver had gathered as much from seeing him imbibe at their club, but the port went around three times before Wraxhall declined. It was a wonder the man was still on his feet.

He wanted to tell Mrs. Wraxhall to take her tipsy husband and get on the next ship for South America or at least

Italy, far away from blackmailers, far away from snobs who looked down at her for her lack of breeding. Far away from whatever lawlessness and chaos she was inadvertently about to dip her expensively shod toe into.

Of course Mrs. Wraxhall did not recognize Oliver from that afternoon in Turner's study. He had been well concealed in the shadows and she had scarcely turned towards him anyway. And likely she wouldn't believe that Oliver could have anything to do with a reprobate like Jack Turner.

Oliver could scarcely believe it himself.

When, finally, it came time to leave, he decided to walk the short distance back to Rutland House rather than hail a hackney. He was restless, and besides, hackneys always made him feel vaguely itchy and in need of a bath.

He was going to have to buy a carriage and a couple of horses, there was no way around it. It was a frightful expense, but his leg couldn't take much more of this. Moreover, if he intended to go to dinners and balls and whatnot, he couldn't keep arriving on foot. It was settled, then: he would go to Tattersall's. He felt satisfied out of all proportion by the prospect of accomplishing something, even though the task itself would be an act of unmitigated self-indulgence.

The night was perfect for walking—still and moonless—and cool for early June. But his leg was tired before he even reached Piccadilly. He decided to cut down one of those lanes that sliced across the network of streets at an angle. Calling it a lane or even an alleyway was making too much of such a place—it was a sort of emptiness that occurred during the process of knocking a few buildings down and replacing them with something shiny and new.

The alleyway was empty, apart from some rubble and debris. The sound of his uneven steps and his walking stick clacking against cobblestones echoed dismally off the walls of the surrounding buildings. It was so quiet here, you wouldn't guess that within a mile there were half a dozen balls and God only knew how many dinners going on. And that wasn't even counting the gentlemen headed off to their clubs or in search of less refined entertainment.

It was the silence that alerted him to something being wrong, that gave him a crucial second to act. No alleyway ought to be quite so deserted. Not unless somebody was being deliberately quiet. No sooner had the thought crossed his mind than he saw shapes emerge from the shadows.

Three or four people appeared—he could hardly tell, they moved so fast to surround him. The wise thing to do was to hand over all one's money and any valuables. He knew that. Everyone knew that. But Oliver had spent too long in the army to ignore his instinct to fight. He raised his walking stick, but someone must have approached him from behind, because the next thing he knew he was falling, his vision going dark around the edges.

Oh, for the love of God. Jack had half a mind to go home and leave Rivington to his fate, to let him learn a valuable lesson about venturing into badly lit lanes. That alley practically had a sign over it announcing that thieves were waiting within and would be only too happy to knock any stray gentlemen over the head and relieve them of their valuables. But then he saw that there were four thieves setting on Rivington, and one of them had something flashing in his hand. A knife. No, that would not do at all. The penalty for being a bloody fool wasn't brutal death. And it really would be a pity for anything to happen to that handsome face.

Jack had a knife too, but this situation called for something that could be wielded with less precision. He scanned his surroundings and saw a pile of rubble that must have been left over from when they knocked down the building that used to stand here. Sticking out was a promising piece of wood. It looked like the post from a banister and felt solid in his hand.

Rivington hit the ground with a heavy thud and Jack knew he had to act quickly, while the thieves thought they were out of harm's way. Staying close to the wall, Jack edged nearer. Right when two of the attackers were bent over Rivington, he stepped out of the shadows.

Swinging the post, he hit one of the thieves in the shoulder, hard enough to get his point across but not as hard as he could. It would be lovely to get through another twenty-four hours without blood on his hands, or at least not any more than was absolutely necessary.

Suddenly, Rivington was back on his feet. He, apparently, had no reservations about committing murder tonight, because he wasted no time in coshing one of the men over the head with that bloody great cane of his.

The scene devolved into a melee at that point. Rivington, with more strength than Jack would have expected from a man who had been on the ground an instant earlier, knocked out the man with the knife and deftly pocketed the weapon for himself.

A brute of a man Jack recognized from the old days in St. Giles landed a punch on Jack's jaw and sent the banister post clattering out of reach.

Rivington cudgeled that man too.

Jack was dangerously close to being impressed with Rivington, but he supposed he'd get over it.

Maybe he got too distracted watching Rivington fight off his attackers. Or maybe the years were catching up with Jack and he wasn't as fast on his feet as he once had been. Whatever the reason, Jack wasn't prepared for the blow to his wrist. He had nearly gotten the banister post within his reach when he saw a man charging at him, wielding a broken off bottle.

Jack did not like his odds at that moment, not one bit. He chanced a look at Rivington, not sure whether he was begging for help or checking to see whether the man was all right. But Rivington didn't hesitate a moment before tossing his walking stick to Jack.

Jack caught it, as if they had been fighting together for years. As if the two of them had practiced that move until they had it down perfectly, like a pair of dancers.

He used the stick on the man with the broken bottle and then tossed it back to Rivington, who didn't waste any time before putting it to good use. The two remaining assailants looked at their fallen comrades, glanced at one another, and then ran.

"Well," Jack said after he had caught his breath, "are you going to throw the bodies into the Thames? What do you usually do after you murder people in alleyways?"

"Nonsense," Rivington countered, but he sounded shaken. "They'll be right as rain in the morning." He poked one of the men with his walking stick, eliciting a faint groan. "They will, won't they? At least I hope—"

"Where the bloody hell did you learn to fight like that?"

Rivington retrieved his hat from the ground and put it back on his head. "You know I was in the army. What do you suppose we do in the army, if not fight?"

"Christ." He pitied the French. "But your leg . . ."

He couldn't quite see Rivington's expression in the gloom, but thought the man was smiling. "I fought in Waterloo with my leg like this. I can handle a couple of thieves."

"Apparently so."

Rivington bent down to brush the dirt off his breeches. "Were you following me?"

Jack hesitated. "Only a little."

"Oh." Rivington's eyes were wide. He looked like he wanted to step forward. But then he abruptly shook his head as if dismissing the thought. "If you were hoping to catch me doing anything worthy of blackmail, you're out of luck. I'm afraid my dealings are all very boring."

"Oh, believe me, I know," Jack replied.

In truth he'd only followed Rivington a few times, partly to discover whether he knew anything of Wraxhall, but also wanting to know whether this proper gentleman frequented the establishments that quietly catered to men of their proclivities. Not out of any intent to blackmail, but rather from idle curiosity and maybe something a little . . . warmer than that.

"You go to your sister's house and your club and bloody Almack's. Sometimes the theater."

Jack had, admittedly, been disappointed. The idea of Rivington blushing as he slipped into some den of iniquity had been frankly thrilling. And Jack wasn't above seeking out whatever random sources of titillation came his way these days. "We ought to leave these fellows alone so their friends can come back and haul them away home."

But Rivington didn't budge. "You think they'll be all right?" He was standing over one of the thieves.

Jack prodded at one of the men with his boot. "This one's more drunk than anything else. He's best left to sleep it off." He moved to the other man, examining him, resisting the old urge to check for gold teeth "This bastard will have a nasty bump in the morning, but I can't see what we're to do about it." He wanted to go home, not play nurse to a pair of thieves.

"I shouldn't have been quite so forceful."

Did this man feel guilty about having defended himself from attackers? "No, you should have let them kill you." Jack tapped his chin in a parody of thoughtfulness. "That would be the gentlemanly way to comport oneself, I'm certain. They'll take back your voucher to Almack's now, no way around it."

Rivington made a dismissive sound. "Still. I don't know." But he walked away from the fallen men nonetheless.

Jack followed him out of the alley. Rivington's step was faltering, and when a gaslight illuminated his face, Jack could see traces of blood. The man had to be in agony. If climbing a flight of stairs left him ragged with pain, what must he be feeling now? And he was worried about the thieves? Jack would never understand gentlemen.

"You're a mess," Jack said. "Blood and God knows what else. My rooms are only a few blocks away. Come with me and get yourself tidied up, that way you don't set your servants to gossiping." *And rest your blasted leg*, he wanted to say, but felt that wouldn't go over well.

Rivington let out a crack of laughter. "Too right." He shook his head. "Can't scandalize the servants." He leaned against the brick wall and fell silent. Jack could see enough of the other man's face to know he wasn't smiling anymore. "Who hired you to follow me, then? I'd say it had to be my father, but now I'm doubting it—he wouldn't give a damn who knew I was in a fistfight."

Jack regarded the man carefully. It would take a hell of a lot more than blood and bruises to make Rivington anything less than handsome, and when he laughed it proved a fair sight, indeed. "I already told you I don't have gentlemen as clients, and that includes your father. Nobody hired me to follow you. I was following the Wraxhalls and saw you come out." This was partly true: he had been following the Wraxhalls, but when he saw Rivington, he sort of allowed himself to become distracted.

Rivington stared down at Jack, plainly disbelieving him. But when their eyes met, Rivington did not look away and neither did Jack. "Thank you for getting me out of that jam," he said after a moment.

"Bollocks. You had the situation well in hand." Jack reached into his pocket, pulled out a handkerchief, and set about rubbing a spot of blood off the other man's cheek. Rivington seemed to soften under Jack's touch, melting against the wall as he submitted to Jack's ministrations. Jack returned the cloth to his pocket and now touched Rivington's jaw with his bare hand. There was the faintest hint of coarseness. Rivington's valet hadn't shaved him quite close enough.

Jack nearly said so aloud, before deciding that criticizing a man's valet had no part in a seduction.

At this point he wasn't even trying to tell himself that all this touching and sighing and staring was anything other than a seduction. Even Rivington had to know. There he was, eyes closed in obvious pleasure, inches away from a man whose finger he had licked only a few days earlier. This was not a subtle situation.

But then Rivington's eyes shot open. "I'll tell you what I've learned about the Wraxhalls, if you like," he blurted out. Without waiting for an answer, he went on. "She has hardly any friends, none of them intimate. Fashionable people openly sneer at her because of her low birth, but her manners really aren't terrible at all. Her husband drinks." The words were coming out in a rush, as if he wanted to unload all this information before he could think better of it. "I don't think it's a good marriage. Not that I'm an expert on marriage, far from it. But they don't look at one another."

Jack only stared.

Rivington's cheeks went red. "You know, the way married couples look at one another, where you can tell they can't wait to be alone and laugh and gossip and do the other things that married people do."

*The other things that married people do?* If Jack hadn't seen Rivington in the orangery he might have thought him a total innocent.

Jack kept on staring. If Rivington wanted to see what a man looked like when thinking of *what married people do*, Jack would go right ahead and show him. But first there was something he had to set straight as a matter of pride. "I already know all of that." What did this man take him for? "I knew most of those things before Mrs. Wraxhall even left my office, and now I know a great deal more besides. If you're sniffing around after the Wraxhalls because you think you'll learn something useful, then you can bloody well stop." Another explanation suggested itself to Jack. "And if you're telling me this as some sort of quid pro quo for having saved you tonight, then you can piss right off."

Now Jack was angry, his fingers clenched into fists, as if he weren't accustomed to being paid in information, or used to a little bloodshed in a night's work, for that matter.

"No!" Rivington looked flummoxed, and a little offended. "I told you because I wanted to do you a kindness after rescuing me, not as a payment."

Jack decided not to argue to the point. From a man so high-minded as Rivington, any insinuation that Jack traded in secrets and sometimes blood would have been an insult, and Jack wasn't able to stomach an insult from this man.

"What exactly is it that you think I do for a living, Mr. Rivington, if not find out information and then put it to use? The last thing in the world that I need is somebody fumbling along and making people suspicious."

As he spoke, he inched closer to Rivington, who was still leaning against the wall.

"I'm unclear as to what it is you do for a living, Mr. Turner." Rivington's voice was only as loud as it needed to be for Jack to hear a few inches away, transforming the statement from an accusation to something more intimate.

It was pride and a little arrogance that made Jack say what came next. He was good at what he did and wanted to prove it to this handsome, interfering, aristocratic bastard. "Then allow me to demonstrate. Here's what I know about you, sir. You have no debts, neither to money lenders nor your friends. You have no scandals in your past. You have no mistress nor do you frequent whorehouses. Everything about you is, as you said, drearily boring." He paused, let his voice drop. "And therefore highly disappointing."

He was standing too close now, crowding the taller man's body. But Rivington didn't protest, didn't even flinch. His body almost seemed to be yielding, and if Jack hadn't seen him fighting in that alley he might not have known how much raw strength lay underneath those elegant evening clothes—power that the man was deliberately *not* using to distance himself from Jack.

"You've recently spent a great deal of money on clothing." Really, Jack could have fed an orphanage full of children with that sum of money, not that he was in the practice of doing anything so noble. "That either means you're very interested in being fashionable—but the fact that you muss your hair up by rubbing your hands through it suggests that you are not—or it means your old clothes didn't fit anymore."

Jack was cheating—he had seen Rivington wearing a coat that might have fit a man two stone heavier than he was now. He ran one finger down the length of Rivington's sleeve. "You're very thin," Jack continued. "I think you've been ill." He paused with his finger on the cuff of Rivington's sleeve and the man stood perfectly still, as if he had been shackled.

"Not ill." Rivington's voice was scarcely audible. "I have no appetite. Haven't had since my injury."

And he had been injured before Waterloo, he had said. So

he'd been off food for at least a year, possibly several? Lord. Jack had the novel urge to feed this man coddled eggs and pie.

Jack could hardly see Rivington's face in the shadows, but he was close enough to smell whatever poncy soap his laundress had used on his shirt. That's what Rivington smelled of—expensive laundry soap and the wine he had with his dinner. Jack couldn't think of any two scents less likely to make his heart pound in his chest, but here he was, wondering what would happen if he got to his knees.

"Somebody went to a great deal of trouble to get you looking like that." He slid his finger beneath Rivington's cuff, feeling the smooth underside of the taller man's wrist. "Your boots have been polished to a shocking degree and your cravat is just so." Beneath the blood and grime that spattered Rivington's boots and neck cloth, Jack could see the handiwork of a talented valet, and almost hated the servant for having had his hands on this man's body. "You're at loose ends. That's why you let your valet spend time on you. It's also why you poke your nose into your sister's business and my own."

Rivington pulled his arm away from Jack's touch as if he were flinching. Ah, so that topic was a sore spot, then. And likely Jack had hit the mark, too. "Some helpful advice for you," Jack said, instinctively raising his hands to adjust the man's lapels into some semblance of order. It was a bald excuse to keep touching him as well as the tiresome old habit of making gentlemen look presentable. "You're acting like you're looking for a wife or a mistress. Nobody goes out nearly as much as you unless he has some kind of agenda." He smoothed Rivington's collar, letting his knuckles brush across his jaw and the tender flesh beneath. "You'll wind up married, like it or not, and you're not looking for a wife any more than I am."

He paused with his hands on Rivington's shoulders, letting his words hang in the air. His meaning couldn't be clearer. At least he hoped so. But he didn't dare move any closer—Georgie's words echoed in his ear. Did he really want to have anything to do with this man who smelled of costly laundry soap and even more costly wine? Not so long ago Jack had straightened the collars of Rivington's brother-in-law, a service then performed for wages and now from lust, but it all shook out the same in the end as far as Jack could tell.

"Your accent started to slip at the end of that speech." Rivington's face was still hidden in the shadows, but his voice scarcely betrayed that anything interesting had just happened. The man's feathers were hardly ruffled, but Jack had felt Rivington's heart pound under the superfine wool of his dinner coat. He wished he had tried something more brazen, more offensive.

Rivington continued. "Before that, I had been under the impression that you were . . . I don't know, something along the lines of a solicitor's clerk. Not quite a gentleman, you know, but perhaps two degrees removed from that."

Of course the fellow had thought so. That was precisely the effect Jack had set out to achieve. "That's excellent news." He affected a level of cheer he hoped was obviously facetious. "It's been ages since I've been able to remember my real accent." That too was true. "I'll have to yell at aristocrats more often, see if I can get the rest of it back."

"I liked hearing it." Rivington pushed off the wall, that action bringing him briefly nearer. Jack didn't dare so much as breathe, lest he end the moment sooner than necessary. "Until we meet again, Mr. Turner," he said, his lips so close that Jack could feel the words on his skin. Rivington headed east on Piccadilly, where Jack hoped he would have the sense to get a hackney.

Jack didn't even bother to say that they wouldn't be meeting again. He didn't mind lying, but hated making predictions that time would certainly prove false.

# CHAPTER FIVE

If you want to take the measure of a person, Jack always said—or rather thought, since it wasn't as if this topic arose often in conversation—search their servants' quarters. Kitchen maids and boot boys were little more than children. A man who allowed children to sleep in filth under his own roof was likely capable of greater sins besides.

In the Wraxhalls' house, even the lowliest scullery maid slept on a tidy pallet near the fire. Her apron and gray dimity work dress—both tolerably clean—hung on a hook in a nearby cupboard, a pair of stout boots beneath. It was Sunday morning, so the child was at church wearing her best clothes. The fact that she had more than one dress and, more startling, a pair of shoes she considered finer than this perfectly serviceable pair of boots, told Jack all he needed to know about the Wraxhalls. He'd finish his search, but it was almost impossible to believe that anything was amiss in this household.

He relied on instinct. "Heathenry," Sarah called it, no matter how often Jack protested that he always had reasons for the conclusions he drew. "I don't doubt it," Sarah would counter, her voice suspicious, "but you reach your conclusions first and your reasons second, which is a backwards way of doing things."

Since it was Sunday morning, the Wraxhall house was as deserted as it ever would be in daylight. There wasn't even a kitchen maid left behind to stir the midday soup, so Jack hadn't had any trouble letting himself in through the garden door Molly Wilkins had left unlocked for him. He climbed the kitchen stairs to the upper story that held the Wraxhalls' bedchambers.

Mr. Wraxhall's own bedchamber was almost aggressively tidy—the work of a good servant rather than a finicky master, Jack guessed. Whenever Jack got a glimpse of the man, Wraxhall had something askew—hat or cravat, at the very least.

Jack gingerly checked under the mattress, then checked the mattress itself for any seams that had been picked apart to create a hiding place. He peeled back the carpet, checked for loose floorboards, looked behind the few bits of art that hung on the walls, and examined the contents of the wardrobe. He turned up nothing. This was the room of a man who went to sleep, woke up, and left to spend his day elsewhere—whether in other parts of the house or other parts of the city, Jack could not yet tell. But the room itself held no comfort besides the bed. There was one chair before a looking glass, where Wraxhall likely shaved or had his valet shave him.

On one wall was a door that likely led to Mrs. Wraxhall's bedchamber. Jack tried the knob and found that it was unlocked, but the door couldn't swing entirely open because of how the shaving chair was placed. Jack was able to pass through, albeit awkwardly, but a man who made the journey often wouldn't keep his chair in so inconvenient a place—especially since such a trip was likely to be made in the dark, when the chair would only be tripped over.

Jack remembered what Rivington had said about the couple not looking at each other, and felt bad for these people who paid their scullery maid lavishly and apparently rarely shared a bed.

Mrs. Wraxhall's bedchamber was more comfortable, and consequently took a great deal longer to search. Jack even debated whether he ought to search it—surely if the woman had stolen her own letters she wouldn't hide them in her own bedchamber. Nor would anyone else who had stolen them. But still, he searched, not for the letters so much as for a clue as to who might have taken them or who might want to do Mrs. Wraxhall harm.

Naturally, he hadn't told his client of his intent to search her home. He never did. First of all, they would only hide anything remotely interesting. Secondly, they would feel intruded upon, almost violated, knowing someone had pawed through their things. And while Jack didn't give a farthing for the finer feelings of the upper classes, he knew he earned clients through word of mouth, and a client who felt uncomfortable with Jack's involvement was less likely to recommend him to a friend.

He knew how to perform a thorough search without leaving any sign that he had been present, a trick he'd learned during his years of service. Cleaning and searching had a good deal in common, after all. Also, it was a fine trick to nick a couple teaspoons, hide them somewhere in the house, and sell them after everybody had stopped wondering where the missing silver had got to. He had done that sort of thing almost tediously often before deciding to go after larger game.

Mrs. Wraxhall's jewel box proved to have a lock that was pitiably easy to pick. He had half a mind to leave a note inside advising her to get a better box, but that would defeat the purpose of this secretive search. At any rate, there was nothing in the box other than jewels and an empty place where the letters used to be. The jewels looked real, too. So, it couldn't have been Molly who took the letters. He could rule her out, if nothing else. If she wanted money, she could have taken the jewels and replaced them with paste. She had done it before, he was fairly certain. A girl of her skills would have had no trouble picking the lock, either.

The other bedchamber on this floor was empty—a guest room that was as easy to search as Wraxhall's room, and equally devoid of secrets. Really, the whole house seemed like a place that couldn't hold anything untoward. The scullery maid had two pairs of shoes. There were jewels virtually lying about for the taking. He was certain the letters hadn't been taken by a servant.

He was equally certain that the motive wasn't money, or at least not only that. When there were jewels, why take letters instead? Blackmail was riskier than jewel theft, and uglier besides. No, you only blackmailed a person if you'd be as glad to ruin them as you would to get their money.

Still, he went upstairs to the servants' quarters. The rooms were clean—even the room that housed three footmen—and there wasn't a pin out of place. The head housemaid had a wilted posy in a jar on her bedside table. One of the footmen received regular letters from a brother in the navy. The valet apparently had enough time on his hands to read sensational novels.

The house was sickeningly well run. No expense had been spared, and Jack could have told Mrs. Wraxhall half a dozen ways to save her money, but of course he wouldn't. That wasn't what he had been hired to do, and besides, he vastly preferred seeing money flow from the absurdly rich to servants and tradesmen. And who could find fault with a woman who paid the scullery maid enough for her to keep two clean dresses and two pairs of boots? He found that his mind kept coming back to that simple fact.

The faint clack of a door and the echo of voices intruded on his thoughts. The servants were returning from church. The drawing room and library would have to wait until nightfall, so he slipped into the attic to wait out the hours of daylight. Even the attic seemed devoid of secrets, housing only a few boxes and trunks. The Wraxhalls hadn't been at this address long enough to accumulate much in the way of dust or debris. It seemed for all the world that this was a house without secrets, a house without unsavoriness, even.

This mellow orderliness was not what he expected in the house of a person who was so distressed as to resort to hiring him. Jack knew that appearances could be deceiving, but as he sat alone in the attic waiting for darkness, he tried to pinpoint exactly what it was that didn't add up about this case.

Oliver feared there could be no happy reason for Anne Sutherland's presence in the seldom-used morning salon at

Rutland House. When Oliver had taken up residence this spring, his father—who, as far as Oliver knew, hadn't set foot farther south than Cambridge in the fifteen years since his wife had died—had insisted that all the main rooms of the house be opened up, even though Oliver had protested that he would never use the dining room and certainly not any of the parlors. He had no intention of receiving guests—anyone he wanted to see could be found at his club or Charlotte's house.

And yet, here was Miss Sutherland, seated on a settee that Oliver's mother had likely chosen when a new bride, and which had not been replaced in thirty-odd years. Oliver's elder brother's wife would doubtless oversee a refurbishment after Father died, but meanwhile the house was left to genteelly stagnate. The Earl of Rutland had better things to do than worry about upholstery, this room said.

"What a pleasant surprise to see you," Oliver remarked. Even more ominous than her presence in this house was that she was wearing a traveling costume. Where was she going? Charlotte had said nothing about either of them leaving town. Was there an emergency of some kind? And if so, why had Charlotte not sent a footman with a note? He reached for the bell to ring for tea.

"No, please don't," Miss Sutherland said. "In fact, you might want to shut the door. I know this is quite irregular." She took a breath, apparently steadying herself. "But, you see, Lord Montbray has returned."

Oliver didn't see. Or maybe he didn't want to see. He was still not entirely clear about whatever events had led his sister to hire Turner to rid herself of the man she had married, or why his return was the sort of thing only discussed behind closed doors. Whenever he tried to broach the topic with his sister, she dismissed his questions with a wave of the hand, as if he were a gnat flying around her head.

"Is Charlotte in any danger?" he asked slowly, lowering himself onto a chair opposite his guest.

Miss Sutherland pressed her lips together. "He is not a kind man."

"Did he raise his hand to her?" But he already knew the answer. He had not wanted to think of it, but Charlotte's actions—and Turner's involvement—made little sense unless Montbray posed a threat.

"On a few occasions." Her face was pale beneath her hat.

Oliver digested this. "Can she go to stay with my father at Alder Court? He would welcome Charlotte and her son making their home there."

"Before Lord Montbray . . . departed, he once told Charlotte that if she left his house he would petition to take William away from her. William was only a baby then, and now he's two, of course, but still too young to be in the hands of a man like Montbray."

He was aghast. "Can Montbray do that?" One heard of such situations, but usually when the wife had left home with a lover.

"Apparently so." Miss Sutherland's face was colorless, her mouth tight. "Charlotte has consulted with her solicitor."

"When did Montbray return?"

"Last night. He smelled of drink," she said, her nose wrinkling in disgust. "I spent the morning having locks put on the doors to the housemaids' bedchambers."

She . . . oh. Realization dawned. Oliver felt his face flush. "Did he cause that kind of trouble before?"

"Yes," was all she said, but her nails were digging into the faded upholstery of the settee.

There was something about her tone of voice that made him ask, "And you, Miss Sutherland? Will you be safe?"

She laughed, a dry and bitter sound. "I had three brothers, Mr. Rivington. I can handle myself. I'm worried about Charlotte and the child."

"I don't know what I can do." He felt worse than useless. "Why did you come to me?"

"Would you consult with Mr. Turner?" she asked without hesitation.

"What?" His voice was a hoarse whisper.

"Mr. Turner addressed the problem before. He promised that if Montbray returned, he would renew his efforts."

Good God. His *efforts*? What did that mean, precisely? He felt a shiver go down his spine. Were they talking about murder? Was Turner to murder Charlotte's husband? Not that Oliver had any better idea of what to do with Montbray. Hell, a younger Oliver would have volunteered to murder Montbray himself, but now he knew only too well that killing a man was the kind of transgression that lived in your soul. "Turner is a scoundrel, Miss Sutherland."

She gave a quick shake of her head, as if Mr. Turner's being a scoundrel was the least of her concerns. Which, likely, it was. "If you don't go to him, then I will. In fact, I stopped by his office before thinking to come here, but he wasn't in." Her voice was matter-of-fact. Oliver had heard generals talk that way about battle strategy, with a detached focus on organization rather than the horror that lay beneath. "I can try again tomorrow, but I would rather be near Charlotte and William. They left before dawn to visit a friend in Richmond for the next week, and I plan to follow as soon as possible."

"But you said Montbray won't allow that!" The idea of Montbray taking the child from Charlotte—he couldn't even think of it.

"That won't matter if Turner deals with Montbray before he has a chance to act," she said darkly. "But if you don't want to go then I'll find a way."

"No, no, I'll go myself. Of course." He would not send Miss Sutherland to strike a bargain with Turner. If any hands were to be dirtied, they would be his own. He would go to Turner himself and find out exactly how a violent, threatening husband could be gotten rid of in ways that didn't involve felony. Was it even possible? Whatever Turner had done last time had kept Montbray away for two years. But it hadn't been enough.

She thanked him somberly, leaving him alone in his late mother's parlor. For one ludicrous moment he thought he ought to marry Anne Sutherland. In doing so he would save at least one person from Montbray, and it wasn't as if she had any other prospects. Marriage to a man with a small but safe income would be better than she could reasonably hope for otherwise. She would have a home and a place in society. Possibly she would even have children, although how he would contrive to make that happen was not something he wanted to dwell on.

Oh, what a fool he was. He had nearly convinced himself that it was his charitable duty to marry some spinster—the first one who walked through his door, in fact—just to confer on her all the status and standing and security that he had to offer. Conveniently, he had ignored those things that he couldn't give to a wife—love, desire, passion. Well, those were things he wasn't going to have for himself, either, so it was no wonder that he let them slip from his mind. Marriage, indeed.

Besides, marrying Miss Sutherland would protect her from Montbray, but it wouldn't do a damn thing for Charlotte. Rousing himself from his delusional reverie, he hailed a hackney and went immediately to Turner's office, but it was Sunday, and the dressmaker on the ground floor was closed for business. When he knocked, nobody came to the door. Oliver thought Turner lived as well as worked there, so the man would have to return at some point. Well, it wasn't as if Oliver had anything better to do than wait, so he made himself as comfortable as possible on the front steps of the building, ignoring glances from passersby.

Charlotte's situation was horrible. He knew, in the abstract, that some women were mistreated by their husbands, but the idea that his own sister was living under such a threat was shocking and painful. When he shut his eyes he could almost hear musket balls whizzing past his ear, could almost smell gunpowder and blood. It seemed that there was violence and lawlessness no matter which way he looked.

He opened his eyes and saw the well-maintained buildings of Sackville Street; when he took a deep breath he smelled horses and baking bread. When one was fortunate enough to live in a place and time with laws, it was one's duty to follow them. There had to be another way out of this mess. But still he waited.

Jack had brought a book to keep himself occupied while waiting for night to fall. It was some nonsense Georgie had recommended, about an orphan and a great deal of hijinks. So much silliness, really. But after the household returned from church, he had retreated to the attic to spend the daylight hours hiding among the empty trunks, waiting for darkness so he could resume his search. This was the closest he was ever likely to come to a holiday, so he tried to enjoy it.

There were two full hours during which it was too dark to read but before the household retired. Rich people could always be counted on to spend money to show the world exactly how rich they were, which was probably why they burned candles and lamps to light their revels and then slept through several perfectly good daylight hours the next morning.

Finally, though, the house was quiet. Jack crept down the servants' stairs to the main floor. He really only had to search the drawing room, back parlor and library. This was a more modest establishment than many in this neighborhood, so there were no music rooms or ballrooms or morning salons or any other such madness. And Jack was glad of it, because he was well and truly tired of being in a rich man's house, even for this one day. The sight of all those pointless urns and gilded picture frames almost made him nostalgic for the days of the guillotine—even though he had only been a child then and one with more pressing problems than who killed whom in France. But all these acres of impossibly soft carpets gave his thoughts a dark turn.

And none of those carpets lay atop a single loose

floorboard; none of the picture frames concealed a secret compartment; the urns were all depressingly empty of secrets and scandal. He had turned up nothing in either the drawing room or the back parlor except for a big, stupid dog who followed him around as if they'd known one another their whole lives. In these rooms the curtains were drawn, allowing Jack to light a single candle without any concern that he would be noticed from the street. He gingerly opened the door into the hall—of course the doors didn't so much as squeak in this house—and crossed to the library.

He really didn't want to shake out every book in this place. It would take all night and make a mountain of dust that would be noticed by the housemaids in the morning. "What do you think?" he whispered to the dog, who was wagging his tail and slobbering. No bad man could own a dog this stupidly affectionate. Jack was certain of it.

Before he could decide what to do with this room, he was interrupted by the sound of carriage wheels rolling up in front of the house. The front door opened and a few words were exchanged, too quiet for him to catch. In all likelihood, this was Wraxhall returned from a night at the club. Jack didn't know if Wraxhall planned to visit the library or head straight to bed, but he couldn't take the chance.

Footsteps ascended the stairs. Quickly extinguishing his candle, Jack made his way to the window, which overlooked Grosvenor Square. *Damn.* No housebreaker wanted to make his escape into a well-lit street. The mews would have been better, but he wasn't in a place to choose. He opened the window, swung himself over the sill, and jumped.

Oliver watched in amazement as Turner all but fell out of the hackney. It was well past midnight and Oliver had been sitting on the steps for hours, leaving only to get a pint of ale and attempt a few bites of sludgy-looking stew at a nearby public house. When the carriage had rolled up, he was on the verge of heading home, planning on sending over a footman with a message first thing the next morning. But then Turner stumbled to the steps. With an instinct born of too many years on the battlefield, Oliver rose to his feet and got an arm around Turner's shoulders.

"What in God's name happened to you?" He steered the man towards the building. Even in the moonlight he could see that Turner's breeches were ripped.

"Rivington? Christ. What in hell are you doing here? It's two in the morning. You'll give a fellow ideas."

He ignored that last remark but couldn't quite ignore the deep and gravelly voice it was delivered in. But for heaven's sake. This situation was awkward enough without a cock-stand. "I'll tell you inside."

"Inside? Like hell you will. Go home." Turner attempted to shrug out of Oliver's grasp, but Oliver held fast.

"You have no chance getting up the stairs without help. Trust me on this." If there was anything Oliver knew, it was what a man looked like when he was trying not to put any weight on an injured leg.

"I hurt my ankle. It's nothing."

"How?" The man looked like he had been attacked by a lion, or dragged through the streets behind a cart. A fellow didn't tear his breeches and ruin his shirt for no reason.

"By being a fucking idiot, that's how." Turner fumbled in his pocket and even that small effort made him visibly wince in pain. "If you want to help me up the stairs, then fine. Have at it. For my part, I'd have thought a gentleman of your tendencies might worry about where he was seen at this hour and in whose company."

There it was again, another hint that Turner knew about Oliver. *Tendencies.* "Is that blackmail?" He didn't think it was, but he honestly couldn't tell with this man.

"God, are you that dim?"

"Probably." When it came to some things, definitely.

Turner unlocked the front door and they stepped inside a tiny pitch-dark vestibule. "Then let me clear things up." His voice was harsh and rasping and Oliver thought he could feel the vibration low in his belly. "Because I am not going to blackmail you, you bloody interfering toff. For a lot of reasons, not least of which is that it's a nasty fucking thing to do, but also, you daft bastard, because if I blackmailed you for happening to prefer men, you could blackmail me right back. Did you somehow not notice that I nearly fucked you against a building on Piccadilly the other night?"

Oliver didn't know how to answer that, so he stood silently in the dark, waiting for whatever might happen next. And then he felt it—Turner's big hand skimming up his arm, then along his neck, before resting on his jaw. Only then did Oliver realize Turner was trying to find Oliver's mouth in the dark. He had only a half second of waiting for the kiss to come before he felt the other man's lips brush against his own.

It was only the subtlest touch, something he might have

imagined here in the darkness—except for how his lips were now hot and tingling, his pulse roaring in his ears.

Except for how even in his more debased fantasies, he hadn't considered that one innocent kiss could make him feel this way. Although, *innocent* seemed a ludicrous word to describe any activity that occurred with Jack Turner, confessed thief and unashamed scoundrel.

Turner was still tantalizingly close. Their boots were actually touching, their chests nearly so. Oliver's heart was beating too fast for him to collect his thoughts. He wanted to reach out, smooth his hands over Turner's strong body. Instead he simply pressed his cheek into the other man's ungloved palm. Turner laughed softly, a single huff that balanced on the knife's edge between amusement and desire. But still he didn't step away. Oliver leaned forward, brushing his lips against the other man's in the same way Turner had done. A gentle pressure, the merest taste of a kiss.

But now Turner's body was pressing him against the wall, the man's lips punishingly hot and hard against his own. Tasting, exploring, taking exactly what he wanted—and Oliver wanted him to keep on taking. All too soon, though, Turner pulled away. They stood in the darkness for a moment, catching their breaths, heavily breathing the same air, before Turner spoke.

"Just so we're perfectly clear," Turner said in his gritty baritone before taking his hand from Oliver's jaw. "Now, up we go."

They made it up the stairs slowly. Turner was heavy, for one thing, and grumpily uncooperative, for another. And Oliver was nearly driven to distraction by the sensation of hard muscles bunching and moving beneath Turner's coat. Those muscles were the sort of thing Oliver would have noticed under any circumstance, but after that kiss, dear God. However, there was a job to be done. Between them they had two good legs and a walking stick and eventually they managed to make it to the top of the stairs.

When they reached Turner's door, a girl appeared on the landing above. "Miss Sarah wants to know what the ruckus is," she whispered.

"The ruckus is me coming home after earning my daily bread. And Betsy?" He reached into his pocket and held up a coin. "Sarah does not need to know that I have a gentleman with me."

Oliver blushed at the implication, but he was the only one who seemed embarrassed. The girl simply nodded in agreement, deftly catching the coin Turner tossed her, before returning to wherever she came from.

"Who is Miss Sarah?" Oliver asked, following Turner into his rooms. He didn't expect an answer.

"My sister." Turner stumbled across the room that served as his office and passed through a door. "She owns the dress shop and lives upstairs."

Turner lived with his *sister*? That seemed disconcertingly cozy for a man one might be hiring to commit a crime. A man who had kissed him not five minutes earlier.

Oliver didn't know what to do with himself in this strange, dark room, but it felt wrong to follow Turner into the room beyond without being told to.

Then Turner called out. "In the top drawer of my desk you'll find brandy. Bring me some. Only the bottle, don't bother with a glass."

Oliver did as he was told and carried the bottle through the door Turner had just disappeared through. He found himself in a small sitting room that contained mismatched chairs and a deal table but no Turner. He passed through yet another doorway and realized he was now in Turner's bedchamber. The room contained little more than a bed, a washstand and a small wardrobe. Turner stood by the window, struggling to unfasten his shirt.

"You'll never manage it like that," Oliver pointed out. A man did not spend ten years in the army during wartime without learning the finer points of dressing and undressing while encumbered by minor injuries. "Let me," he said, tucking the bottle under his arm and tugging off his gloves.

Turner said nothing. He put his hands by his sides, giving Oliver access to the shirt closures. Mercifully, Oliver's hands did not shake, even as he worked the shirt open, revealing skin that he did not allow himself to look at. He kept his eyes focused on his own fingers, his mind trained on the task at hand, not even letting himself so much as think about the heat of Turner's gaze. Even without looking—he dared not meet Turner's eyes—he could feel the intensity of the other man's gaze on him.

"My hands are scraped and I couldn't seem to get hold of the studs," Turner said, sounding apologetic.

Oliver worked free the last closure and then reached for one of Turner's hands, half expecting the other man to stop him, to remind him that he didn't belong here, that he ought to go home. But he didn't. Instead Turner held his hands out, palms up, almost meekly. Oliver took one in his own hand. Scrapes everywhere, but nothing too deep. He darted a glance at Turner's face, and saw a similar scrape on one of his cheekbones. "It looks like you were worked over with a rasp." He released Turner's hand and gave him the brandy.

Turner took a swig from the bottle. "It was a windowsill."

"A windowsill?" Oliver repeated, incredulous. "Did you fall out a window?"

"Jumped." He took another drink. Oliver could see Turner's throat work as he swallowed the brandy. "I didn't have time to put on my gloves, so I had to hang onto the sill with bare hands. Then I must have grazed my face along the bricks on the way down. And *then* I landed like a sack of laundry."

Oliver found that he was surprised, not that Turner was involved in any kind of cloak-and-dagger enterprise that required leaping out of windows under cover of darkest night, but rather that he wasn't apparently very good at it.

As if reading his thoughts, Turner laughed, low and rumbling. It was the first time Oliver had heard him laugh, and he couldn't help but smile foolishly back. "I might be too old to clamber out windows like a cat burglar at this point in my career. Alas. My father will be rolling in his grave, knowing I learned so little at his knee."

His *father* taught him to—but never mind that. "Is that what you were doing? Robbing someone?"

Turner was silent for a moment, and Oliver realized he had insulted the man. He probably ought to be relieved to have ruined their fleeting moment of intimacy, but instead he felt unaccountably disappointed. "I was searching a client's house, if you must know," Turner answered, his voice tight. "But I suppose I committed a few crimes along the way." He took another drink. "I tend to do so."

"I only asked because—" but Oliver was distracted by the sight of the other man tugging his shirt over his head. He knew he ought to take a step backwards, or turn around, or leave the room, or really do anything other than stare open-mouthed at Turner's torso, yet here he was. Ogling.

Turner was lit only by the moonlight that managed to make its way through the room's one sooty window. Which was to say barely lit at all. Yet Oliver could see every muscle and sinew in Turner's chest and arms, in the same broad shoulders that had moved under his hand earlier. Had he been a prizefighter? Some kind of laborer? Where had he come from?

"Feel free to watch. Believe me, it's not a problem." Turner had managed to work open the closure of his breeches. "I'm enjoying it. In a moment, though, I'm going to start enjoying it a bit more, if you catch my meaning." He made a lewd gesture suggesting a hardening prick. "And I need to put on an untorn pair of breeches before I go out again, so—"

Oliver whipped around, embarrassed. And then he was embarrassed to be embarrassed, and wished he had gone home hours ago and sent Turner a note. He expected to hear Turner laughing at him and was relieved not to.

It wasn't that Oliver was inexperienced, precisely, only that most of his experiences had been rather transactional in nature. A couple shillings in exchange for a bit of this and a bit of that. Sometimes an arranged and rushed-through meeting with a like-minded gentleman. Tender kisses of the sort that village maidens received on May Day and that Jack Turner bestowed in his vestibule had never entered into the picture. Oliver was very much out of his depth.

"Go out again?" he asked, suddenly struck by the insanity of the idea. "You've only just jumped out a window. Something might be broken. It's past two in the morning and surely you ought to go to bed." Because Oliver was evidently playing the role of the nursemaid in tonight's performance.

"I'm half starved, though," Turner said, as if that settled the matter.

"Have you nothing to eat here?" Oliver could hear the all too familiar sounds of a man shoving an injured leg into a boot and decided it was safe to turn back around.

"There's some bread upstairs at my sister's but I don't want to wake her. She'll give me hell over my bruises. And besides, I don't want day-old bread and drippings. I want hot food."

Oliver felt his mouth water at the idea. That stew had been hours and hours ago. "Where on earth are you going to get hot food at this hour?"

"Are you hungry? Because you look like you ought to be. I'll swear you're thinner now than you were the first day you walked into my office."

"I told you. I'm off my appetite." His voice sounded peevish even to his own ears.

"Well, you won't be after you taste what happens when Mrs. Madrigal has her way with a potato and a couple of leeks."

"I'm not—"

"Yes you are. You had something to discuss with me, remember? I'm going out for supper. If you want to talk to me, then so are you."

"Fine. Where are we going?" What kind of filthy, greasy establishment would serve supper at this hour?

"We're going to a whorehouse, Mr. Rivington."

---

# CHAPTER SIX

Jack Turner was the sort of man who could make a hackney materialize out of thin air even on a side street in the small hours of the morning. Oliver couldn't help but be impressed. After getting down the stairs, they hardly needed to walk three yards before climbing into the carriage, which was a good thing because by that point it was anyone's guess which of them was limping more.

"I've never been to a whorehouse," Oliver said, breaking the silence in the carriage.

"Am I supposed to act surprised?" Turner retorted, his face hidden by shadows.

The hackney stopped after only a few minutes, and they entered a narrow building through the back door. "Tell Mrs. Madrigal I'm here with a companion and that we want whatever she has cooking," Turner told the boy who opened the door to them.

"You can tell her yourself, Jack," the boy said in an accent Oliver found almost unintelligible. "I'm not a bloody butler."

"A thousand fucking pardons, Alfie." Turner's voice had the coarse edge Oliver had heard in the alley.

Oliver followed Turner down a corridor to the kitchen where they found a woman stirring a pot over the range. He watched in fascination as she threw down her spoon, wiped her hands on her apron and crossed the room to embrace Turner.

"Jack! What happened to you?" She was somewhere between forty and fifty, plump, with graying hair tucked into a cap.

"I had a run-in with a building."

"You haven't been here in weeks and now you turn up at this hour. I have a roast on the spit and some soup in the pot, but hardly anything else. Go take your friend and sit in my room. I'll bring you something in a tick."

Oliver followed Turner down a narrow corridor to a small room that was crammed with comfortable-looking furniture, the walls decorated with seaside prints. Turner immediately dropped into the chair facing the door. Oliver froze on the threshold, momentarily paralyzed by the decision of whether to sit across the small, round table from Turner or beside him, but Turner used his leg to push out the chair next to his.

"Sit," he ordered.

Oliver sat. "She didn't ask who I was."

"It's a whorehouse kitchen, not the queen's drawing room." Turner was leaning back, his chair tipped onto the rear legs. "Visitors aren't customarily announced. Although I should have introduced you. If it were known that you frequent brothels it would only do good things for your reputation."

"Very humorous," Oliver grumbled. "What's the name of this place?"

"Madame Louise's." Jack removed his hat and tossed it onto the sideboard.

Oliver knew the name from his club. Madame Louise's was considered to be the best establishment of its kind in London. Indeed, he had heard its cook had been stolen from some or another great house. And the woman had greeted Turner like a long lost son.

Turner, the same man Oliver was about to hire to commit some variety of misdeed.

He decided to broach the topic. "So, the reason I wanted to speak with you—"

"No, stop right there." Turner brought the front legs of his chair down with a bang. "Wait for her to bring the food and then we'll shut the door."

Oliver nodded. Today was to be a day of shut doors, it would seem. He recoiled at the notion, not wanting to be the sort of man whose conduct required secrecy. He wanted to be morally upright, a model citizen, firmly on the side of good in a world where good and evil were separated by a clear line.

But that ship had sailed around the time he resolved to hire Turner to commit a crime. There was a part of Oliver that didn't give a damn whether what he was doing was right as long as it kept Charlotte and his nephew safe. But Oliver knew only too well how important it was to keep that part of him—of anyone—well in check.

The food came shortly thereafter, though, and all other thoughts were driven from his mind. All he could do for a moment was savor it. The roast was seasoned with—honestly, he had no idea what. Unicorn tears? Fairy dust? And the soup. He nearly moaned. Turner hadn't been exaggerating—and Oliver hadn't enjoyed food so much in ages.

"I told you." Turner refilled both of their wine glasses. He was watching Oliver with evident satisfaction, a wolfish smile playing on his lips. How had Oliver gotten the impression that Turner was ordinary-looking? Because when the man smiled he was paralyzingly gorgeous. "Wait until she brings out the pudding."

"She said she only had roast and soup." Oliver found that he wanted his pudding as badly as any child in the nursery.

"She lied. She'll come up with something. Meanwhile . . ." Turner gestured to the door, and Oliver reached out with his walking stick to push it shut.

"Lord Montbray has returned."

Turner went still for an instant, his wine glass halfway to his mouth. "Oh he has, has he?"

"My sister wishes to engage your services." Oliver hoped the other man would not ask him to spell out exactly what services he required.

"Why didn't she contact me herself, then?"

"She's staying at friend's house in Richmond."

"Good. But first—" He cut himself off and glanced at Oliver, his expression going hard. "I was his valet, you know." His voice held a challenge.

"Montbray's?" Oliver was astonished to think that this gruff rogue had been anyone's valet. Servants were usually so meek, so mild, nearly invisible. Turner was about the farthest thing from invisibility Oliver could imagine. He seemed the only thing in the world Oliver could manage to think of.

Turner was looking closely at Oliver, as if waiting for him to react. "For a few years. I saw how cruel he was to your sister after they were married, and once things reached a certain point I offered to help."

"Help," Oliver repeated. Turner made it sound so innocent.

"It was only a question of my paying an acquaintance of mine to hit your brother-in-law on the head. That, and drag him onto a ship." Turner spoke as if he were describing how he brewed a pot of tea or some other everyday task. "I imagine Montbray bribed or thwarted the man I employed. This time I believe I'll hire two such men."

Abduction was certainly a crime, but not as serious as murder. That sort of balancing was repellent, but still he was relieved. Had he truly been ready to tacitly agree to something worse?

"In the spirit of full disclosure"—Turner shot Oliver a faintly mocking smile—"it was when I was Montbray's valet that I learned of your preference for gentlemen. I saw you in the orangery at Alder Court with . . ." He tapped the table. "I can't remember his name."

Oliver groaned. He had been home on leave, staying with his father at Alder Court. Charlotte had been there, too, along with her husband. Turner, as Montbray's valet, would have come with his employer as a matter of course. He was mortified to think that Turner had witnessed one of the few times he had thrown caution to the wind and indulged himself at his father's house. He wanted to sink into the earth.

"It felt like the sort of thing I ought to share with you in the name of honesty. Or something to that effect. It's not often I'm moved to honesty, Mr. Rivington, so when I feel the urge, I tend to obey it."

Oliver had no response to make, opting instead to drain his wineglass. When he dared look at Turner he saw that the man was returning his gaze. There was more than a day's worth of stubble darkening his jaw and some equally dark hair revealed by his open collar—he had hardly gotten himself dressed and tidied at all, only throwing the shirt over his head and tossing a waistcoat and coat over it. He still had dried blood on his face. In short, he was a shambles.

And Oliver wanted him nevertheless, or maybe because of that.

It was the sense of possibility more than anything else. To be sharing a meal with a man he wanted to bed—and to know that feeling was shared—felt like a gift.

"Oh, don't start with that." Turner jerked back in his chair so abruptly that Oliver could hear the wood creak. "Don't look at me like you're going to start leaving posies by my door." It was the tone one would use to scold a cat who had dropped a dead animal at one's feet. "Did you miss the part where I admitted to being habitually dishonest and told you that I used to be a servant in your sister's house? And when I wasn't a servant, I was a thief. Sometimes I was both at the same time. Sometimes I was a good deal worse than any of those things."

Oliver kept his gaze on the table. "Posies don't enter into it," he whispered, and then he felt his cheeks get hot.

Turner must have noticed his blush, because he fell silent for a moment. When Oliver did look up, he found Turner's eyes dark and intent.

"There's more disgrace in my family than you can even wrap your honorable little mind around. My father was a petty crook and a confidence man and my mother was . . ." His voice trailed off.

"What was your mother?" Oliver tried to make it sound

like a normal bit of conversation. He didn't care what Turner's mother had been. Likely the man came from a long line of scoundrels and worse. But Oliver found that he cared very much about the fact that Turner was telling him something about himself, something important enough to make the man hesitate.

"A different kind of criminal." He had shaken off that air of intimacy and reverted to his usual distant terseness. "My point is, since you're the type of gentleman who needs this sort of thing spelled out for him, I'm more than game for a roll in the hay, a mutual scratching of backs, as early and as often as you like, but I'm not interested even slightly in, ah, an affair of the heart."

"I'll keep that in mind," Oliver managed to say. All Oliver wanted was to drink in the possibility of the moment, and Jack seemed intent on making even that much into something seedy.

The door opened then, and Oliver thought this must be the arrival of the sweets. Too bad his appetite was quite gone by now.

But there were no sweets. Instead a vaguely familiar and highly dashing young man entered the room.

"Georgie, what the bloody hell?" Turner shot to his feet.

"No need for that." The new arrival planted his hands on Turner's shoulders in order to shove him back into his chair before bending to drop a kiss on his cheek. "I come bearing information." He lowered himself gracefully into the seat next to Turner, across from Oliver.

Oliver was astonished by this. He had never seen gentlemen behave like this. Kissing? Lord. He also felt a mortifying but undeniable surge of jealousy.

"Don't worry," said the new arrival. Oliver realized with a start this comment was addressed to him. "Jack's my brother."

Oliver was relieved and embarrassed in equal parts—relieved to have an explanation for Turner's intimacy with this brazen young man, embarrassed that his own envy was so obvious.

Turner seemed amused. "Rivington, this is Georgie."

"Charmed, charmed," Georgie drawled. "Mr. Rivington, is it?" He flicked a knowing glance at his brother before returning his gaze to Oliver. "You should call me Georgie, otherwise we'll have too many Mr. Turners in the room and it'll be too dreary to sort it all out."

"Then you must call me Oliver," he managed to say. This debonair gentleman, whom he had surely seen at a soiree or ball, and who was dressed in clothing that could have come from the same tailor Oliver himself had patronized, was Turner's brother? Turner, who had been a valet and a thief?

"You're quite right. I must," Georgie said, spearing the last piece of roast off of Jack's plate. "And you'll have to call my brother Jack and then we'll all be fast friends." Oliver was not sure why such breezy familiarity didn't seem like insolence. "See how cleverly I managed that, Jack?" Georgie asked, with a louche grin. "I've saved you a great deal of trouble."

"You've done nothing of the kind," Turner—*Jack*—replied, his voice stern. "Look at how he's blushing."

"I know, but he's adorable, don't you think? All pink and white, like a Dresden shepherdess."

Jack only looked at his brother. "I think you'd better tell me why you've come before you give him an apoplexy."

Georgie bent forward, using the candle to light his cheroot. "May I speak freely or should I invent a cunning code?"

"Mr. Rivington is aware of the matter, so you can speak freely." Jack didn't use Oliver's Christian name, and Oliver didn't know whether to be relieved or disappointed.

"Mr. Wraxhall—Francis, when he's at home—has no debts, no mistress, no expensive tastes. In short, he's a dead bore." Georgie took a drag from his cheroot. "His wife brought with her a sizable dowry, which came with no strings attached, as far as I can tell. The entire sum was made over to her husband with precious little left for her own use. In other words, your Mr. Wraxhall is a rich man and has no apparent need for ready money."

"What about before he was married?" Jack asked.

"He had the usual dull career at Oxford. The family had some idea that he would go into the church but that was before he met the current Mrs. Wraxhall while at Brighton recovering from a winter cold. Marrying her quite obviated the need for obtaining some piddling post as vicar. But nobody ever considered him a fortune hunter. Before his marriage, Wraxhall never so much as set foot in London or Bath or any of the places you'd think to find a rich wife. But find one, he did."

Oliver was not pleased to hear Wraxhall discussed in this light manner in the sitting room of a whorehouse cook. What had Wraxhall ever done to deserve this treatment, other than marry a woman who had the bad sense to get blackmailed?

"There was something untoward about the engagement," Georgie added after another puff on his cheroot. "The happy couple was found in a compromising situation at a ball. Not so compromising as to actually be interesting, but compromising enough to require a man of honor to do right by the lady. Wraxhall, being lamentably honorable, married the lady as soon as the banns had been read three times."

"You know," Oliver said impatiently, "I could have told you as much." He turned to Jack. "In fact, I think I did tell you as much and you dismissed me. Wraxhall is the most obviously decent fellow I've met in ages. He's harmless."

He found two pairs of almost identical brown eyes staring at him.

"No," Jack said after a moment. "That is *not* how it works. With all due respect," he remarked, managing to convey no respect whatsoever, "you wouldn't know whether or not he was decent. You couldn't, in fact. You play cards with him, maybe drink or make idle conversation. He has no power over you to be anything other than decent. It's his wife and servants who know the truth. You would likely have thought your brother-in-law a decent fellow had you met him at your club."

Oliver bristled at the mention of Montbray. In truth he had only met the man that one time, during that visit to Alder Court several years ago. And Oliver had spent that visit getting seduced by the Honorable Freddie Cavendish, not assessing the character of his sister's husband. "That's a bleak picture of marriage," was all he could think to say.

"It's a bleak picture of life," Jack corrected. "And an accurate one."

"Oh, God." Georgie rose to his feet. "If you want to know what's bleak, it's all this griping when there's pleasure to be had. I'm heading upstairs to pay my respects to Madame Louise and see what the night brings."

And with that, he slipped out the door, leaving Oliver alone with Jack.

After finishing the jam tart, Jack could see the first hints of dawn through Mrs. Madrigal's windows. He needed to get back to his rooms and attempt a few hours of sleep before starting his day's work.

"Write your sister a note telling her to stay in Richmond for two weeks, or until you send word that Montbray is gone, whichever is longer." He would need the extra time to set his plans in motion. "I'll put out word that I have a job for a pair of men with the requisite qualifications." The primary qualification was the ability to cosh a man on the head as hard and as often as necessary. "But the day after tomorrow I plan to leave London on another matter."

"Where are you going?" Rivington asked, pushing bits of pastry crust around his plate, as if that would disguise the fact that he hadn't eaten a bite.

Jack considered not answering. He had given this man altogether too much information tonight. Rivington now knew about Jack's past, about Georgie and Sarah. Hell, Jack had even mentioned his mother. But Rivington was regarding him with those clear blue eyes, as innocent as a kitten's, and Jack wanted to tell him even more. He wanted to confess all his crimes, all his dishonor, all the sordidness that sometimes woke him up at night. He wanted to lay his soul bare and see if Rivington still looked at him like that.

Rivington—like that poor bastard Wraxhall—considered himself a man of honor, a notion that Jack usually laughed at.

Honor was a luxury item, like hair pomade and snuff. Its only purpose was to show the world that you could afford to be impractical, that you had enough money to behave in a way that was compatible with some ludicrous code instead of acting out of self-preservation like the rest of humanity.

Jack remembered how squeamish Rivington had been that day he had tried to give Jack money, as if a few banknotes would untangle Jack from his family's affairs and wash away the stain of such an association. That had been humiliating. Or, rather, it would have been if Jack could bring himself to give one rat's ass about what a toff like Rivington thought about anything. Which, he reminded himself, he did not.

"Why do you care where I'm going?" Rudeness might do the trick. A dose of horrible manners might shake Rivington loose, might send him packing back to the drawing rooms and tea parties of Mayfair.

And yet, Rivington had waited outside Jack's building in order to ask for help, and he hadn't balked at taking supper in a whorehouse. He had heard about Jack's background and not raised so much as an eyebrow. The demands of respectability had their limits, it would seem.

"Good God, man. I'm making conversation." Rivington seemed amused rather than put off, damn him. Those eyes were fairly twinkling.

"I'm headed north," he said, to stop his thoughts from getting away from him. "To visit the village where Mrs. Wraxhall lived as a child."

"That's in Yorkshire, is it not?"

"Yes. Near Dewsbury." Unfortunately. Why could the woman not have hailed from someplace nearer to London?

Perhaps Surrey. Somerset at the utmost. But Yorkshire? That meant at least two days of travel by the mail and another two back. But he had been unable to turn up anything useful in London, so he had no choice but to look farther afield.

"I was thinking of traveling north myself," Rivington said, studying his wineglass.

An obvious lie. He had the shifty look of a man not accustomed to outright dishonesty, as if he expected to be struck down at any moment. "Were you, now?"

"I was thinking of buying a house in that area." Now his gaze was fixed on some point on the wall behind Jack's head. "It would be a day's ride from my father's house."

"A house. What, for your wife and all the children you plan to sire on her?"

He blushed. Of course he did. Rivington's blushes were a delight. A grown man, a former soldier no less, blushing like a bride. Georgie had been right that he looked like a Dresden shepherdess, although that wasn't what Jack liked about these displays of embarrassment. No, what he appreciated was that a blush couldn't be counterfeited. It was like when a pawnbroker took a piece of gold between his teeth to test whether it was the real thing. For all Rivington's aristocratic polish, his courtly composure, he couldn't stop those blushes.

"Would that be so strange?" Rivington protested. "I wouldn't be the first man to marry a woman without, ah, appreciating female companionship."

"No, indeed." Jack wondered what it would take to get the man to speak of these matters without euphemism. "But you wouldn't marry a woman under false pretenses."

"False pretenses? That's laying it on a bit thick. I have a

modest income." He scrubbed his hand along the back of his neck. "I could give a woman a good life."

He had his eye on someone in particular, did he? A woman in straitened circumstances, by the sound of it. "So. The lucky lady is to have a house in Yorkshire. How delightful for you both." Jack officially did not give a damn who Rivington married or for what reasons or in what county they decided to reside. He needed to go home, do something about the scrape on his face, and try to catch a few hours of sleep.

"I have a new curricle," Rivington said, and Jack would have bet ten guineas that it was another lie. "I could drive you to Yorkshire. The curricle is sprung a good deal better than any post chaise or stagecoach. And while we wouldn't travel as fast as the mail, I daresay it would be more comfortable."

It wasn't often that Jack found himself completely at a loss, but this was one of those times. On the one hand, he did not need Rivington interfering in the Wraxhall matter any more than he already had. But on the other hand, his instincts told him he ought to keep Rivington away from Montbray, lest the fellow bungle everything by approaching his brother-in-law with threats and accusations. And if that meant Jack had to spend a couple of nights with Rivington in coaching inns, so be it. He wouldn't mind that at all.

"I could help." Rivington leaned a bit forward in his chair. "My father is well known in the area. A good many doors would open for Lord Rutland's son."

Jack had to concede that there was truth in that. It didn't even matter who his father was, the fact was that all it took was one look at Oliver Rivington, with his aristocratic features and expensively tailored coat to know that you were dealing with quality. There were people for whom costly clothes, a fine accent, and a disarming smile worked like a magical combination of skeleton key and truth serum. Jack's own talents were more along the lines of seeing what people didn't want seen. Snooping. Observing. He couldn't do any of that unless he had a way in, and he didn't know any servants to bribe in the wilds of Yorkshire.

"What would our pretense be?" Jack knew he was admitting defeat. "What's our excuse for being in Yorkshire? For traveling together?"

"Like I said, I'm considering buying an estate."

"No you're not. Don't be nonsensical. You don't have nearly enough money to be purchasing estates."

"How do you know how much money I have?" Rivington had the nerve to look surprised.

"Please." Had this man figured nothing out? Jack made it his business to know everything.

"I have twenty thousand pounds! At five percent interest that's a thousand a year. That's more than enough to live on."

Jack burst out laughing. Oh God. Yes, yes, a thousand a year was enough to live on. It would outfit all the urchins of St. Giles in shirts and shoes for the rest of their lives, with some money left over for bread. But when men bought curricles and outfitted themselves like Rivington did, a thousand pounds wouldn't leave much left over for a wife, let alone children. "Yes, you're rich," he said, striving to compose himself. "No doubt about it."

"You were trying to distract me," Rivington cried, but he was smiling. "Now. Back to the matter at hand. Our pretense."

Jack emptied the wine bottle into Rivington's glass. "We're seeing a man about a horse."

"You're not serious. That's an old cliché." At some point Rivington had lost the shifty dishonest look and settled back in his chair. This was likely how he looked at his club—his long limbs loose and relaxed, his glass casually propped in his hand. That thought was an unwelcome reminder of who Rivington really was.

"It's a cliché for a reason," Jack said, his voice harsh. "Men are always buying horses. It's completely unremarkable." The best lie was the one that sounded like a truth too boring to merit discussion.

"Whose horse?"

"How the hell would I know? We'll figure that out when we get there, and then we'll look at his bloody horse. That's the easy part. The more difficult question is why the Earl of Rutland's son would be traveling with plain Jack Turner."

Rivington took a slow sip of his wine. "You could pose as my valet. You were a valet in the past, after all, so it wouldn't be a challenge."

"You must be cracked." Jack shoved his own glass away from him. "I'm not pretending to be your servant or anybody else's servant either." Jack realized belatedly that he was nearly shouting. "Not ever," he added, bringing his voice to a calmer register.

Rivington seemed unperturbed by Jack's loss of temper. He rubbed his hand along his jaw. "In that case, we could pretend to be cousins by marriage. And then we can both act appalled by the connection."

Jack laughed, feeling his anger dissipate. But Rivington's

blithe assumption that Jack wouldn't object to posing as a servant—as *his* servant, no less—reminded him of the gap that lay between them. He would have to tread carefully here. Because he very, very much wanted to strip every stitch of pricey clothing off Rivington's back and see what it felt like to get that man's lean body beneath his own. He wanted to know how many different ways he could make that handsome face flush with color. But he didn't want it so much that he was willing to sacrifice his self-respect.

# CHAPTER SEVEN

Since Oliver had been meaning to purchase a curricle anyway, he hadn't felt too bad about fibbing that he already had one. An afternoon spent at the carriage seller's and Tattersall's, and he was practically an honest man. Ordinarily he would balk at the notion of spending so much in a single day, but he had recently received the proceeds from the sale of his commission. There was probably some irony in the fact that the funds that had once made him a soldier were now equipping him for life as a frivolous man about town.

But he didn't care. Irony be damned. He had a purpose, and while he wasn't sure whether his purpose was to protect the Wraxhalls, buy an estate to house the wife he would likely never have, or get seduced by Turner, that purpose required a carriage and horses.

No. Get seduced by *Jack*. He was quite determined on that score. There were hardly any men alive whom Oliver addressed by their Christian names. Even his older brother had always been called by his courtesy title, even when they were children.

But you couldn't call a man by his surname when you were in bed with him. Or at least that was Oliver's best guess. His previous encounters had not, as a rule, involved beds or much conversation beyond the strictly logistical. He wanted to know what it was like when relations weren't hasty and shameful and soon forgotten.

He suspected that nothing about Jack Turner was hasty or shameful or soon forgotten.

Surely, his conscience ought to have something to say about this. At the very least Oliver might have expected a pang of concern about spending a week in the company of a man who, a few days earlier, he had found morally questionable in the extreme. But his scruples had begun to disappear around the time he learned that Charlotte needed precisely the kind of help that Jack could offer. By the time of their chaste little kiss, Oliver's conscience was nearly silent.

On Wednesday morning he turned his curricle up Sackville Street toward Turner's rooms. Jack emerged from the building with his brows knit together and dark circles under his eyes. The stubble on his jaw was visible at a distance of five yards and the scrape on his cheek looked angry. He couldn't look less reputable, Oliver thought. "Tie your case onto the back," Oliver called down, "and then hop up."

"What have you done with your valet?" Jack asked, climbing into the conveyance. "Tell me you haven't had him follow behind in another vehicle." His voice was laced through with scorn.

"I've done nothing of the sort." Not that it would be such an outrageous thing to do, though. Gentlemen frequently had their valets and sometimes their grooms travel separately

with the luggage. A curricle only comfortably sat two men
and wouldn't hold too much luggage strapped behind. Oliver,
however, had left his servants at Rutland House for a holiday,
because a man couldn't very well get himself seduced with his
valet looking on, could he? "I can fend for myself for a few
days, you know."

"Can you?" Jack slouched sullenly against the side of the
curricle.

"I was in the siege of Badajoz, for God's sake. I didn't have
a valet then."

"You were in Badajoz?" Jack asked. Of course he would
know what a bloodbath *that* had been. Everyone knew.

"Yes, and a number of other places besides," Oliver said
lightly, having no intention of summarizing his war record.
The sun was shining, the birds were singing, and it would
take a bigger fool than Oliver to let that nightmare intrude
into their day. "I don't care to talk about it."

"Why in hell would you?" Jack's tone managed to convey
sympathy for Oliver's experiences and scorn for anyone who
expected him to talk about them, while somehow giving the
impression that if Oliver were indeed looking to unburden
himself he need look no further. Or perhaps that last bit was
only Oliver's imagination run wild.

The farther they got from Sackville Street, the lower Jack's
spirits seemed to get, however. His occasional grumbles and
snide comments decreased in frequency until he was silent,
slumped despondently against the corner of the curricle seat,
his hat pulled low over his forehead.

It took Oliver another mile to realize what was bothering
Jack. It wasn't the company—if Jack hadn't wanted to make

this journey with Oliver he could have come up with any number of excuses. "Are you going to be sick?" Oliver asked cheerfully.

"Bugger off. No, I'm not going to be sick." After a moment he added, "I only *feel* like I'm going to be sick. But it never actually comes to pass."

"Oh, bad luck. I get seasick myself. Every time. Without fail, there I am, casting up my accounts over the side of the ship. It's only the puking that makes you feel better, you know."

Jack groaned and covered his face in his hands. "Are you trying to make it worse? Puking, indeed. Who raised you?"

That was rich, coming from a man who had confessed to having two criminals for parents. "Do I need to remind you for the second time in an hour that I spent the past ten years in the army, not flitting between tea parties and soirees?" He kept his voice easy, as if that distinction were of no import to him at all.

Jack grumbled incoherently.

Now that they were well north of London and the road was clear, Oliver decided to give the horses their heads and see what they were capable of. He kept the ribbons light in his hands and let the horses do the rest. Before long they were practically flying down the straight country road, and Oliver didn't regret a penny he had spent on them.

He realized Jack was sitting bolt upright, his ornery expression gone and replaced by something Oliver never thought he'd see in Jack Turner's face: bewilderment.

"I've never gone this fast," Jack said after a minute.

"Do you want me to rein them in?" He hoped not, but he'd do it anyway.

Jack seemed to be considering that option. "No."

"Do you want to hold the ribbons for a bit?"

Jack shuddered. "God no."

Oliver laughed. Well, well. Jack didn't like horses, or traveling, or some combination of the two. This was the first time in their dealings that Oliver felt he had the upper hand. He wasn't sure what he would do with this sense of power, but the possibilities seemed very promising indeed.

"Look at that sheep." Rivington gestured with his chin. "It looks like it hasn't been shorn in two years." He had one arm slung along the back of the curricle bench and was using the other to hold the ribbons.

"Don't you think you ought to keep both hands on that thing?" Jack didn't know which had him more disconcerted, the proximity of Rivington's arm or the apparent disregard he had for either of their lives.

The problem with travel—apart from the fact that it took you increasingly farther from London, which was bad enough, really—was the horses. Horrible animals. They could kill you as fast as a pistol and with less warning, too. All it took was for the beast to hear a clap of thunder or catch wind of smoke and it would lose all sense, and the next thing you knew you were in a ditch, or kicked in the head. Or at least that was Jack's understanding of the situation.

"Bugger the sheep," Jack grumbled, which caused Rivington to burst into a riot of laughter.

Jack had been born and raised—in so far as a child who was left up to his own devices from the age of mobility can be said to have been raised—in London. As far as he cared, there was little that he wanted to see that wasn't within walking distance of Charing Cross. He hired a hackney if absolutely necessary and if a client was paying for it, because while his pockets weren't totally empty, he still wasn't going to pay for the privilege of being killed by a mad horse. No, if he were going to meet an untimely end there were plenty of people who would gladly stick a knife in his back or unload a pistol in his general direction—the way of his forefathers, as it were.

A little after midday they arrived at an inn. While Rivington set about hiring a fresh pair of horses and arranging for his own animals to be sent back to London, Jack stumbled into to the taproom and ordered a tankard of ale. He was halfway done when he heard Rivington come up behind him—the sound of the walking stick always gave him away.

"Did it ever occur to you, Rivington," Jack asked without turning his head, "that the world would be a better place if we could use dogs to pull carriages?"

Rivington slid into the seat next to Jack's. "I can't say that it has."

Jack would give Rivington credit for not treating him like an escaped bedlamite. "Dogs are reasonable, predictable creatures." He tried to sound very sane. "Give them some meat, scratch them behind the ears, refrain from kicking them, and you have a friend for life. Horses, on the other hand, are a roll of the dice."

There was a lengthy silence, during which Jack supposed Rivington was deciding whether to summon the authorities. "Are you afraid of horses, Jack?" His voice hovered in that careful middle ground between merry riposte and gentle query. Rivington was no novice at dealing with men who were out of their heads, then.

He supposed he had Georgie to thank for this "Jack" business, but there was no unringing that bell. "It's not fear, Rivington." He deliberately used the man's surname, glad to score a single point that day. "I see horses every day. I'm not a hermit, nor do I live on some desert isle. Horses are a fact of life. It is, however, an objectively terrible idea to let yourself be dragged around the country at breakneck speeds by an animal that can't be trusted to behave reasonably."

"Ah," was all he got by way of response.

On the next leg of the journey, Rivington was evidently feeling chatty. He talked as if under a spell in the sort of fairy story you told to only the naughtiest of children: the sad tale of a child who couldn't hold his tongue and was subsequently put under a witch's hex, to the effect that the brat could never stop talking unless he wanted his tongue to shrivel and fall off. Except in this case, Rivington produced easy chatter with the same effortless composure with which he did everything else.

The man seemed to have an endless supply of anecdotes about far-flung parts of the world. Cairo and Argentina and New Orleans, to say nothing of all the places in Spain and Portugal that Jack had read about during the recent war. At first all Jack could think was that there were so many places in the world that were Not London, an observation he did not say out loud, knowing that Rivington already likely thought him weak in the head after this morning's fit of nerves.

But then something changed—perhaps it was the easy cadence of Rivington's speech, or the obvious fascination the man had for all these foreign parts, or the way he made those places come to life with a few words. Hell, maybe it was the two pints of ale Jack had consumed on an empty stomach, or the fact that Rivington's neatly tailored clothes and handsome face were covered in a healthy layer of dust from the road, giving him an unexpectedly raffish look. But whatever the cause, Jack started asking questions, and it changed from a monologue to a conversation.

"Do you think you'll visit any of those places again?" Jack asked, almost without realizing what he was doing.

"I hope I do." Rivington kept eyes fixed on the road ahead of them. "And without war to get in the way of seeing things properly this time."

Jack would rather not travel so far as Greenwich, let alone anyplace he'd be hard-pressed to find on a map. "When I think of the world as being as big as it truly is, I feel like I'm going to be sick," he confessed, which was likely the stupidest statement ever made by a man who relied on his wits to earn a living.

But Rivington only blandly agreed, and, as if sensing Jack's discomfort, launched into a description of a meal he had eaten in the ruins of a fort in some place Jack had never heard of and would likely never hear of again.

There were worse companions for this sort of voyage than Rivington—that much was obvious. That was something else Jack couldn't stand about travel, the endless stretches of time with nothing to do but chatter. But with Rivington it was no burden. On the contrary, he was better company than you'd think the son of an earl would be. It was almost . . . pleasant to sit next to him on the curricle bench, occasionally catching a whiff of that pricey laundry soap, sometimes stealing a glimpse at his perfect profile.

The next time they hit a bad stretch of road, Rivington shot him a reassuring smile. Jack realized then that Rivington was deliberately using this steady stream of chatter to soothe Jack's nerves. Blast the man. Jack would not tolerate being managed like a tiresome child.

So he did the only thing he could to even the score. He set about making things difficult for Rivington. When Rivington expertly brought the horses around a curve, Jack exaggerated the movement caused by the sway of the carriage and leaned into Rivington's arm. Glancing over, he saw that Rivington had a faint blush on his cheeks.

He couldn't help but feel triumphant every time he saw that blush.

When they stopped at the next inn and ordered supper, Jack caused his arm to brush Rivington's when he reached for the salt cellar. He adjusted Rivington's cravat, leered at his breeches, raised his eyebrows suggestively, made every double entendre he could think of, and in general made a nuisance of himself. By the time the meal was over and they were climbing back into the curricle, Rivington's face was permanently flushed. But Jack wasn't done.

"You know," he said, as if the idea had only just occurred to him, "I think I'll take you up on that offer to hold the ribbons for a while." He paused, so his next request would have greater impact. "But do you think you could contrive not to let go of the ribbons yourself?"

Rivington likely knew exactly what Jack was about, of course, but he was too much the bloody gentleman to retract his offer. So he handed over the ribbons and then reached an arm around Jack. Now Rivington's chest was pressed against Jack's back, his hands touching Jack's, his breath ruffling the hair beneath the brim of Jack's hat.

Jack was quite enjoying this. He nearly forgot that he was handling giant murderous beasts, so focused was he on the presence of Rivington's body next to his, the wiry arms entangled with his own, the scent of laundry soap and wine that was fast becoming something that made his cock leap to attention.

But then Rivington spoke, his voice a hoarse and thready murmur in Jack's ear, and Jack nearly dropped the ribbons. All he was saying was horse-related piffle that Jack paid no attention to because he had no intention of ever driving a curricle again. But his voice. God help him, his voice was something Jack would never forget. This was how the man would sound in bed, when he was at the edge of not being able to hold out any longer. His voice was low and urgent and Jack didn't trust himself to say anything at all in response.

Instead he dropped the ribbons entirely, leaving Rivington to sort them out, and spent the rest of the drive silent and painfully aroused. The fact that Rivington was likely in the same state did nothing to make Jack feel like he had won a victory.

Try as he might, Oliver couldn't get his left boot off. Usually he could contrive to manage it, but his knee was stiff and his leg more swollen than usual after a day spent mostly sitting, to say nothing of how fashionably snug these boots were to begin with. He rang for a servant but either the bell pull was broken or standards were lacking at this rural inn, because he had pulled the cord no fewer than twelve times, but still no servant came.

The more he thought about it the more desperate the situation seemed. He wanted this boot off and he wanted it now. Wasn't it bad enough that he had to spend every day ignoring pain and living in a world that was damned hard to manage if you didn't have two working legs? Now he couldn't get his own blasted boot off and couldn't summon anyone to help him? If he had to put his right boot back on, shuffle down the stairs, speak to the innkeeper, and then climb the stairs again, he would be spitting mad.

"Damnation!" He flung his right boot against the wall. "Damn, piss, and hell!" It wasn't often that he let his temper get the better of him, so perhaps he was only out of practice, because throwing things and cursing didn't bring nearly as much relief as he had hoped.

Next thing he heard a tapping at the door. About time. "Come in," he grumbled, embarrassed that the inn servant heard him swear.

But it wasn't a servant. It was Jack, the last person on earth he wanted to witness him in such a state. Jack shut the door behind him but didn't step any further into the room.

"What can I help you with, Turner?" he asked, knowing he sounded peevish and not caring a bit.

"It sounded like you were wrestling a bear in here." Jack's hands were jammed in his pockets as he leaned against the closed door. On his face there was an inscrutable half smile. "Whatever it was, I didn't want to miss out on a good show."

Oh, so Jack had come to make sport, had he? Well, to hell with that. "It's my boot," he said from between gritted teeth. "I can't get it off myself."

"I should think not," Jack said, his voice infuriatingly calm. "They're cut so close."

"It's not the cut," Oliver ground out. Although that was certainly part of it, and he wished he hadn't let Charlotte talk him into this particular pair, no matter how dashing they looked. "It's my damned leg. And apparently the servants here do not understand the concept of a bell pull."

"Let me." Jack crossed the room and knelt before Oliver's chair.

Oliver couldn't bear to even look. "Quite unnecessary." He wanted this man to leave, not help. "If you wouldn't mind fetching me a servant, though, I'd be very much in your debt." So help him, if Jack made a rude comment about Oliver's dependence on a valet he'd set something on fire.

"Bollocks." The swear was low but emphatic. "I've pulled off a good many boots in my life."

"Oh, pity for a cripple?"

"Don't be an idiot. Pity, my arse. I can't imagine a world where I feel pity for the likes of the Honorable Captain Rivington, with his thousand pounds a year and his family connections." There it was again, that trace of . . . *something* in his accent. Something guttural and unrefined and real. "I only meant that it's hard to take your own boots off even if you haven't been shot in the leg. It's not pity, only reality. You helped me with my shirt the other night and I didn't act like it was an insult, did I?"

"Fine," he said, not able to summon up anything that

resembled gratitude. He shut his eyes, overwhelmed by the wonderfully filthy sight of Jack kneeling on the floor before him. Oliver was afraid that as soon as Jack laid a hand on him he'd embarrass himself. That would be the final humiliation.

But Jack made fast work of the boot, relying on a few efficient movements and not burdening Oliver's leg with a single unnecessary touch. That was a surprise and maybe a disappointment after the way he had carried on in the carriage. But still, Oliver nearly groaned with relief once the boot was off. As soon as he was alone he would slather his leg with the liniment the apothecary had given him. It smelled like peppermint mixed with goose fat and cheap gin but it worked like the hand of God.

"Better?" Jack asked.

"Yes." Oliver opened his eyes. "Thank you," he added belatedly.

"Good," Jack said, but he didn't rise to his feet. He remained on the floor, tantalizingly close to Oliver's ever-hardening cock. "Are we quite done with the cranky and resentful portion of this evening?" His voice was gravelly and serious.

"Mmmm," was all Oliver trusted himself to say.

Jack touched Oliver's knee with one big hand, sliding it ever so slowly up.

"Oh God," Oliver said, the words sounding wrenched from his gut. He watched Jack's hand slide further up his thigh, heard the low rumble of his laugh. Oliver had never done this—whatever precisely this turned out to be—without having to ask, and seldom without having to pay for it. He had wondered so often what it might be like in different circumstances, if he had the luxury of letting physical relief come only after the slow simmer of desire. But now he changed his mind. He didn't think he could take the suspense.

"You ought to get on with it." Oliver sounded needy and desperate to his own ears. "Unless you want me to have an apoplexy. Just so you know."

"No, I don't think I will get on with it." Jack slid his hand an inch closer to where Oliver wanted it. "I'm going to take my time with you, Rivington."

Oliver groaned. "Well, I'll be dead soon, so you're going to run out of time."

Jack paid this no heed. "Look," he said wonderingly. "You're so hard and I've scarcely touched you." With that, he let his knuckles graze Oliver's rigid cock.

As if Oliver needed to be told to look. There was no chance he could look anywhere on earth besides Jack's hand resting on his thigh. "God help me," Oliver breathed.

"This is going to be *fun*," Jack said, rising to his feet and planting a hand on each of the arms of Oliver's chair. Oliver made a sound of protest at the loss of contact. "I'm going to *enjoy* this." He bent and brushed his lips over Oliver's. "So are you." It sounded more like a threat than a promise.

Oliver needed more, though. This faint touch of lips against lips was not going to do. He reached his hands up to tangle in Jack's dark hair, tugging his head closer and pressing their lips together with greater urgency.

He felt Jack's tongue slide between his own lips, exploring, touching. Maddening. Oliver responded by drawing Jack's tongue into his mouth, and felt triumphant when he heard the other man groan helplessly. Good. Two could play at this. Oliver would be damned if he was the only one panting with desire.

Oliver took advantage of the moment by pulling Jack down onto his lap—onto his good leg, really. Jack came willingly, without breaking the kiss, and while his weight ought to have been too much for Oliver's leg, he relished the solid pressure of Jack's body so close to his own. The next thing Oliver knew his cravat was gone, simply vanished to God knew where, and Jack was pressing kisses along his neck. He let his own hands explore the other man's broad shoulders and strong back, his own desire ramping up every time he felt those bulky muscles move and shift. He flicked open the buttons of Jack's waistcoat and started working on the closures of his shirt.

"No," Jack murmured into Oliver's neck. "Not tonight."

Impossible. "You cannot be serious."

"Oh, I'm perfectly serious." His voice was wonderfully rough. "I meant it when I said I was going to take my time with you. I'm not rushing this."

*Time.* That was what Oliver wanted too, even more than he wanted immediate relief from the desire that was consuming all his senses. He wanted something that wasn't hurried and soon forgotten.

"Fine," he whispered. "Take your time, then."

Jack leaned back and Oliver could see the pulse throbbing in his neck. "It'll make it that much better when I finally do fuck you, you know." He made that word sound like a caress. Oliver felt like he heard it with his cock instead of his ears.

Oliver let out a breath that sounded like a whimper. He only sat still, his erection throbbing in his breeches. "You ought to call me Oliver," was all he could think to say.

"Hmmm. Maybe I ought to, but I don't think I will." And after one more lingering kiss Jack rose to his feet and left the room.

## CHAPTER EIGHT

Jack's heart sank as the curricle rolled into Pickworth.

"This is quite charming," Rivington said approvingly. "Very picturesque."

And so it was. "I know," Jack agreed glumly. The place was as bad as he had imagined. Passersby stopped to chat with one another. Pinafore-clad girls carried market baskets along the main street. This was likely the sort of village in which everyone knew one another. There would be no way for Jack to safely disappear into a crowd, no network of back alleys that he knew by heart, no trusted confederates or willing accomplices. Well, one confederate, if he could be called that.

He'd been to a hundred such places with former employers or on previous investigations. As far as he cared they were all alike. Even the inhabitants seemed to look alike, with their countrified clothes and pointlessly friendly manners. He missed the whores and the urchins. He even missed the ridiculous toffs, although he supposed he had brought his own ridiculous toff along with him.

The ridiculous toff in question deftly wheeled the curricle

into the inn yard. Jack grimaced. He could now add skill with horses to the list of items he reluctantly found arousing, right behind ludicrously scented laundry soap. Which only went to show that all that time bouncing along in a carriage addled one's brains. After two and a half days of watching Rivington handle pair after pair of horses—which he insisted on referring to by their color, as if their feelings might be hurt if they realized they weren't any different from all the other stupid fucking horses in the world—he now knew that his pulse sped up every time the man masterfully rounded a corner or avoided a ditch with no more effort than a flick of one elegant hand.

"You all right, Jack?" Rivington asked, and Jack couldn't tell if he was poking fun or genuinely concerned.

It seemed safe to assume a lack of concern. At least—didn't it? Jack pretty much took it as an article of faith that aristocrats were not inclined to care whether any mere commoners lived or died, let alone whether they were bothered by a fancy bit of curricle driving. But when Jack looked over at Rivington, he didn't see a high-handed aristocrat. He only saw the man he wanted to have in his arms.

"I'm bloody fantastic," Jack responded with as much acid as he could manage, which wasn't much at all. Deplorable, really.

The other night Jack had barely been able to calm himself down after those shenanigans in Rivington's room. By all rights that should only have been the first act in a mightily filthy three-act play. Hell, Rivington certainly seemed more than game. It was Jack himself who wasn't ready yet. But he had a plan and he was keeping to it. He thought he had figured out a way to thoroughly enjoy Rivington, without ever losing the upper hand. First, he'd wait until Rivington was positively begging for it. Second, he was going to remain in total control over the encounter. So, when they had arrived late last night in a hamlet located somewhere between the middle of nowhere and the gates of hell, Jack made sure a servant was sent to Rivington's room to help him with his boots and then took himself directly off to bed.

Now, as Jack looked on, a pair of stable boys jostled one another across the inn yard for the privilege of tending to Rivington's horses. It was impossible to forget who and what Rivington was—barkeeps kept his glass filled, boot boys bowed and scraped. Rivington responded to the lot of them with an endless supply of shiny coins and a sunny nonchalance, as if it never occurred to him that a person might be met with any other treatment.

Jack needed to breathe for a minute. "I'll meet you back in the taproom in half an hour," he called over his shoulder as he hopped out of the curricle. He headed across the inn yard without waiting for a response. A walk always cleared his head.

Even though this village likely consisted of little more than a row of cottages, a church, and an inn serving watered-down ale, it would be a relief to spend a few days in the same place. Jack had relied utterly on Rivington for all things related to navigation—the geography of the north of England was nothing more than an ominous question mark to Jack. This morning, as plain as day, he had seen mountains to the west, mountains that he was certain had no business being in England at all, and yet there they were, which only went to show how completely unreliable everything became the farther one got from London.

He located the church steeple at the opposite end of the high street and decided to make that the destination of his walk. Before beginning his investigations he wanted to get the lay of the land. On the way to the church he passed a couple of modest-looking houses and the sort of shops you'd expect to see in a village of this size—a chandler, an apothecary, a drygoods merchant. Some smaller roads bisected the high road at any and all angles other than perpendicular.

The church was situated at the top of a small rise. Jack passed through the lynch gate and saw that the churchyard spilled down the hill toward a stream, the gravestones looking for all the world like they were about to tumble into the water. But if they had managed to survive a couple hundred years without landing in the stream—and according to the dates on some of the stones they had done precisely that—he guessed they'd survive a couple hundred more. The effect was still unsettling.

Beyond the churchyard, a wooden bridge crossed the stream, leading to a house that had to be the vicarage. Also on the other side of the stream was a hill that was the mirror image of the one Jack stood on, on top of which was a very large house. That had to be Pickworth Hall, the house where Mrs. Wraxhall had grown up. Her father had bought it from an impoverished gentleman after making a pile of money building canals, and even more investing in the mills and mines that used the canals.

He could see how another person might find this place charming, with its crooked streets and profusions of ivy, but

Jack felt like a fish in a bowl—nothing to look at, little to do, altogether too visible and too vulnerable.

When he returned to the inn, he found Rivington already waiting for him in the taproom, conversing easily with a man about his own age. So, he had run into a friend. Not a surprise—the gentry made it their business to know people in towns and villages all over the globe. The richer the man, the more likely it was that he had gone to a school whose only purpose was to introduce him to other rich lads and make all of them unfit for the company of anyone but themselves.

He pushed aside the thought of exactly how companionable he had found Rivington over the past few days. Well, that was done with. Now that Rivington had found one of his own he'd be uneasy about the connection with Jack, he'd be reminded of how totally unsuitable it was for them to be so much as traveling together, never even mind anything else. As he watched them, Jack felt something alarmingly close to jealousy seeping into the edges of his thoughts.

But then Rivington caught sight of Jack and his face broke into a grin that caused Jack's breath to catch. "Turner!" he called, waving him over. "This is Nicholas Peale, formerly of His Majesty's Army. We were in Belgium together."

Peale rose and shook Jack's hand. "Belgium—that much is true. I can't remember half the other places."

Jack wondered if they had already performed the British upper class ritual of listing everyone they knew in common or if he'd have to sit through that. Rivington and his friend were wearing nearly identical country attire, which did nothing to assuage Jack's feelings that he was an outsider. That was another thing these rich bastards did, all these costume changes. All the better to keep the club exclusive, he supposed. He had spent enough years as a valet to know the rules governing what to wear and when to wear it, but he never failed to be amazed by the sheer expense of the wardrobe required to be rich.

To be fair, though, Rivington looked damned well in his riding coat. Whatever outrageous sum he had paid for it had been money well spent. However much Jack detested the class it signified, he wouldn't mind peeling it off Rivington's shoulders later on.

"You know," Rivington was saying, "my sister has a friend who lives somewhere around here but I can't remember her name. You remember Charlotte, she has friends from every town and village in the kingdom. So when she heard I was coming to Pickworth she was quite insistent that I call on her friend. But I'm afraid I wasn't paying the least bit of attention to what the lady's name was. I'm going to be in frightful trouble, aren't I?"

Now, what the devil was this? Rivington hadn't said anything about using this line to get information, and Jack didn't like to see the script changed without his consent.

"Well, you're in luck," Peale said, "because I know all the ladies in a five-mile radius."

Rivington laughed dutifully. Jack resisted the urge to fold his arms across his chest in impatience.

"There's Miss Barrow at the cottage. Old Mrs. Durbin lives at Pickworth Hall but she spends most of her time at Tunbridge Wells or Bath or wherever it is old ladies go. I have to say that I doubt whether she ever crossed paths with any sister of yours, Rivington, although her daughter married a man with some or another connection to respectable people so it's not out of the question."

Mrs. Durbin was Mrs. Wraxhall's mother. Jack was impressed that Rivington didn't show so much as a flicker of interest when the name was mentioned.

"The vicar's sister, Miss Ingleby, died last year, quite suddenly," Peale continued. "He's been at sixes and sevens since then with no one to keep his house, but that's neither here nor there. Let's see, who else is there? There's Lady de Vere but I think she and Sir John spend so much time in London your sister would simply call on them herself rather than foist the job on you. And I suppose it could be Mrs. Lewis," he added with obvious doubt. "She's a gentlewoman, but her husband, Hector Lewis, is one of the mill owners near Dewsbury. Which sounds very sordid, believe me I know, but they're quite rich and one never knows." He shrugged, as if apologizing for a world where mill owners ran free among the gentry.

Hector Lewis was the man who wrote the letters that were stolen from Mrs. Wraxhall. Once again Jack was impressed with Rivington's sangfroid.

"It has to be one of them, I daresay." Rivington swirled the ale in his glass. "After all, how many ladies can a village this size possibly hold?"

When Peale took his leave a few minutes later Jack looked closely at his companion. "You lie much better than I would have thought." As he said it, he didn't know whether it was a compliment or an insult. And by the looks of things, neither did Rivington.

"**W**hy are we starting with this Miss Barrow?" Oliver asked. Had they truly needed to choose the person who lived farthest from the inn? And why hadn't he thought to use the curricle? He had hoped, against all reason, that walking in the countryside might be more manageable than walking in London, despite years of evidence that—contrary to what surgeons liked to advise—fresh air and a verdant setting in fact did nothing to ease his pain.

"Because she's the first person your Mr. Peale mentioned." Jack was silent for a few more paces. "Also because she was Mrs. Wraxhall's governess until two years before her marriage."

Oliver stopped walking and swung around to face Jack. He had known the identity of Mrs. Wraxhall's likeliest confidante and hadn't said anything about it? Oliver wasn't under the impression that he was owed any information—this was Jack's matter, not his. But still, he had liked the thought that this trip was, to some extent, a joint undertaking.

"How much more are you not telling me?" Oliver could almost taste the coldness of his tone.

"Heaps," Jack said in an infuriatingly offhand manner that was all the more annoying since Oliver was looking for a reason to be uncivil.

"We were in the same carriage for days. You might have told me you knew where to find the lady's governess, you know." Even as he spoke he knew he was being petty—it wasn't as if Oliver had been in a position to do anything with the information even if Jack had seen fit to tell him. He just didn't like the sensation of having been kept in the dark, of not being trusted.

"But I *didn't* know where to find her, not until half an hour ago, when your Mr. Peale said she lived in the village. My understanding was that she had found another post after Mrs. Wraxhall—Miss Durbin at the time—reached an age where she no longer required a governess. But for whatever reason, she returned to Pickworth, and now we're going to see her."

They resumed their walk in silence until turning onto the lane that led to the cottage.

"Look, Oliver. I'm a right bastard but you knew that already." Jack's voice was gruff, but his hand brushed against Oliver's in a way seemed deliberate, almost conciliatory. "You're not going to hold it against me, are you?" As far as apologies went, it was lacking, but it was the first time Jack had addressed him by his Christian name and Oliver fully intended to savor it.

Before Oliver had to come up with a suitable response, he caught sight of the cottage.

Jack whistled low under his breath.

"I can hardly believe this place is real," Oliver said, pausing in order to better admire the sight. The cottage itself was made of the same grayish brown stone as most of the buildings they had seen in this part of the country. He didn't know why the building was referred to by locals simply as "the cottage." It looked rather like it had once been a dower house or hunting lodge or some other outbuilding associated with nearby Pickworth Hall.

While the cottage itself was pretty, what made this place astonishing was the garden. There was a profusion of flowers—vivid purple Canterbury bells and soft yellow primroses, foxgloves in every shade of pink and a carpet of violets. He caught the clove scent of sweet William before he saw the clusters of tiny red flowers. Every square inch of soil had been planted and carefully tended by someone with an almost preternatural ability to make things grow.

Oliver knew nothing about gardening. What he did know was that he might sell his soul at a crossroads to live in a place half so lovely. A man could forget about war and evil in a place like this.

Suddenly, his walking stick caught in between two stones and he lost his footing. Damn it, he was going to fall and tear up his breeches right on this lady's doorstep. But then he felt Jack's arm around him, supporting him as easily as if Oliver weighed no more than a kitten.

"Steady now," Jack said easily, as if half-crippled men fell into his arms as a normal occurrence. They stood there for a minute, Jack's arm around Oliver's waist, their mouths only inches apart. "I'm going to let go if you're all right," Jack finally said, his voice rough.

Oliver murmured something suitable and stood up straight. His leg—to say nothing of his mind—would never let him forget about war and evil, not even in such a pretty place as this. But damn it if he wouldn't like a chance to try.

He picked his way more carefully along the stone walkway as it wound through the garden, arriving at the cottage's front door, which was painted a shade of green that made it fade into the ivy-covered walls. A neatly dressed maid answered the door and took Oliver's calling card.

"Cottage, my arse," Jack said, as they stood in the small vestibule awaiting the maid's return. Indeed, most cottages did not have Hepplewhite chairs littered about the entryway, nor were most cottages freshly plastered and painted.

The maid directed them into an adjacent sitting room. Oliver had to duck his head to pass under the lintel. On the settee sat a lady of about thirty, a book opened spine-up on her lap, her hand raised to her mouth to cover a yawn. Three books were in similar positions on nearby tables. A tea cup was balanced on top of a stack of books, and one of the walls was lined with bookcases holding dozens of volumes.

"Mr. Rivington?" She was wearing a white muslin day dress and her pale brown hair was falling out of what had this morning likely been a tidy arrangement. "Do sit, if you can find a place. To what do I owe the honor?" Her voice sounded rusty, as if she had only now woken from a nap.

Oliver removed a shawl from one chair and watched Jack try to rouse a sleeping kitten from another. "Thank you so much," he said, smiling apologetically. "I couldn't have walked another step, I'm afraid." He gestured to his walking stick. "And Mr. Turner here was positively done in by your bluebells, Miss Barrow, and insisted on meeting the—what did you say, Mr. Turner—ah, yes, the artist responsible for such a bewitching creation. That was it." He liked this fictional Mr. Turner, and liked even more that the real Jack probably did not.

Miss Barrow laughed, a genteel tinkle of a sound. "My gardener is the artist, I'm afraid. I do nothing but agree to whatever schemes he comes up with. He's been here longer than I have and I'm loathe to ruffle his feathers."

"Are you not originally from Pickworth, then, Miss Barrow? I was rather hoping you were. You see, my sister,

Lady Montbray, instructed me to call on an acquaintance of hers in this neighborhood." He smiled ruefully. "But the trouble is I forgot her name." He supposed they ought to keep to the same story throughout their visit in case the villagers compared notes. Besides, it was hardly a lie at all: if he had in fact told Charlotte that he was coming to Pickworth, she would doubtless have dragged out someone or another for him to visit, and likely as not he would have promptly forgotten the name. So it was, if not precisely the truth, at least a close second.

"Oh, you gentlemen, never writing things down," she said indulgently. "No, I haven't had the pleasure of meeting your sister."

Tea arrived, carried by the same maid who had answered the door. The tea was very good and the china was of a quality that even Charlotte wouldn't be embarrassed to possess. That, compounded with the proliferation of calf-bound books and the abundance of very fine furniture meant only one thing: Miss Barrow was no impoverished gentlewoman, regardless of having once been a governess. Had she come into an inheritance, perhaps? Jack would want to know.

But when Jack spoke, it seemed to have nothing to do with their purpose in coming here. "Is your gardener here today, Miss Barrow?" Jack asked, speaking for the first time since entering the room. "I wonder if I could speak to him."

"I daresay he's pottering in the back garden. Be careful or he'll talk your ear off."

Jack was gone instantly.

"He's plant-mad," Oliver offered by way of explanation. "Can't make him think of anything else."

"Well, he and Norris will be equally matched, then."

"The family that owns the house on the hill is called Durbin, are they not? A friend of mine, Francis Wraxhall, married a Miss Durbin last year some time. Can't remember when, because I was still on the Continent. But I'm wondering if it's the same family."

For an instant too long the lady stared at him in surprise. "Oh, yes, you're talking about Lydia Durbin. I was her governess for some time, in fact." After an awkward pause, she added, "Lovely girl," and Oliver supposed she couldn't say anything else.

"But what I don't understand," Oliver went on, "is what Wraxhall was doing in Yorkshire. His people are from Norfolk." He could thank Debrett's for that piece of knowledge.

"You're quite right, of course. The Durbins went to Brighton for Mr. Durbin's health, and the next thing anyone knew Lydia was engaged. She never came back to Pickworth, not even for the wedding. She was married in Brighton and they went to London directly after. It caused quite the uproar." She leaned forward and brushed one of the stray tendrils of hair behind her ear. "Because, you see, everyone thought she was going to marry—" She stopped abruptly, apparently realizing she was speaking to a stranger.

"I never heard her called a jilt, or anything like that," Oliver said in between sips of tea, as if there was nothing remarkable about this conversation, just two well-bred people talking about the antics of someone less refined.

"That's because she wasn't truly engaged to the other man. The banns were never read. It was simply understood in both households that Lydia would marry Mr. Lewis."

It was simply understood that they would marry. An odd way of referring to a youthful dalliance, he thought.

Odder still when you considered what Charlotte had said about Wraxhall and Lydia Durbin having been caught in a compromising situation before their marriage. Had Lewis refused to marry her after she was compromised? Or was there some other explanation?

They were interrupted by the vicar, who entered the room without being announced by the maid. Oliver rose to greet the man and take his leave from Miss Barrow. "Thank you for tea and for giving shelter to a pair of weary travelers, Miss Barrow."

"Nonsense," she replied distractedly, giving Oliver her hand while looking at the vicar. "I hope you find your sister's friend."

He found Jack in the back garden talking with the gardener. The midsummer sun was only beginning to set, glinting off Jack's overlong hair in a way that brought out flecks of colors he hadn't expected to find there—gold and copper and brass and maybe even the first strands of silver.

In London they had mainly seen one another at night or indoors; Turner was a man who preferred to hide his face in shadows and darkness. This was not Jack Turner's natural habitat, as it were, these green hills and extravagant blooms. And yet, the setting seemed to crystallize a thought that had been lurking in the recesses of Oliver's mind for days.

It was more than attraction. Seeing Jack like this was the first inkling Oliver had that he could feel more for him than interest in a passing dalliance. Jack Turner's face was one that could be dear to him.

# CHAPTER NINE

How long had Rivington been standing there watching him? Jack scowled but received a smile in return. He had needed to leave that house with all its reminders of this world he didn't belong to, didn't want to belong to. In fact, he very much wanted to have nothing to do with anyone in that world, except take their money in exchange for honest—and occasionally dishonest—work. It was Oliver Rivington, blast him, who seemed to constitute the single exception to that rule.

Georgie had been right of course, but it was too late to wring hands. He had known better than to get mixed up with the son of an earl. But now he wanted Rivington, with his too-handsome face and his too-polished manners more than he'd wanted anything or anyone in a good while. And he would have him. But then he would be done with Rivington—with gentlemen—for good.

"Come on," he said, his voice gruff, "let's get back before dark." He wanted to ask if Oliver would be able to make the walk home, but knew he'd only embarrass the man—and himself—with any show of solicitude. So he kept his peace, but made sure he matched his pace to Rivington's slower one.

"Did you learn anything from the lady?" Jack asked as they walked.

"Perhaps," Rivington said, as if considering the matter. "Are we sharing information now?"

So he was going to be like that, was he? "Oh, sod off."

But Oliver laughed and flashed him a wicked smile before sharing what Miss Barrow had told him of the former Miss Durbin. "It turns out I have a talent for making conversation with ladies." He gave his walking stick a twirl in the air. "It's quite wasted on me, of course, but it's a talent nonetheless."

Jack would *not* be charmed by how proud the man sounded. "Talent, my arse." But it was true. At every inn Rivington found a baby to coo at or an old woman to prattle with. Yesterday Jack had watched him listen raptly to a farmer's lecture on hop yields, a subject Rivington couldn't possibly care about. "As for your talents with the ladies," Jack continued, "I've already told you that you need to watch out or you'll find yourself married by Michaelmas. But I think you're safe as far as Miss Barrow goes. She'll marry Ingleby."

"The vicar?" He sounded surprised. Would he never grasp the extent of Jack's knowledge? "Did the gardener tell you that?"

"No." Jack sighed impatiently. "The vicar walked into her house through the garden door without knocking, which suggests intimacy. He needs a wife—your friend Peale said the man's been a mess since his sister died, and you can see for yourself that he needs looking after. He missed a spot on his chin when he was shaving and his coat is covered in lint and God knows what else. Those are things that anyone can see."

Rivington made a noise of protest.

"Or, rather, that anyone could see if they looked," Jack amended. "To those facts, I'd add the following suppositions. Miss Barrow was likely friends with the vicar's late sister, and I wouldn't be shocked if Miss Ingleby's will left a small income to Miss Barrow. Ingleby clearly has connections—this parish likely gives him a good living without much work—so it follows that his sister might have had money of her own."

Now Rivington shot him a skeptical look, as if he thought Jack was spinning a yarn. Insulting. He supposed they could verify the terms of Miss Ingleby's will, but he wouldn't go to that kind of trouble simply to earn this man's respect.

"It's too bad we didn't learn anything about Mrs. Wraxhall's letters," Rivington said after a moment, in a bald attempt to change the topic. Jack did *not* appreciate being on the receiving end of Rivington's bloody perfect manners.

"But we did," Jack said. "Miss Barrow is no blackmailer. She's utterly shiftless and was certainly a very bad governess, which goes some distance toward explaining why her charge was so wayward. Nobody that disorganized and lazy could manage blackmail. She probably can scarcely manage to order meat from the butcher." The lady obviously spent her days reading, napping, and eating biscuits. He didn't know whether to be disgusted or jealous. "Come to think of it, I'd lay even odds that the little maid we saw is robbing her mistress whenever she gets a chance, and I can hardly fault her. But never mind that. It's not our affair, and besides, I expect Ingleby is the sort of man who manages his accounts with some precision, so the pilfering will stop after they are married." He kept his gaze fixed resolutely ahead, not wanting to know what expressions were crossing Rivington's face.

"Are you having me on? You can't possibly know even half that much." They had crossed the footbridge and were now in the churchyard. The sun had set behind the hills and darkness was coming fast. "Show me." Rivington demanded. "What do you know about me?"

He should have said no, in the clearest and most expletive-ridden terms. He did not perform parlor tricks for the amusement of the aristocracy, for people who were too lazy or too inept to do what he did. But he wanted to prove himself, he wanted this man to know who he was dealing with.

He wanted to lay Rivington bare, let him know exactly how exposed he was.

He wanted to scare the man away, before it was too late.

Jack stopped walking. "Fine." He turned to face Oliver in the middle of the graveyard. "Fine," he repeated, as if convincing himself. "We've already established that you're bored. That's why you're here. No, don't interrupt. You're lonely."

He touched Rivington's shoulder, as if to soften the blow. Maybe to let him know he wasn't the only lonely one in this quickly darkening boneyard, not that Jack would ever say so out loud. "You were never particularly close with your sister," he went on. "She didn't tell you why she needed my services. But I know you're fond of her because you were livid when you came to see me that first day, but since then I've hardly seen you anything other than calm, even when you fought off those ruffians in the alley. You're not close at all to your older brother—you've never so much as mentioned him."

Jack paused in his recitation, looking intently at Rivington. Not for confirmation—he needed no confirmation to know he had spoken the truth. No, he wanted permission to go on. Rivington gave a quick nod and Jack continued.

"That's all very easy. Here's what interests me." Oh God, was he really going to do this? Could he even stop if he wanted? "Who did Oliver Rivington play with as a child? You were lonely then too, I think. How happy you must have been to go away to school. You liked school for the same reason you liked the army—there were people everywhere. Of course you had to hide your . . . proclivities or risk being hated." He took a step closer, and Rivington backed up. "Shunned." Another step, and now Rivington was backed up against a monument. "Expelled. Cashiered." Jack kept inching forward even though there was no place left for Rivington to go. "Arrested. Pilloried." He braced his hands on the cold stone behind the other man's shoulders. "Hanged." A sigh escaped from Rivington's chest and his shoulders dropped. "Believe me, I know. The loneliness is always there for you, isn't it?"

Rivington made no sound, but even in the darkness Jack could see that his eyes were wide. There was more he could have told the man but that was enough. Instead he leaned forward. With a pang he saw Rivington tip his head forward. He was expecting a kiss. Too bad. Jack brought his mouth closer to Rivington's ear. "What will you do with the remainder of your years, Oliver? So many days to fill without anything to do, without anyone who knows you for who you really are, too afraid to let anyone close?"

There wasn't a lot that actually surprised Jack. Sometimes he wondered whether he was even capable of the sensation. But when Oliver Rivington hit him with a neat right hook in the middle of a West Yorkshire graveyard, he was truly astonished.

He sat there on the ground where he landed, fully intending to let Rivington hit him again. Likely he deserved it, even though he hadn't said anything that wasn't the truth. But instead he saw the silhouette of the other man's lean frame as he limped out of the churchyard and down the street towards the inn.

Oliver paid for the entire bottle of brandy and tucked it under his arm to take upstairs, much to the consternation of the innkeeper. But he was not about to get foxed in the public taproom of the Crown and Lion. One little glass was not going to do the job. Nor would two, for that matter. There wasn't enough brandy in the world to make sense of tonight.

Turner had been right, damn him, when he said that Oliver didn't get angry often. He knew how to keep his head, even when thoroughly provoked. But if any man had ever needed to be punched in the face it was Jack Turner. Of course everything he had said was true, which only made it worse to hear. Those were the fears that assailed Oliver in the dark of night, when he couldn't sleep and his leg hurt too much for him to do anything but lie there and worry: he would live a pointless life; he would always be alone, isolated by deep-rooted secrecy about his desires, haunted by shame about his past.

But to know that those fears were visible to another person—that was beyond the limit. He didn't know or even care what kinds of tricks Turner had used to read the secrets of his heart. Likely he only had a knack for guesswork, but even if he had struck a deal with the devil, it didn't matter. What mattered was that he tried to frighten Oliver with secrets and fears that belonged only to Oliver himself.

He climbed the stairs at the inn with little trouble from his leg. That was something surgeons never thought to suggest—the restorative properties of a towering rage. He lowered himself into a chair by the hearth and knocked back a few mouthfuls of brandy.

No, he realized, Jack hadn't tried to frighten him. That wasn't it at all. Jack had said all of that to provoke Oliver. To push him away. And he would only have done that if he was worried about Oliver getting too close.

Oliver took another swig of brandy and felt the beginnings of a satisfied smile curve his lips. When he heard a knock at the door, he didn't know whether or not he hoped it was an inn servant come to help with his boots. "Come in!" he called.

Jack stood in the doorway, his hands jammed into his pockets. "I'm an idiot," he said without preamble and without stepping any closer.

"You are," Oliver agreed, tipping the bottle back for another sip without taking his eyes from the other man. "Are you some kind of fortune-teller?" He had never felt as ignorant as he did when he asked that question. A fortune-teller, indeed. He was no rustic who hung bundles of weeds from the eaves to ward off evil spirits or the sort of fellow who paid ladies in turbans to read his tea leaves.

Jack's face darkened. "No. Nothing like that. I see hints and I put facts together. Sometimes I'm wrong, but it's not often." Jack ran a hand along his stubble-darkened jaw, and the room was so quiet that Oliver thought he could hear the scratch of rough fingers against new beard. "My father was a confidence man and a crook. He taught me how to read people's faces." His jaw was set in a grim line. "I was an apt pupil, you see."

"And now you use those skills to insult people in graveyards. I see." Oliver knew Jack also used his skills to help people, but now was not the time for patient understanding.

"Like I said, I'm an idiot," he said gruffly.

Oliver gestured for Jack to sit in the chair across from his. Remaining seated while talking to a man who was standing made Oliver feel like an invalid, or like he was talking to a servant. And he didn't want either of those thoughts to intrude at the moment.

Jack approached, but instead of sitting he went to his knees and put a hand on Oliver's boot. Oliver thought his heart might stop. "I only told you the bad things." Jack's voice was somewhere between a grumble and a whisper. He looked like a supplicant and sounded like a sinner. "I could have told you that you're loyal and honorable and just sickeningly decent. I could have said that the way you care about such a poor sap as Wraxhall, the way you would do anything for your sister, including dirtying your hands by hiring me—no, don't try to tell me it was otherwise—those things say more about who you are and what you mean to the people around you than any of that shite I told you in the graveyard." He kissed the inside of Oliver's knee and then looked up, not needing to ask the question out loud.

Not needing—or not able? What Oliver saw in the other man's eyes was a mess of confusion. Jack Turner was not a man on whom confusion rested easily. Oliver was touched and also terrified to realize that he was not the only one out of his depth.

Oliver swallowed. "Not as an apology." He hoped Jack understood. He didn't want this—whatever was about to happen between them—to be recompense for what Jack had said earlier. Oliver had come this far wanting something like a seduction, and he still wanted it. He wasn't going to let Jack pass this off as a way to even the score.

Jack's eyes darkened and one corner of his mouth turned up in something that could almost be mistaken for a smile. He tugged off one of Oliver's boots. "Not as an apology." He pulled off the other boot. "But because I've been thinking about this for days." His big hands slid slowly up Oliver's thighs. "Years, even, if I'm being honest. Thinking about how your cock would feel in my mouth. How you would taste. The sounds you'd make when I sucked you."

"Oh Christ." He could listen to Jack talk like that all night.

"I think it was watching you handle the horses," Jack continued. "I've never been able to resist a man with talent." He worked open the fastenings of Oliver's breeches, and even that glancing touch was enough to force Oliver to bite back a moan. "I can't remember the last time I wanted to do this so badly."

It was an unexpected torture to hear Jack's words of desire but not have his touch. Oliver wanted to tilt his hips towards Jack, but that would be shameless, maybe even pathetic. Desperate with need, he forced his body to remain still, to wait. And when Jack threw him a sly look he knew this was part of the man's plan.

"Cruel," Oliver murmured. He took hold of Jack's collar and bent down for a kiss. With each stroke of his tongue he thought, *This is ours.* It wasn't something he was doing to Jack, or Jack was doing to him. Neither of them owned it. It was theirs. This was what he had wanted; as much as the physical pleasure he wanted the sense of shared desire, mutual longing. This was no frantic, embarrassed effort to satisfy a need.

He stroked his hands along Jack's broad shoulders, savoring every ridge and furrow he could feel beneath too many layers of wool and linen. It would be lovely to see as well as feel those muscles, to touch that darkly curling chest hair he had once glimpsed.

But then Jack slid his hand inside Oliver's breeches and pulled out his erection, and all Oliver could do was watch as the other man leaned forward to lick the already wet head. And then—oh God—all at once he sucked Oliver's cock deep, deep into his throat. The wet heat of Jack's mouth, the slide of his tongue, the slight moan he made when he had taken Oliver to the hilt—it was all too much. It was going to be over too soon. He wanted to tell Jack to make it last, but he was too out of his mind with lust to find the words.

Instead he brushed back the strand of hair that had fallen onto Jack's forehead, threading his fingers in that too-long hair, not guiding Jack's movements so much as trying to experience this moment with as much of his body as possible. Only once did Jack glance up at Oliver's face, and he tugged his gaze away immediately, as fast as you'd pull your hand away from a hot stove.

Oliver tried to hold back his release in order to earn himself a few more seconds in Jack's mouth, but Jack was relentlessly stroking the underside of Oliver's cock with his tongue and there was nothing Oliver could do to delay his climax. Stammered blasphemy was all he managed by way of warning, and then he came in a surge of pleasure and regret.

Jack froze, his head still bent over Rivington's lap.

"Holy Jesus," Rivington mumbled. He was sprawled in his chair, legs wide, head thrown back. Jack had been telling the truth when he admitted to having dreamt about this for years, the chance to bring Oliver to this incoherent, boneless satisfaction.

Jack raised his eyes to the other man's face. This was what he had seen in the orangery all those years ago: Oliver Rivington stripped of all his fine polish, lips parted, eyes half closed, cheeks pink with lust. He had longed to know how it would feel to utterly undo a man like Rivington. But now he knew that it wasn't *a man like Rivington* who caused his heart to beat so riotously, it was Rivington himself. Oliver. And Jack was in terrible danger of becoming foolishly fond of the man.

Jack flicked out his tongue one last time, reveled in the final shudder that passed through Oliver's sated body. When Jack rose to his feet, he had to adjust his trousers to accommodate his aching prick.

"Come here." Rivington looped a lazy finger into Jack's waistband and tugged him close. "Let me." His voice was gravelly with pleasure.

"No." Jack set his jaw, clenched his fists at his sides, a stance better suited to a brawl than a lover's bedside, but he'd feel safer in a boxing ring than in any proximity to Rivington's languorous grin.

"I want to." Oliver licked his lips, and Jack had to suppress a groan.

"I don't," he ground out. "I can't."

Oliver stared pointedly at the part of Jack's body that argued otherwise.

"That isn't what I meant." Jack meant that he couldn't do *this*—feelings and tenderness and all the other fine things he was never meant to have. He couldn't have those things with anyone, let alone Oliver Rivington. He couldn't let himself even think about those things, and, at the moment, that meant not putting his prick anywhere near Rivington's mouth. Summoning up a cool disinterest he didn't feel, he said, "Perhaps I don't feel like tutoring a nobleman's son in the finer points of cocksucking."

"And what makes you think I need tutoring?" A flash of amusement glimmered in the man's absurd blue eyes. He shot Jack a filthy smile that landed like a cudgel to the side of Jack's head. "Give it to me and I'll show you how wrong you are." He reached up and took hold of Jack's cravat, pulling him down for a kiss. Helpless, Jack groaned into the other man's mouth.

Oliver unfastened Jack's trousers and curled his palm around Jack's cock, giving it a few slow strokes. But he didn't lean forward to take in his mouth, perhaps sensing that this was a line Jack wouldn't cross tonight. Instead, he rubbed his thumb over the head, then spread the moisture down the shaft.

"Come for me, Jack," Oliver murmured, his voice low and entreating. "Let me see." The need in his voice transformed this act into a favor Jack was doing Oliver, which was absurd and also exactly what Jack needed.

Jack braced himself on the back of Oliver's chair and squeezed his eyes shut. He wrapped his hand around Oliver's fist, showing him the pressure and rhythm he needed.

There shouldn't have been anything special about it, it was just an ordinary cock-stroking. There was no reason for it to be any different from any of the dozens he had gotten over the years, in back alleys and spare rooms. It wasn't even so very different from when he took pleasure in his own hand.

But when he finally came, it was with the sound of Oliver's whispered encouragement, the feel of Oliver's warm hand. He felt exposed and helpless, caught unawares as a trespasser, a poacher, the basest kind of lowlife.

Jack Turner knew he was in deep, deep trouble, and he didn't know what to do about it.

# CHAPTER TEN

Oliver took a deep breath before rapping on the door to Jack's room. Last night, Jack had left Oliver with hardly a word, eyes averted as he awkwardly readjusted his clothes. Now Oliver feared that Jack meant to avoid him, the all-too-familiar ritual of pretending an ill-advised encounter had never happened. But Oliver had deliberately arrived at Jack's door at an hour that was too early for the man to have conceivably left the inn.

Jack came to the door in only trousers and a shirt, the latter of which he had obviously thrown over his head when he heard Oliver's knock. Oliver tried to keep his gaze from lingering on Jack's chest, bulky muscles almost visible through overlaundered linen. That tiny glimpse made him blush as if he hadn't spent most of his life changing and bathing around men in far less clothing.

When he finally dragged his gaze up to Jack's face, Oliver realized that he could see the bruise on his jaw from where he had hit him yesterday. Between that bruise and the still-unhealed scrape from his mishap escaping that building earlier in the week, he looked like a prizefighter or a pirate.

"I'm sorry about that," he said, vaguely gesturing at Jack's face.

"Don't be," Jack muttered.

"Did you put anything on it?"

"Shut up about it." Jack hadn't shaved or brushed his hair, and his shirt, while clean, was wrinkled. That only added to the piratical quality of the man's appearance this morning.

Oliver tore his gaze away from Jack and took in his surroundings. Jack had only brought one valise with him but it appeared that he had strewn its contents around the room in a single layer of detritus. Jack's office hadn't been like this, and Oliver realized with satisfaction that the office's tidiness likely owed more to the skills of Jack's servant than it did to any of the man's own habits. And he had had the nerve to suggest that it was Oliver who couldn't survive without a servant? Ha! That bit of information was getting filed away for later.

"Are you certain you were once a valet?" he asked, striving for a light tone. "You must be the most slovenly person I've ever met." Stranger still, Oliver recalled Jack's expression of distaste when he referenced the vicar's linty coat and Miss Barrow's untidy parlor.

"I've earned the right to be slovenly," Jack growled, hastily shoving aside what looked like dirty linens in order to clear a chair for Oliver.

"I daresay you have."

He hadn't planned on sitting—more like collecting Jack and bringing him to visit the next person on their list. But now that Jack had gone to the trouble of clearing the chair he felt like he ought to sit, so he did. "What are these?" He gestured at the table beside him, where cards were laid out as if for a game of solitaire. But these weren't playing cards. They appeared to be blank calling cards, with lines of handwriting on them.

"Nothing." Jack swept the cards away and stuffed them haphazardly into his coat pocket.

"Oh, you're in a fine fettle this morning." Slovenly *and* not a morning person. The Crown and Lion was a place of revelations today.

Jack looked like he wanted to say something, likely something very rude, but he held his tongue and went back to getting dressed.

"Your cravat is on the pillow," Oliver pointed out, "if that's what you're looking for."

Evidently it was, because Turner wrapped it around his neck and tied it. Oliver had seen fishing lines tied with more care and style.

"Those cards are where I write what I've learned in an investigation. Notes," Jack said.

That seemed a reasonably orderly process, and Oliver approved. "May I take a look?"

Jack hesitated, so predictable in how he rationed out motes of trust.

"Come now, another set of eyes can't be a bad thing," Oliver wheedled.

"Fine," he said, digging into his pocket and tossing the cards back onto the table. "I spread them out like this, so I can see everything at once and see if any patterns come out."

In the bright early-morning light slanting through the windows, Oliver could see that Jack was pale. He likely had freckles as a child. He would turn red in the sun, so it was just as well that he preferred shadows and darkness.

Oliver turned his attention back to the cards Jack had arranged before him, and wasn't surprised to find that the handwriting was a bold but barely legible scrawl that unraveled like so much tangled yarn across each card. Nor was he surprised to note the level of painstaking detail. Even the absence of information was included: "Wraxhall. No debts, no secrets." And "Servants overpaid," followed, amazingly, by "Very friendly dog."

As Oliver scanned the cards, he saw nothing interesting or even unsavory. Certainly nothing that indicated a source of the blackmail.

"I know," Jack said as he stepped into his boots. "As completely unobjectionable a pair of people as I've ever come across." He said this with a note of disgust in his voice. "With any luck we'll find some hint of depravity today."

"You don't think Miss Barrow knows anything?" Oliver remembered her sitting room, filled with half-read books and dozing cats.

"Oh, she definitely knows something." Jack took out his shaving kit, and then evidently thought better of it, tossing the case back into his valise. "The gardener told me that the cottage belongs to Mrs. Durbin. Miss Barrow has free use of it. Why else would Mrs. Wraxhall's mother give her a home if not to keep watch on the lady and provide a bit of an incentive for her silence?"

Oliver opened his mouth to protest, then decided he had no horse in this race. Whether the unknown Mrs. Durbin gave Miss Barrow a home—and such a home as that cottage—out of charity or from baser motives was not something Oliver gave one fig about.

"But Miss Barrow and the vicar aren't our blackmailers." Jack slid a knife into his boot. "They're happy young fools in love. And happy people don't engage in blackmail."

"They don't?" This was not something Oliver had ever thought about. "What crimes do happy people commit, then?"

"Other than fornication and sodomy, you mean?" He caught Oliver's eye in a way that made his meaning clear and caused Oliver's skin to flush. "There are plenty of otherwise decent, happy, hardworking criminals. Smugglers, forgers, whores. Pillars of society, every last one of them."

Oliver opened his mouth to protest—smugglers as pillars of society, indeed. But he stopped himself. He wanted to hear more of these misguided notions. At that moment he wanted to hear just about anything Jack Turner had to say.

Jack turned away from Oliver and began throwing stray objects helter-skelter into his valise in what looked like a child's attempt to tidy the nursery. "My father was a perfectly happy criminal," he continued, "at least when he wasn't starving. Georgie too. But some crimes are just nasty. Arson, blackmail, anything involving children. You'll only see the worst kinds of miserable bastards doing those things."

Oliver recalled that Jack had once said he'd have no compunctions about blackmailing blackmailers, and wondered whether he considered himself the worst kind of miserable bastard.

Oliver found that he hoped not. Worse than that, he disagreed. And the idea that he might have a better opinion of self-avowed scoundrel Jack Turner than the man had of himself was unsettling, to say the least.

They took the curricle to the house of Mrs. Wraxhall's former lover. And thank God for it, because Oliver didn't think his leg could take much more after yesterday. The Lewises lived just outside Pickworth, close to Mr. Lewis's Dewsbury mill but still in the country.

Hector Lewis's father had been in business with Mrs. Wraxhall's father. According to Jack's note cards, the Lewises and the Durbins had both stood to profit handsomely by a marriage between Miss Durbin and young Hector Lewis. Instead, Lewis was running the enterprise.

Oliver, for his part, was eager to discover what kind of house a Yorkshire mill owner lived in. He was conscious of a curiosity that did him no credit, as if he were off to gawk at those people who drove reindeer around, whatever they were called.

Sadly, the Lewises' house turned out to be the sort of rigidly symmetrical affair that everybody insisted on building a generation ago. There were the requisite portico and columns, a neatly graveled semicircular drive, and a soporifically regular facade. Oliver suspected they'd find faux-Roman sculpture strewn about the premises.

Jack's thoughts turned out to be along similar lines. "Even odds the door is opened by some poor bastard wearing a powdered wig and velvet breeches."

Oliver let out a bark of laughter. But when they rolled up to the front of the house and handed off the curricle to a servant, the door was opened by a very somber and ordinary-looking butler who gravely took their calling cards before disappearing.

"They're checking Debrett's, I'd wager." Jack tweaked the nose of a marble statue and Oliver swatted his hand away.

When the butler returned and bade them follow him to the morning room, Jack murmured, "I ought to always have an aristocrat when I want to look into other people's houses. It's a hell of a lot easier than climbing drainpipes and shimmying through garret windows."

That, Oliver knew, was the closest he was going to get to an expression of thanks. Which was fine, he supposed, since all he had done was get fathered by a peer.

They found Mrs. Lewis bent over her embroidery hoop. She glanced up at the two men with sharp black eyes. She was older than Oliver had expected—closer to thirty than twenty—and visibly with child. Oliver supposed she was pretty enough, but not agreeable-looking. She pressed her narrow, pale lips together in a way that suggested habitual disapproval. Her dark hair had been dressed in an aggressively fashionable manner, with an abundance of ringlets and twists.

Oliver made the usual apologies about dropping by uninvited and without an introduction, and then launched into his story. This time he couldn't use the story about Charlotte's fictitious friend—Lady Montbray being unlikely to make the acquaintance of a mill owner's wife—so he and Jack had come up with something else.

"I've come to Yorkshire with my man of business to find a location for a home for wounded soldiers." He knew she would infer that he was also after a donation for this fictitious charity. "The vicar mentioned that you might be capable of helping with this endeavor." Something flickered in her expression that made Oliver think he had hit his mark with that bit of flattery.

"You would need to speak to my husband about any charitable interests, Mr. Rivington." Her voice was flat and unapologetic.

If they really had been collecting for a charity they could hardly have done better than the Lewises. Plenty of money here. No expense had been spared in furnishing this house, and it was all done in the latest fashion. A trifle vulgar, this strict adherence to fashion, but nothing outlandishly crass. Oliver guessed Mrs. Lewis had redecorated the place soon after her marriage.

"When is Mr. Lewis expected home?" Oliver asked.

"Not until teatime at the earliest." She flicked a glance at the embroidery hoop that still lay on her lap, as if longing to get back to her work.

"Is he ever in London? I can make arrangements to see him there."

"London?" Her dark eyes went wide before narrowing again. "No, he never travels that far."

Oliver thought she was suspicious, but also thought she would err on the side of humoring the Earl of Rutland's son.

A footman came in with tea and nearly dropped it when startled by the emergence of an angry little dog from under Mrs. Lewis's chair. What ensued ought to have been one of those trifling domestic farces that happen in all households—absurdly tiny dog endeavors to defend mistress from tea—but instead it was a tense moment. The footman was highly nervous and apologetic, Mrs. Lewis was plainly irritated, and out of the corner of his eye Oliver noticed Jack watching the scene carefully.

Oliver did his best to engage Mrs. Lewis in conversation that might be of use in the investigation. He complimented the lady's embroidery, made a remark about the unusually cool summer—all the mainstays of drawing-room conversation. But he couldn't quite draw her out. She regarded him with that wintry little smile and said as little as possible.

There was something oppressive about the room, despite the care that had been taken in furnishing it. Oliver was almost nauseated. Was it the bilious shade of yellow in the wallpaper, or was it the heavy scent of rose water? And why did the figurines on the chimney piece look quite so . . . menacing?

Mrs. Lewis started glancing at the gilt clock that sat on the chimney piece, and Oliver decided to end the performance.

On the way to the front door Oliver watched in astonishment as Jack, pretending to be lost in admiration of the friezes, walked directly into a housemaid who had been polishing furniture. Both the maid and the footman who was escorting them to the door went quite pale, and then the girl rushed away close to tears.

"What was that about?" Oliver asked Jack after they were in the curricle, speeding down the gravel drive.

"The Lewises are terrors to work for. All the servants we saw were jumpy. Everyone in that house was strung too tight for comfort."

Oliver couldn't see what that had to do with Mrs. Wraxhall, but out of the corner of his eye he could see Jack looking very smug. "Do you think she's the blackmailer, then?"

"I don't think she'd hesitate to blackmail," Jack said immediately. "She's ruthless. I'd have hated to work in that house."

"I'm glad you got your dose of sordidness."

"Christ, so am I." And he sounded like he meant it. "But whatever she's capable of, she didn't take our client's letters."

Oliver heard that "our" but decided it would be unwise to comment on it. "Why? Because she doesn't travel to London? I don't suppose a woman in her condition would make a very effective burglar."

Jack shook his head. "No, no. Because she cares too much for her reputation to want to expose an affair her husband had before marrying her. You saw how her face lit up when you said the vicar mentioned her." He spoke with the thread-bare patience of a man used to the rest of the world being two steps behind him. "Lewis himself would appear to be an unlikely culprit for the same reason."

"Wouldn't the Lewises have a reason to steal the letters and then destroy them, to prevent their contents from being known?" Oliver asked.

"Yes, absolutely. But why leave a blackmail note, then?"

"Unless Mrs. Wraxhall was lying about having received a blackmail note," Oliver suggested.

Jack cast him an approving glance. Oliver felt his cheeks flush, and then heard the other man's soft rumble of laughter.

"That house was hellish," Oliver said in an effort to change the subject.

"So it was," Jack said thoughtfully. "I'm glad you saw it too. You know, I'm inclined to think Mrs. Wraxhall made a lucky escape." And with that, he pulled out some of those cards of his and began scribbling on them with the stump of a pencil.

Jack wasn't fool enough to assume his clients told the truth when they engaged his services. During the first few cases after he set up his business two years ago, he had been offended by his clients' lies and omissions, but now he sometimes wished they would simply walk into his office, throw a wad of banknotes onto his desk, and leave him to untangle their lives without any distractions.

The picture he now was forming of Mrs. Wraxhall's situation didn't map onto the one she had presented him with. It was difficult to imagine a man who lived in such a cold mausoleum of a house, a man who had as skittish a crew of servants as Jack had ever laid eyes on, penning the sort of love letter a woman would treasure. True, there were instances when people changed. But a forbidding house, a long-faced wife, and a crew of terrified servants were not circumstances that Jack could ignore.

With that in mind, he flipped through his cards again, more out of habit than thinking he'd see anything.

They were traveling along a stretch of road that was badly out of repair. One side had sunk to the level of the adjacent field and the other side was pitted with ruts and holes. Ordinarily Jack would have awaited certain calamity, his only question being which ditch his body would ultimately be found in, but Rivington managed the task with easy confidence. He kept up a steady stream of soothing chatter that might have been directed either at the horses or at Jack himself.

Jack had to tear his gaze away from the sight of Rivington's long fingers in their kidskin gloves skillfully managing the ribbons. When he made the mistake of turning his head, Rivington's face was boyishly happy, bits of golden hair curling from under the brim of his hat.

This morning, confused and frustrated by his reaction to what should have been a perfectly commonplace bit of fun, Jack had woken up in a right foul mood. But then Rivington sailed into his room like a bright ray of bloody sunshine and Jack let himself be coaxed back to his usual not-too-horrible humor. There was an alarmingly large part of Jack's mind that would have done far worse than putting on a happy face if that's what Rivington wanted. He was a lost cause.

Suddenly the curricle lurched to the side and his cards spilled off his lap. A breeze carried a few out of the vehicle and onto the road outside.

"Damn!" Jack muttered. "Damn, damn, damn!" He should have known better than to risk losing his cards in such a stupid way.

Without Jack having to ask, Rivington immediately brought the horses to a stop. Jack hopped out, scrambling to retrieve the cards. When he looked up he found that Rivington had looped the horses' ribbons over a low tree branch and climbed down from the carriage as well. Presently he was bent over, attempting to use his walking stick to retrieve some cards that had blown under a bush.

"You don't need to do that." Jack knelt beside him and attempted to take over the task. Over the past few days he had seen how difficult it was for Rivington to bend his injured knee. And while the man was very good at concealing his discomfort and wearing that mask of bland politeness, sometimes an expression of pain and annoyance would flit across his face even when he did something as ordinary as rise from a chair.

"It was my own bad driving that caused the cards to tumble, so it's the least I can do," he said, and proceeded to drop to one knee to get close to the cards.

"Bullshit. I ought to have kept them tied up in string, like I usually do. I should have known better." That might have been the first game of "No, It Was My Fault" that Jack had played in his life, to say nothing of the fact that they were now both kneeling in the mud, which was a waste of at least one pair of breeches.

Rivington handed him the cards he had retrieved, which Jack jammed into his pocket before extending his hand to help the other man up. It seemed crucially important that Rivington not incur any additional suffering on Jack's behalf or for any other reason. The urgency of that need must have been why Jack forgot to rise to his own feet before offering his hand. So when Rivington, an amused half-smile playing on his mouth, peeled off his muddy glove before grasping Jack's own bare hand, the result was that instead of Jack being able to tug the other man to his feet, he found himself being pulled against Rivington's chest.

"You ran out on me last night." Rivington's voice was low in Jack's ear, his arms tight around Jack's back.

Jack caught the familiar scent of Oliver's laundry soap. The bush hid them from anyone who might chance to come along the road, so Jack let himself relax against Oliver's chest. He took a deep breath, and the warm June air felt cold in his lungs. "I'm an idiot," he said for the second time in as many days. A pair of wiry arms tightened around him.

"Is that what you're going to say every time you try to push me away?"

Every time? *Every time?* What could Rivington possibly be thinking? Jack ought to get away, say something cutting, something true and ruthless about how there wasn't going to even be another time, let alone a sequence of events that could be described as *every time*.

But instead, when Rivington leaned in, Jack let himself be kissed. Rivington tipped Jack's chin back and kissed him and Jack just let it happen, as if he weren't watching his peace of mind and dignity slip farther away. Every sweep of Rivington's tongue, every caress and every sigh loosened Jack's resolve.

And Jack had half a mind to simply let everything else unfold however Rivington wanted. Kissing on the road, falling stupidly in love, why the hell not?

"Everything's so easy with you," Jack said, pulling back from the kiss. "It's as if you don't know what a bad idea this all is."

Rivington didn't answer, he only reeled Jack in for another kiss, soft and needy and dangerous. They had shared so few kisses but already Jack had memorized the feel of Rivington's lips against his own. The sweet taste of Rivington's mouth now felt familiar, expected. And when Rivington tugged him closer, the press of their bodies was relief from an absence he hadn't known existed.

He ought to stand up. Hell, he ought to go back to London. Alone. He had no business feeling warm and safe in such proximity to a nobleman. This was like losing a hand of cards in a game where he had bet too much. But Jack didn't gamble and he didn't like the sick feeling that was growing in the pit of his stomach. But still, he let Rivington kiss him. He let the sensations sweep over him, as if this wouldn't be the unmaking of him.

"Oliver," he said against the other man's lips. He didn't know when they had slipped into using Christian names, only that it was a bad idea and that he would keep doing it.

"Hmmm?" Oliver's lips lingered on Jack's jaw.

This was the moment, his last clear chance to get out of here unscathed. He ought to say something cutting, something utterly offensive, something even worse than the words he had spoken in the graveyard last night. But all he said was, "We need to get out of the road." He supposed this was the moment that sealed his fate.

"I know, I know," Oliver said in the same tone of voice he had used to calm the horses, and Jack was struck by the fear that Oliver knew exactly what Jack was feeling.

With a sigh, Jack stood and extended his hand as he should have done minutes ago. He hauled Oliver to his feet, and the two of them climbed back into the curricle.

"I'm helping you with your boots tonight," Jack growled after Oliver had set the horses in motion.

Oliver was silent long enough that Jack knew he had made his meaning clear. "Is that so?"

"It most definitely is." Jack fixed his eyes on the road ahead.

"But what if I don't want help with my boots?" Jack didn't need to turn his head to know that Oliver was smiling as he spoke. "What if I prefer a servant to assist me?"

Jack snorted. "If after less than two days in a sleepy village you've managed to find someone willing to do what I have in mind, I'll tip my cap to you."

Oliver turned his head to look directly at Jack, a mischievous smile playing on his lips. "You don't think I know how to find someone willing to . . . remove my boots or perform whatever other services I require?"

"Services, eh?" How very coy. He made up his mind right then that before the night was through he'd hear Oliver beg for Jack's attentions with lascivious clarity. He would hear the filthiest words come out of that pink mouth. To hell with euphemisms.

"Whatever you prefer to call it, then. I haven't lived like a monk, you know. I've managed to . . . have my needs met on four continents. Anything can be gotten for money."

Was that a hint of chagrin Jack detected? The man's very kissable mouth was now quirked up in a sad little smile barely visible under the brim of his hat. Not for the first time, Jack wondered if he had underestimated Oliver Rivington. "Four continents?" he scoffed. "You paid to have your cock sucked on four continents?"

"Well, I was there for other reasons, of course. War, you know. Not exclusively for, ah, untoward purposes."

Oh, Jack was definitely going to enjoy hearing him say the filthiest things. "Naturally. I never assumed you had made some kind of Grand Tour of cocksucking and buggery. But still, four continents? And you paid? A man who looks like you?" He glanced over again, and even in the fading sunlight he could see Oliver blush. "You gentlemen have no sense of what money is worth. It's madness to pay for something that many men would willingly do for free."

"Let me understand." Oliver's voice was faint, whether with amusement or injured pride Jack could not tell. "You're taking issue with my spending habits? Not my moral character?"

"Yes." No. The truth was that Jack felt strangely discomposed imagining Oliver in compromising situations in cities circling the globe. While he should only have felt aroused—which he most certainly did—he also wanted to punch all those foreign bastards in the stomach. He decided he was not going to investigate that urge overmuch.

"For what it's worth, none of them did half the job you did." Oliver's voice was so quiet that Jack could hardly hear him.

Jack tried to sound like someone who wasn't half mad with arousal. "So you paid to have your cock sucked inadequately? That's even worse."

Oliver laughed at that, he laughed so hard Jack was worried that the horses would startle. Then Jack started laughing too, and by the time they reached the inn it was anybody's guess which of them was in a greater hurry to get upstairs.

"Christ, you're handsome when you smile," Oliver said as soon as they reached Jack's room and the door was safely closed behind them.

Jack didn't know what kind of response to make to such arrant nonsense. Instead he pushed Oliver onto the bed and climbed over him and pinned him in place, pressing himself against the other man's hardening arousal. "I want to know what else you paid for on four continents. I want to know what else you like." Other than being manhandled, that was, because Jack could feel Oliver's cock stiffening more and more, even as he spoke.

"I'm not certain I ought to tell you. You'll only scold me for being a spendthrift." Oliver wriggled a little under Jack's body to let him know exactly how much he might like being scolded.

Jack felt himself growl, a rumble in the back of his throat. No, no, no. He needed to stay in control of this encounter. Turning into a mess of base desires wouldn't achieve that. After the past few days he was in a sorry state of arousal, but Oliver's cock was hard too. "Do you want me to fuck you? Is that something you'd like?" He had tried to keep his voice casually filthy but instead the question came out as an entreaty. *Please say yes.*

"God, yes," Oliver whispered, and it was a hair's breadth away from begging.

"Say it."

But Oliver's eyes only widened.

"I'd like to know how you managed to debauch yourself on four continents without being able to say *cock* or *fuck*."

"Gestures, for the most part," Oliver said softly.

Jack took hold of Oliver's wrists and pressed them into the mattress on either side of the other man's head. "Hear me now, Oliver Rivington. You will not use gestures with me." And then he bent his head to take his lover's mouth in a hard kiss.

## CHAPTER ELEVEN

There wasn't even time for Oliver to wonder whether he ought to feel self-conscious about his scars. Without so much as breaking their kiss, Jack's hands deftly undid buttons and pushed aside fabric until Oliver was quite comprehensively naked. Jack knelt on the bed, staring down at Oliver with a look that was utterly indecent. Whatever the condition of Oliver's leg, it certainly wasn't causing Jack any misgivings.

Feeling bold, Oliver reached up to untie Jack's cravat, only to find his hands mercilessly clamped down on either side of his head once again. "I'm not done looking at you," Jack growled.

Oliver nearly whimpered. He felt shameless, like he had been waiting his entire life to have his body pressed ruthlessly into the mattress by a self-confessed reformed criminal in a Yorkshire inn. And maybe he had, because lying here, exposed and willing, he felt more himself than he had in months. "We can both look at one another." He halfheartedly strained against Jack's grip.

He was rewarded with another growling sound and

a stronger grip on his hands. Jack's murmurs of desire and approval were nearly enough to bring Oliver off. But he was damned if he was going to let another night pass him by without seeing what was under Jack Turner's clothes. He had been thinking about it for weeks. Every hint of solid muscle had ramped up his desire.

In one swift movement, Oliver reversed their positions so that Jack was beneath him. He grabbed both Jack's wrists in one hand and started untying the cravat with his free hand.

"How in hell did you do that?" Jack breathed. "I have two stone on you and you have a lame leg."

Oliver laughed into the soft skin and rough stubble of Jack's neck. "I was trained in hand-to-hand combat, you know."

"Right, but I grew up on the streets of St. Giles, which amounts to much the same thing."

"Then you ought to be able to do better than that," Oliver said when Jack made an ineffective attempt to wrestle him back over. "If you're holding out on me because of my leg, I'll never forgive you." He was only half kidding.

Oliver wasn't sure if he slackened his grip or if Jack stopped going easy on him, because an instant later he was flat on his back once again. He couldn't suppress his sigh of pleasure.

"You like that," Jack said, almost wonderingly. "That's what you wanted all along. Hold onto the bedpost."

"Mmmm," was all Oliver would say, admitting nothing, but he raised his arms to take hold of the bedpost.

"I'll remember that for next time."

*Next time.* Yes. Oliver watched in fascination as Jack pulled off his cravat and started unfastening his shirt, all the while never letting his dark eyes stray from Oliver. That gaze alone was more than Oliver had ever hoped to find in a bed partner. He looked like he was barely holding back, like he was ready to eat Oliver alive.

Heaven help him, but Oliver wanted that too.

Jack pulled his shirt over his head and rose to his feet long enough to tug off his boots and breeches, before kneeling over Oliver.

Oliver groaned, tightening his fingers around the smooth posts of the bed frame. The man was muscled like a Greek statue of an angry, brutal god. Not Apollo or anyone half so well-behaved, but rather the sort of god who spent his time at a forge or smiting enemies. His shoulders were broad and his arms were thick, thoroughly corded with muscles. His powerful chest was covered with a dusting of dark hair that led down to an impressive erection. Oliver licked his lips and heard Jack groan in response.

The sun was low in the sky and in their haste to get their hands on one another they had neglected to light a candle or a lamp. Oliver strained his eyes, trying to memorize every sinew, every furrow, in case *next time* never materialized.

Oliver let go of the bedpost and sat up, placing his hands flat against Jack's chest. He kissed the soft skin below Jack's collarbone and felt the other man's shiver of response. But Jack didn't make any move to stop him, so Oliver continued to explore the planes and furrows of Jack's chest with his mouth and hands, letting his lips drift over to a hard nipple and his hands skim down to brush against Jack's cock.

Jack grunted in—what? Protest? Approval? It didn't matter, though, because Oliver found himself flat on his back, his body covered by Jack's, their limbs tangled and their mouths joined. The feel of Jack's arousal rubbing against his own nearly pushed Oliver over the edge. "Jack," he said, desperate.

In answer, Jack turned him over onto his stomach. Oliver could hear the sound of a bag being rummaged through. "Jack?"

"Right here." Jack said, and kissed him first on the neck and then at the top of his spine. "I'm not going anywhere."

There was the sound of a bottle being uncorked and a thrill of anticipation sizzled along Oliver's spine, along with the gratifying realization that Jack had packed his valise in London with the intent of doing exactly this. Jack's oiled fingers slid along the cleft of his arse. Oliver pushed back in answer, wanting more, needing more.

Jack kissed him again on the neck, sucking in counterpoint to the slow slide and thrust of his finger. Then there was another finger and Oliver helplessly bucked against the mattress beneath him, trying to give his cock some pressure while also thrusting onto Jack's fingers.

"Please," he begged.

"What do you want?" Jack's voice was pure gravel.

"I want you inside me."

"But I am." He moved his fingers inside Oliver, as if to prove the point.

Oliver shivered. Oh, this was malice. "Bastard."

Jack laughed, soft and low. "Is there something specific you want?"

Oliver took a deep breath. "Your cock. Inside me."

"Say it," Jack rumbled.

"Fuck me. Please, God, fuck me, Jack."

The noise Jack made was fierce, and Oliver instinctively turned his head to see the man's face, which looked as desperate and unhinged as Oliver felt. His jaw was set, his chest heaving, his eyes so very dark.

Oliver whimpered at the loss of those fingers, but then was distracted by the feel of strong hands on his hips, tugging him up and back. Then he felt Jack shove some pillows under his hips. He was momentarily confused by that, then realized Jack was trying to accommodate Oliver's injured leg. If Oliver had any sanity left, he might have been able to explain that his leg was the least of his concerns at the moment. But he didn't, and besides, the unasked-for kindness of the gesture made his heart turn over. Then was more oil, and Oliver shivered at the sensation of Jack's cock brushing against his entrance.

"Is this all right?" Jack had begun to push in.

"Yes," Oliver begged. He needed this—his body stretching, Jack's grunt of satisfaction when his hips were flush against Oliver's body. "More."

"God, I've been wanting to do this," Jack murmured. He pulled back and entered him at a different angle, hitting that spot inside Oliver that felt like it was connected to his cock.

Oliver wailed in pleasure, then heard Jack's breathless laugh at the same time he felt Jack's hand clamp down over his mouth.

"Do it again," he pleaded against Jack's hand. "Don't stop."

"Why the hell would I stop?" And he didn't stop. He pounded relentlessly into Oliver, murmuring words and phrases that Oliver was too out of his mind with pleasure to comprehend. This was what Oliver had wanted, this feeling of shared pleasure. They hadn't been brought to this point by mere convenience. No, this moment now, the sweat and swearing, the grasping hands and frantic rhythm, was the only possible outcome of the past few weeks.

"Can you come like this?" Jack's voice was rough, hoarse. It was the voice of a man who had spent too many minutes uttering profanities into his lover's ear.

"Almost," Oliver whispered. Jack slipped a hand under Oliver's body, grasping Oliver's cock in one strong hand. That was all it took, that single stroke, and Oliver felt his climax bearing down on him.

He cried out into the pillow as the pleasure overtook him. A moment later he heard Jack let loose a volley of expletives, felt the man's body go stiff on top of his own, and then felt the rush of warmth inside him.

For a moment, the silence was only broken by their ragged breathing.

When Jack spoke his voice was raspy. "Christ, Rivington. Fuck." He dragged that last word out into several more syllables than it rightfully deserved. "If I'd have known it was to be like that, I'd have bent you over my desk the first time I saw you. How the hell am I supposed to get anything done, now that I know?"

Oliver turned his face into the pillow to hide his smile.

Jack didn't know whether he was relieved or irritated to find Oliver still in his bed at dawn. On the one hand, the man ought to have finished the night in his own bed. A servant might notice that Oliver's bed hadn't been slept in and it wouldn't take much to figure out where he had spent the night. On the other hand, he wasn't going to complain about getting to see Oliver spread out, golden and beautiful in the early-morning sunlight. Jack propped himself on his elbow to get a better look. Tentatively, he reached out and smoothed a few pale curls off Oliver's forehead. Asleep, he looked young. Or, rather, he looked his actual age—not quite thirty—with his face at rest, stripped of its usual mask of well-bred manners.

Jack loved that he held the power to strip away that mask, to reduce this fine gentleman to embarrassed blushes or lusty incoherence. And unless he was mistaken, Oliver wanted that as much as Jack did.

Jack trailed his hand down Oliver's arm, which was flung out on the mattress beside him. Oliver was stronger than he looked. His muscles were lean and wiry but powerful. He realized that Oliver's eyes were now open, regarding him from beneath sleep-heavy eyelids.

"Hush," Jack said. "It's not time to wake yet." Which was a stupid thing to say since hadn't he just decided that Oliver belonged back in his own bed? But the fact was that Jack wanted a few more minutes to appreciate the man's frankly excessive beauty without having to hide his admiration behind a veil of grumpiness or displeasure. Stupid, stupid.

He made a move to get out of bed, only to find that one of those wiry arms had wrapped itself around his waist, dragging him back to the mattress.

"Wait." Oliver pressed Jack's back against his own chest and held him there.

"I should go downstairs," Jack protested, his voice gruff. "I need the local gossip about the Durbins and Lewises."

"Later." Oliver kissed Jack's shoulder while trailing his hand down Jack's abdomen.

"What are you doing?" he asked, because he felt like he ought to make some effort to wrest control of this situation.

Oliver ignored the question, which was only right because it couldn't be clearer what he was doing. "You have scars too," he said, to Jack's surprise. More surprising was the way that *too* made Jack's heart clench.

Jack most certainly did have scars, though. He had never had what he would call a serious injury but nonetheless had a good half dozen marks on his chest and arms and likely a few on his back as well. "I wouldn't have survived as Georgie's brother without seeing myself through a few friendly knife fights."

"Your brother stabbed you?" Oliver sounded shocked and his hand went still.

Jack smiled at the idea of Georgie stabbing anyone. "No, it was other blokes trying to stab Georgie, and having to deal with me instead."

"Ah." Oliver said, almost breathing the sound into Jack's neck. "You have bruises too, but I suppose that's what happens when a man falls out of windows." He was fingering a jagged scar that ran the length of Jack's forearm.

Jack couldn't have said how it happened, but he was now almost cradled in Oliver's arms. He couldn't remember the last time he had been . . . inspected, or fussed over, or whatever this was. He didn't even know whether he liked it. "You don't need to—" But he couldn't even finish that thought, and Oliver paid him no heed, instead reaching his hand lower to stroke Jack's already-hard cock, spreading the wetness from the tip along the shaft. Jack groaned, trying to remember why it was so important that he not lose the upper hand, and that he not let this man take any more than Jack was willing to give. Which was not much at all—a tumble, a fuck, maybe a little flirtation. No more.

When Oliver gently bit Jack's earlobe, all those worries scattered like spiders, retreating to the dark and safe corners of Jack's mind. Helplessly, he thrust into the other man's hand and felt the answering press of Oliver's cock against his hip.

"Yes," Oliver said softly. "Just like this."

Jack managed to reach his hand behind him and grasp Oliver's erection. It was hardly graceful, and the rhythm they achieved was clumsy and frantic, but the solid presence of Oliver behind him and the scent of that godforsaken laundry soap lingering on his skin might have been enough to finish him off with little extra effort.

A moment later they were both spent. Jack rolled over to face Oliver. The other man's cornflower-blue eyes were half closed and his mouth was turned up in a very smug little grin.

"You look like the cat who got the canary," Jack said.

"That's how I feel."

So did Jack. "Good," was all he said though.

"I was thinking," Oliver said, and Jack felt his stomach drop because that phrase never meant anything good. "Instead of stopping near Grantham on the way back, we could perhaps break the journey at Alder Court."

"Alder Court," Jack repeated. "That's your father's house." It was Lord Rutland's principal estate, a fact Jack would not have known had he not had occasion to visit the place in the service of his former employer, Lord Montbray, Oliver's brother-in-law. He had no idea how Oliver thought he was going to explain Jack's presence to the earl.

"I haven't been there since I returned to England, and my father never visits London." He turned his gaze innocently on Jack. "And he's getting old."

"Oh, for God's sake." Jack swung his legs off the bed and reached for a cloth to clean himself up, because this was not a conversation he was prepared to have naked and sticky. "Fine. I'm not going to keep you from seeing your elderly father." But he didn't have to like it, either. And if Rivington thought he was going to bring Jack under his father's roof in the guise of a servant, Jack would give him hell to pay.

He dressed quickly and silently and left Oliver alone in bed.

"You know, if you're trying to prove to yourself that you aren't ashamed of having gotten fucked by a former servant, there are better ways to go about it than doing it under your father's nose," Jack grumbled, once they were situated in the curricle that afternoon.

For the most part, Jack was out of sorts because he had failed to turn up any additional information that morning. Nobody at the inn was willing to say anything about the Lewises that Jack didn't already know. The couple of servants who looked after Pickworth Hall in Mrs. Durbin's absence had nearly slammed the door in Jack's face. Small wonder he felt a bit disgruntled. Whenever he looked at his cards he saw hints of a pattern he did not like one bit. He was going to have to have words with Mrs. Wraxhall as soon as he got back to London.

"I'm not in the least ashamed of having gotten fucked by you," Oliver said lightly, but a telltale blush spread across his cheeks. Jack was too distracted by his tightening trousers to care that Oliver was certainly lying. It hadn't taken Oliver long to figure out how much Jack liked to hear coarse language. "I enjoyed it a great deal and would like to do it again, but if you object to doing so under my father's nose, as you so charmingly put it, I'm certain I can wait."

Jack growled in response.

"Besides," Oliver went on, as if he weren't in danger of getting throttled, "I have a hankering for the pork pie my father's cook makes."

Jack turned his head and stared. "You're a devil," he said, half admiringly. First obscene language, now this? Since meeting the man, Jack had experienced an uncharacteristic mother hen urge to feed him. Maybe it was because Oliver had so plainly lost weight since his injury and looked in need of food. Maybe it was the obvious relish he had for a good meal that made it a pleasure to watch him eat. Whatever the case, he was a manipulative little sod to use that knowledge against Jack. Pork pie, indeed.

"I'll introduce you at Alder Court as a friend," Oliver said firmly, as if daring Jack to object to the designation. "My father seldom leaves his apartments, so there won't be any awkwardness at mealtimes, if that's what you're concerned about," he went on, answering the question Jack hadn't yet brought himself to ask.

That was only half acceptable, though. Jack's main concern wasn't over any difficulties in interacting with Lord Rutland. He cared little enough for inherited privilege to dismiss any discomfort a peer of the realm might feel at dining with a man who had once been a servant. But the idea that the old butler at Alder Court might actually be called on to serve Jack? That was unthinkable. As much as Jack might like to see the order of civilization set on its head, he wasn't going to do anything to put the butler out of countenance, nor the cook or any of the other staff.

However, Jack would be glad to have a chance to talk to the earl about Montbray's return. Rutland might have connections he could call on to dispose of his violent son-in-law less feloniously than Jack was intending to. A diplomatic assignment to China, a grant of property in Barbados—anything to keep Montbray out of England and away from his wife and child.

When they stopped at an inn to change horses and for Jack to send a hastily scrawled letter to an associate in London, Jack noticed Oliver leaning on his walking stick a bit more heavily than usual. He wondered if there could be another motive for this plan to stop for a day. If so, Jack approved. Surely over the past few days Oliver had walked more than usual, and even though the curricle was well sprung as far as carriages went, it still jostled a fair bit. That couldn't be any good for his leg.

And then another idea struck Jack—had he been too rough with Oliver's leg last night? He had tried to take every possible care, but there had been a point when he—

"Take my arm," he offered.

Oliver looked at him askance. "How gallant." He sounded

suspicious but took Jack's arm with the hand not gripping his walking stick. And then he proceeded to touch Jack's elbow with all the vigor one would use to hold a newly hatched chick.

"Lean on me," Jack ordered.

"I can fend for myself," Oliver replied frostily.

"I know that. I'm trying to help."

"I don't need—"

"We've already established that you don't need anything. The Honorable Captain Oliver Rivington doesn't need a bloody thing he can't get with a couple of coins and a twinkle of his pretty eyes. But maybe I can help anyway." Why the devil was he pushing this? It shouldn't matter one jot to Jack whether or not Oliver wanted to limp around on his sore leg or whether he wanted to be carried around like a baby, for that matter. Oliver's comfort, or lack thereof, officially did not matter to Jack, not a bit. "Just take my fucking arm."

Oliver shot Jack an inscrutable glance before gripping the offered arm.

Jack felt momentarily triumphant, having won this battle he didn't want to win in the first place. Likely the amount of discomfort he was relieving was too small for the other man to even notice. But the heavy weight on Jack's arm felt like it belonged there, as if he had been waiting years for the chance to help the son of an earl across a few yards of muddy ground. He was hit with a wave of confusion and self-reproach, and it was all he could do not to push Rivington away, abandoning him in the middle of the inn yard.

## CHAPTER TWELVE

Heavy curtains were drawn across the windows in the Earl of Rutland's private sitting room, blocking out the midmorning sun, but even in the dim light Oliver could see how frail his father had grown. They had arrived at Alder Court too late last night for Oliver to see his father, so this morning he had dragged himself up the two flights of stairs to his father's apartments as soon as he received word that the earl was out of bed.

When, precisely, had his father become an old man? His eyes had once been a brighter blue than even Charlotte's, but now they were clouded over and watery. His hair had been iron gray for as long as Oliver could remember, but now it was white.

"Harris told me you arrived with Montbray's valet." That was how Lord Rutland chose to greet the son he had not seen in two years. So, his mind was the same as ever, Oliver supposed.

"He hasn't been in service for some time," Oliver said, as if that went any distance toward explaining why Turner was here at Alder Court today. He had hoped to avoid explaining precisely how he had come to be traveling with Jack. The truth, of course, was entirely unsuitable. He couldn't very well say that he had insinuated himself into a blackmail inquiry out of some combination of boredom, lust, and a sense that he ought to stop Jack from wreaking havoc on the lives of respectable people. He also couldn't say that he had brought Jack to Alder Court partly out of a nonsensical desire to see his lover in the place Oliver considered his home, and partly to have another uninterrupted day of his company. So he said nothing by way of explanation and hoped his father would move the conversation to other topics.

"Are you in some kind of trouble?" His father leaned forward in his chair with an expression like that of a wolf scenting its prey.

"Trouble?" Oliver asked, honestly surprised. What would make his father ask that? "Not at all." That, at least, was the truth.

With less effort than Oliver would have expected, his father rose to his feet and started pacing the sitting room. "If it's a question of money, I'd rather you come to me than resort to any association with the likes of Jack Turner."

"I have no need of money." Oliver caught a flicker of disappointment in his father's eyes. It was an old bone of contention, that Oliver was financially independent thanks to his mother's small legacy. The earl would have preferred to keep all his children under his thumb. Instead, Oliver's sister had married a wealthy man, his brother had married an heiress with an estate of her own, and Oliver was content to live on his modest income.

"That's even worse, then," the earl said, his slippers shuffling across the thick carpet. "If it's not money, then I'm not sure I even want to know what reason you could possibly have for associating with the man." He looked at Oliver in the way one might examine a bad penny, or an improperly cooked roast, or anything else that could have been decent but was instead a constant source of disappointment.

Oliver felt like he'd been slapped. That was the closest his father would likely ever come to speaking aloud his suspicions about Oliver's proclivities. "Mr. Turner is looking into a matter for a friend of mine, and since I find myself at loose ends, I offered to assist."

"I see." The earl's milky blue eyes were still sharp enough to make Oliver uneasy. He tapped his long fingers together, his heavy signet ring glinting even in the feeble light. "Has Charlotte told you anything about your Mr. Turner?"

"Charlotte?" he asked, his mind reeling from the implication that his father knew of Jack's intervention in Charlotte's affairs.

"Don't play the fool, Oliver. I know perfectly well that he got rid of Montbray, and rightly so."

He fought to retain something that could pass for composure. "Did she tell you that?"

"No," his father said, sounding impatient.

"Then how—"

"Never mind that."

"Montbray has returned," Oliver said, because it occurred to him that if his father knew about the cause for Montbray's removal two years ago, perhaps he ought to be told that the man had come back. Perhaps he could even be of assistance.

The earl whipped his head around to face Oliver. "Where is Charlotte? And the boy?" His voice was low enough to be unheard by any nearby servants.

"With friends. She took William with her. They'll stay until Montbray—"

"Stop!" he hissed. "Don't finish that sentence."

His meaning couldn't be clearer: Oliver shouldn't sully himself or his father by even talking about how this situation might be resolved. They would be debased simply by having the conversation. Lord Rutland and his son did not plan or condone abductions, let alone even worse crimes. They left that to other people, evidently.

"So that's why you brought Turner." The earl had resumed a conversational tone.

"No," Oliver said slowly.

His father ignored him. "A nasty business, but Turner's a nasty fellow. How much did you pay him?"

Oliver's mind reeled as he grasped that his father had concluded that if Montbray needed to be removed permanently, Turner was the man for the job. He wanted to protest, but didn't know how or even why. A few days ago he had believed the same thing, but now it seemed impossible that Jack would—what? Stab Montbray? Poison him? Throw him in a ditch? The same man who had—no. Oliver felt a surge of tenderness and affection and other unbidden, traitorous emotions.

It seemed absurd to think of Jack Turner—gentle, strong, *decent* Jack Turner—in the same breath as murder. It seemed absurd, even though Oliver feared it wasn't.

He could piss out the window, just on the principle of the thing, Jack told himself. Why should the housemaid have to empty a chamber pot when instead there was a perfectly serviceable window? The fact that this sounded both highly reasonable and politically necessary was why he did his best to avoid dealing with aristocrats on any terms but his own. Simply being near them was enough to rattle his brains.

After he and Oliver arrived late last night, a footman brought Jack to a small bedchamber at the end of the family wing, decently furnished and quite comfortable but with no traces of the opulence that characterized the rest of the house. This was the sort of room you'd give a visiting solicitor or a physician who had been forced to stay the night. Ridiculous that Alder Court was grand enough to have rooms dedicated exclusively to recognizing the gap between master and servant. As if anyone who occupied that void could ever forget it. Jack didn't need second-rate bed hangings to know that he didn't belong at Alder Court.

It was, he understood, the people at Alder Court who needed that reassurance. The aristocracy and gentry did whatever they could to keep power and money to themselves. You were either Quality or you were not, and if you weren't, it hardly mattered whether you were a surgeon or a street sweeper. Only look at the treatment Mrs. Wraxhall, with all her money, had received. By the looks of things, Wraxhall's family had cast him off entirely for having married beneath him.

The existence of that gap between servant and master

made the entire structure unsteady. It implied a fluidity that those at the top of the heap didn't like to think about. Worse, it suggested that the difference between the aristocracy and those who emptied their chamber pots wasn't as clear cut as they might prefer.

He dressed even more sloppily than usual and didn't bother shaving, a totally unsatisfactory thumbing of the nose at this entire place. He had his hand on the doorknob when he realized that his careless appearance would reflect poorly on Oliver. It was no comfort to remember that the simple fact of Jack's presence—a former servant and sometime criminal—reflected poorly on Oliver.

"Bugger and fuck," Jack muttered. He took off his coat and cravat and proceeded to shave. When he got dressed again he paid a bit more attention than usual to the tying of his cravat. Never had Jack tied a cravat more resentfully and with more confusion than he did that day.

He was almost presentable when a servant came to inform him that the Earl of Rutland would be willing to grant him an audience.

The earl was sitting in a dark and stuffy parlor. A fire was blazing in the hearth despite it being a tolerably warm June day, and the old man had rugs on his lap. Even with his white hair and crepey skin, he looked disconcertingly like Oliver; it was the way the firmness of his jaw contrasted with the fineness of his nose, Jack thought. He had to remind himself that the earl was nothing more to him than an animate pile of money with useful friends in Whitehall.

"I need to dispose of your son-in-law," Jack said without preamble, as soon as the door shut behind him. "Again."

After Jack had gotten Montbray out of the country two years ago, he had been unceremoniously frog-marched to Lord Rutland's carriage by a pair of knife-wielding ruffians. Rutland had asked questions that Jack refused to answer, offered money that Jack refused to take, and then deposited Jack inconveniently far from his lodgings. Jack hadn't seen the man since.

"Then why are you here instead of wherever that blackguard is?" For all the man's age, his voice was unaffected.

"I have a man watching him and a pair of men watching the house where your daughter and grandson are staying." Jack had not been offered a seat but he sat down anyway, another hollow protest.

"Do you need money?" The older man managed to make it sound like an insult.

"Lady Montbray will pay my fee. However, if I need to resort to any services beyond what I rendered last time, it may be best for the lady to be kept in the dark. In that case, if your lordship would oblige—"

"Yes, yes." He sounded impatient. "Send word and you'll have whatever you need. But I don't want to hear the specifics, and for God's sake don't put any details about it on paper."

Did the man think Jack was a fool? He most certainly thought Jack was a murderer. That much was obvious. "I don't intend to do anything . . . irrevocable to Lord Montbray." Not that Jack didn't think Montbray belonged at the bottom of a river. It was just that he wasn't going to be the man to do it. He drew his own lines, and taking money for ending another man's life was on the wrong side of that line, no matter how much the other man deserved to die. But he couldn't expect the earl to understand that. As far as Lord Rutland knew, Jack was a man whose extra-legal services were for hire, full stop.

"Then what good are you, Turner?" the earl barked. "My understanding," he said, his voice taking on an insinuating tone, "is that you'll do damn near anything for money."

Rutland wanted bloodshed, Jack realized. He didn't want the man who had mistreated his only daughter to be sent to live out the rest of his days luxuriating in a tropical paradise. He wanted the man dead and he thought Jack would do it.

Jack took a steadying breath. "If you want the man to die while cleaning his gun, or to fall into the river while in his cups, there are people who specialize in those accidents. I am not one of them."

The earl made a sound of frustration and fixed Jack with a hard stare. Here in his overheated sitting room with hunting dogs lounging at his feet, Lord Rutland looked like a pleasant, elderly country gentleman. But in an earlier era he would have been one of those fellows who spent his days murdering political rivals and poisoning the hell out of anyone who got in his way. Jack suddenly wanted to back slowly out of the room. He rose to his feet and prepared to take his leave, when the earl spoke.

"What do you want with my son?"

The question shouldn't have unnerved Jack, but it did.

"I don't want anything with him." A week ago that might even have been the truth.

"Then you won't object to taking two hundred pounds in exchange for staying away from him."

Jack forced himself to appear calm. Rutland was trying to

offend him, to punish him for having refused to do the earl's bidding. This had nothing to do with Oliver. He would never tell Oliver that his father had put so low a price on keeping his youngest son safely away from an unseemly acquaintance.

"I'll double whatever he's paying you. Triple, even."

Jack shook his head, wishing he could protest that he had never accepted money for that sort of thing, but he knew it wasn't true. And evidently so did the earl. How long would it be before Lord Rutland told his son about Jack's past?

Jack turned on his heel and left the room, his fists clenched, his face hot with anger and shame. The worst part was that he agreed with Oliver's father. It was unsuitable in every way for the Earl of Rutland's son to have anything to do with Jack Turner, criminal, scoundrel, and general reprobate. Their names being spoken in the same sentence would be enough to tarnish Oliver's name.

As he closed the door behind him, he nearly ran into Oliver, whose eyes were opened wide with surprise and something like betrayal.

Oliver stumbled down the stairs, his father's overheard words ringing in his ears. He wasn't surprised that his father had tried to pay Jack to stay away from Oliver—that was precisely the sort of controlling maneuver the Earl of Rutland delighted in. But Jack's total lack of refusal stung Oliver worse than any insult he had ever received.

He felt sick at the idea of Jack weighing Oliver's company against a sum of money. If Jack even considered the offer, it would transform everything that had happened between them into just another transaction of the sort that Oliver had hoped to avoid. Jack would be just another man for whom Oliver meant nothing more than a payment. He felt foolish for having ever thought it could be something more.

Oliver threw open the garden doors. The sunlight was almost blinding after the cryptlike darkness of his father's apartments as Oliver set out for the lake that lay at the bottom of the garden. Depending on his leg, perhaps he'd manage to make it over to the stables and see if any of the grooms he remembered were still at Alder Court.

Not that it mattered. Oliver had been away for long enough that he was a stranger here. And even if someone did recall the earl's younger son, they didn't *know* him. He remembered Jack's whispered words in the graveyard, about how Oliver was isolated by secrets and shame. And Jack didn't even know the half of it.

The landscape ought to have been comfortingly familiar, but instead it jarred with his memories in small, unsettling ways. The yew trees in the avenue had been aggressively pruned back, and the low wall around the kitchen garden looked to have crumbled and then been repaired. There were dozens of other discordant details that he couldn't quite pin down, but which combined to make the real Alder Court dismayingly different from the memory he had treasured during those long years of endless travel and fighting, bloodshed, and chaos.

There wasn't anything left for him here. He had, in the back of his mind, a vague and half-formed notion of leasing a small property in the country. Not actually on his father's estate—even in Oliver's daydreams that didn't seem like a good idea—but near enough for it to retain a sense of home. Something very small, perhaps nothing more than a hunting lodge or a shooting box. He wouldn't even need servants to live in. That would afford him some privacy, in case he were able to tempt a certain man to spend some time with him.

But now he knew that there would be no tempting Jack Turner to any private retreat. No, Jack belonged in London, in the smoke and fog and shadows, surrounded by miscreants and secrets. Not in the verdant countryside. Not with Oliver.

Nor could Oliver hide in the country. Again, he was haunted by Jack's graveyard whispers: *What will you do with the remainder of your years . . . So many days to fill without anything to do, without anyone who knows you for who you really are.* Retreating to a house in the country now felt like cowardice, like failure, like a prolonging of the loneliness that had always chased him.

He turned back to the house before reaching the lake. The soft grass was harder to walk on than even the uneven cobblestones of London or the muddy lanes of Pickworth.

Jack would make his own decision about whether to accept the earl's money. Oliver couldn't do anything about that. What he could do was show Jack what things might be like between them, so that Jack would know what he was giving up. And if Jack did decide to leave, at least Oliver would know that he tried, that he was honest with himself and with Jack.

Really, your heart shouldn't stir when you watch a man eat pork pie, or eat anything else for that matter. In the interest of brevity, Jack felt he could very well shorten the rule: your heart shouldn't stir, full stop.

But Oliver had eaten his second serving of pork pie and Jack was glad of it, and those were the facts of the matter. If those bare facts were written before him on his cards, he'd know what interpretation to put on them, and he didn't like it one bit. He was in a fair way to losing his heart to Oliver Rivington, and there wasn't a damned thing he could do about it.

Not that he'd need to. It was only a matter of time before Oliver realized what his father already knew, which was that Jack fell pitiably short of Oliver's standards of honor and decency. And then Oliver would be gone and the condition of Jack's heart wouldn't matter in the slightest.

If Oliver was the least bit curious about what Jack had been doing with the earl, he hadn't asked. Instead he invited Jack to join him for supper on the terrace. It was too fine a night to waste indoors, he said, but Jack wondered if he was being spared the awkwardness of dining in Alder Court's dining room.

And so they drank wine from the earl's cellars and ate what Jack had to concede was a first-rate pork pie, all without so much as a single servant to hover over them or listen to their conversation. This was the first time since they left London that Jack understood why some people were forever going on about the charm of the countryside. The air smelled sweet and there was no smoke or fog to obscure his view of the sky. It was quiet enough to create the very pleasant illusion that there was nobody in the world but Oliver and himself.

Total rubbish, but there you had it.

Oliver leaned forward to replenish Jack's wineglass and then stretched out, putting his feet up on a low wall that ran along the terrace and folding his arms behind his head. He was the very picture of long-limbed elegance, and Jack wanted nothing more than to drag him off to bed. But that could wait, preferably until Jack could overcome some of his more egregious feelings and trust himself not to play the fool.

As the sun set, Oliver entertained Jack with the sort of easy chatter that required Jack to do nothing more than supply occasional rejoinders. Ordinarily, Jack had no patience for being on the receiving end of all Oliver's pleasantness and good manners, his infernal drawing-room charm. But tonight he knew Oliver wasn't doing this to manage him or to soothe him into a better mood. He was doing it because he was happy and he wanted to share that with Jack.

More rubbish, but no use denying it.

"It's growing chilly," Oliver observed after they finished the wine. "Join me in the library? Nobody will disturb us," he added, with a blush Jack could detect even in the twilight.

Of course Jack went. He would have gone further than the library, God help him.

In the library Oliver wrote a letter to his sister while Jack reviewed his notes, spreading his cards out on an empty table.

"That reminds me," Oliver said, reaching into his pocket. "You could use this to store your cards. It's sturdier than the string you use to tie them up, and you'd have less danger of any cards going astray." He held out a silver calling-card case.

"I couldn't accept—" Jack started.

"No, it's nothing. I have another." He didn't look like he was lying. Abandoning his letter, he came over to Jack and perched on the edge of the table. Taking one of the cards, he placed it in the case. "It's the right size."

Hell's bells. The man sounded so proud of himself that

Jack couldn't bring himself to refuse the gift. "Thank you," he managed. He took a good look at the case. It was very plain, thank God, with an engraved R as the only embellishment.

"I thought you might not mind the monogram."

"I don't." And he didn't. He had to stop his finger from absently tracing it. Instead he placed his hand on Oliver's knee and gave it a squeeze.

Oliver turned his attention back to the cards that sat on the table beside him. "You know, the other day I thought it looked like a hand of solitaire, the way you arranged the cards, but tonight it strikes me that tarot is the better comparison."

The wine had loosened Jack's tongue, or maybe it was that he was being lulled into a false sense of security. Stupidly, so very stupidly, Jack wanted to tell Oliver all the sordid truths about himself, all the things he never talked about, not to anyone.

Maybe it wasn't such a bad idea. If nothing else, his confessions would hasten the inevitable dawning of Oliver's disgust.

Jack spoke slowly, keeping his eyes fixed on Oliver. "My mother was a fortune-teller. One of the more unscrupulous of a pretty bad lot, as far as I remember. Anyway, that's where I got the idea of laying the cards out to see if they tell a story." Now, when Oliver saw Jack's cards, he'd see deceit and dishonor, as surely as Georgie and Sarah did. He'd understand that it was in Jack's blood, in his soul.

"Quite," was all Oliver said before reaching down to tilt Jack's chin up towards him. Jack's instinct was to shrink from the touch. He felt too exposed, too vulnerable, like there was too much written on his face to let Oliver look at him.

But he didn't move away. Instead he turned his face into Oliver's hand, brushing his lips across Oliver's palm. And when Oliver bent his head to take Jack's mouth in a kiss, he didn't shy away from that either.

But here they were on familiar enough ground. This terrain Jack could navigate without leaving himself too open. He tugged Oliver off the table and onto his lap, cupping his hand around the bulge in the other man's breeches. It likely said no very favorable thing about Jack's character that he somehow thought putting his hand on another man's erection was a suitable way to avoid intimacy, rather than to increase it, but he wasn't going to waste any time figuring that out now. Not when there were other matters needing his attention, such as the fact that he had a beautiful, eager, charming man in his lap, pressing into his touch.

Before he could properly appreciate that circumstance, Oliver wriggled out of his grasp and pulled him to his feet.

"What are you doing?" Jack asked, as Oliver shoved him backwards onto the table.

"For a man who makes his living figuring things out, you're terribly slow sometimes." He pushed Jack back so he was lying flat on the table. The look on his handsome face was positively villainous. "It's a flaw," he murmured, unfastening Jack's trousers.

"You don't—"

"Shut up." Oliver pulled the trousers down only enough to give him access before bending to swipe his tongue over the tip of Jack's prick.

"Jesus." Jack scarcely had the presence of mind to prop himself up on his elbows in order to get a better look. Oliver's cheeks were flushed and his eyes raised to Jack's. He quirked his lips up in a smile before leisurely running his tongue up the length of Jack's shaft. "You're killing me," Jack said.

"Is there something you want me to do?" Oliver inquired, the picture of innocence.

"God damn it, yes," Jack growled. "Take it in your mouth. Please. Now."

And he did. Thank God he did. He sucked Jack down, taking him to the root. It shouldn't feel this good. Nothing should feel this good. Jack shouldn't allow it to feel this good. He had thought to avoid letting Oliver perform this particular act, thought that would somehow keep Jack from being at the young aristocrat's mercy. But that had been a terrible strategy, both because it denied them this pleasure and because it was too late for Jack to avoid being in Oliver's thrall. If Oliver wanted to make Jack his working-class plaything, then so be it. Jack couldn't help himself. Any opposing arguments he could come up with were outweighed by the feel of Oliver's tongue swirling around his cock, to say nothing of the foolish way his heart sped up whenever Oliver was near.

He watched in fascination as Oliver's pink cheeks hollowed each time he drew Jack deep into his throat, his eyes raised to watch Jack watching him.

When Oliver moaned around Jack's shaft, Jack couldn't hold back a stream of mortifying babble, words of praise and want and pleading. He was embarrassed by his loss of control but also beyond caring. Oliver's only acknowledgment was to reach for one of the hands Jack had braced on the desktop, and to place it on his own head. Jack realized he was being offered a measure of control.

Jack leaned back on the desk and twined his fingers in Oliver's hair, only exerting the faintest amount of pressure to guide his head up and down. Oliver then tugged Jack's breeches down farther, began letting his fingers play with Jack's bollocks and—

"Oh, fuck," Jack groaned.

Oliver was stroking his entrance with one wet finger. He must have taken Jack's moan as a sign of consent because he began to gently probe Jack with that one finger.

It was too much. As soon as that finger pushed inside him, he was gone. "Oliver," was all the warning he gave as the pleasure started to gather inside him. He twisted a few locks of the other man's golden hair around his fingertips as he emptied himself into his lover's mouth with a groan.

His hands were still in Oliver's hair a minute later when Oliver slumped beside Jack on the tabletop, resting his head on Jack's shoulder.

"God almighty, Rivington," Jack said, kissing the top of Oliver's head, "that was some professional-quality cocksucking."

"Why, thank you." Oliver's smile was quite smug, and rightly so. "I take it you don't feel that this particular nobleman's son needs to be tutored in that matter?"

Hell, he had remembered that. Jack pulled Oliver close for a kiss. "I'm a fool." He reached for Oliver's erection. "Let's go to bed."

They were interrupted by the unexpected sound of hoof beats on gravel, followed by shouts and footsteps. Both men hurriedly got themselves to their feet and put their clothing in order. Jack smoothed Oliver's hair and saw the look of concern on the other man's face.

"Could something have happened to Charlotte?" Oliver asked, his brow furrowed.

"No," Jack said firmly. "Not with the men I have on her and Montbray. But let's go and see what this ruckus is about so we can put your mind at ease."

They stepped out into the hall, where they found a man covered in the kind of dust that came from a day spent traveling. Jack's heart sank immediately when he realized who the man was.

"Mr. Turner, sir, I came as fast as I could." It was the man who had been shadowing Montbray. "Lord Montbray is dead."

## CHAPTER THIRTEEN

With a sense of dread, Jack forced himself to look at Oliver, watching his expression go from surprise to confusion as his gaze settled on Jack.

"I'll pack my bags," Jack said to the messenger. "Then we'll go back to London on the mail." He headed up the stairs, but heard Oliver's uneven gait behind him. So he wasn't to be spared a scene, after all.

"You mean to go back to London without me?" Oliver asked as soon the door was closed behind them.

"I need to be there before the inquest." That didn't answer Oliver's question, but Jack didn't care. Oliver could hardly intend to leave his father's house in the dead of night, in the company of a pair of ruffians.

"Did you do it? Montbray, I mean." Oliver's arms were folded across his chest, his chin tilted up in patrician displeasure.

Not meeting Oliver's eyes, Jack scooped up his clothes and dumped them into the valise. "I've been with you for the better part of a week. You know I didn't nip off to London to murder a peer."

"I mean, did you . . . arrange for it?" There was a hint of hesitation in Oliver's voice, as if he were embarrassed to find himself in a situation that required such a question.

Jack sighed. It didn't matter that Oliver was wrong in this instance—it was only a matter of time before Jack did in fact commit an act that Oliver was unable to reconcile with his own standards. Jack had been waiting for this moment for days and now that it was here, it almost felt like a relief.

"I haven't had the pleasure of arranging any murders lately." Jack tried to sound like he didn't care how badly Oliver thought of him. He could have given a flat denial. After all, the simple truth was that he had been totally shocked to hear of Montbray's accident—shocked, but not displeased, of course. Oliver still looked skeptical. Jack wanted to cross the room, hold him close, swear up and down that he'd be decent and honest and good, all the things Oliver was and Jack never would be. "Oliver"—Jack's voice held a pleading, desperate quality that he hated—"you must know by now that I'm not an outright villain, even if we don't always agree." But Oliver's face remained impassive, and Jack's heart felt like it was breaking. So much for sincerity.

"A man like Montbray simply begs for killing," Jack said, resuming a glibness he didn't feel. "I'd wager that the house was filled to the rafters with people who had every reason to want him dead. Footmen who were tired of having bottles of gin thrown at their heads, housemaids who resented being interfered with—oh yes, he most certainly did that sort of thing. You forget that I was his valet."

"But he only returned to England a week ago," Oliver protested.

"That's long enough." Jack could only assume that Montbray inspired instantaneous thoughts of murder most places he went.

"One more thing and I'll leave you to your packing." Oliver sounded more dejected than anything else. "Did my father pay you to look after me?"

"To look after—what the devil are you talking about? He tried to pay me to stay away from you, which you already know because you were listening at keyholes."

Oliver didn't rise to the bait. "Before that. Did you let me accompany you to Yorkshire because my father had offered you money to keep me out of trouble in London?" From the blush on his cheeks, there was little doubt as to what trouble Oliver thought his father suspected.

"Jesus Christ. Do I look like a fucking nursemaid? No, I have never taken a single farthing from your father and I never will. God damn it, Oliver. You know perfectly well why I brought you to Yorkshire and it was to fuck you senseless and use you to gain access to people's homes." He had to take a deep breath to tamp down his anger. "Honestly, I'm more offended by this than you accusing me of murder."

"Good."

"Good that I want to throw furniture at you?" Jack growled.

"Good that at least you didn't take my father's money," Oliver retorted.

Jack sucked in a breath of air, trying not to dwell on that *at least*, that sign Oliver hadn't accepted Jack's word that his hands were clean of Montbray's blood. "And really, what kind of man would I be if I accepted a commission to keep you out of trouble and then proceeded as I did?" At this reminder of precisely how they had proceeded, Oliver blushed. Of course he did. "And if you don't know by now that I'm only here with you because I want to be . . ." He shrugged helplessly, and let his voice trail off before he started saying the sort of nonsense he had never before said out loud. When he could trust himself to speak without betraying his thoughts, he continued. "Just get out."

That was the last he saw of Oliver that night.

Black crepe was already tied to the door of Charlotte's house when Oliver arrived. He had driven to London as if he had devils chasing him even though there was no urgency. Montbray was dead, Charlotte was safe, and it was only Oliver's mind that was unsettled, filled with unbidden thoughts of bloodshed, and equally unbidden thoughts of Jack's arms around him.

He found Charlotte sitting in her boudoir, wearing a black day dress that must have been left over from the death of an aunt or cousin he hardly remembered. But she was eating cake and reading a novel, neither of which seemed to go with the mourning attire.

"Oliver!" she cried, throwing herself into his arms.

"Are you holding up all right?" he asked, not sure what the proper thing was to say to a woman whose violent, despised husband had died.

"Holding up? You must be jesting." She pulled back to look at Oliver's face. In a lower voice, she added, "It's over. I can hardly believe it. I'm afraid I'm going to wake and find it was a dream." She was nearly bouncing up and down on her toes, like a child about to have a pony ride or some other promised treat. "William and I came back from Richmond as soon as the footmen finished cleaning up blood from the hall."

Oliver tried to blink back the image of blood puddled on the marble floor of the foyer, its metallic battlefield tang supplanting the scent of furniture oil and fresh flowers. The messenger who had ridden to Alder Court said that Montbray had fallen down the stairs in a drunken stupor. The next morning there would be an inquest. Nobody disputed that falling down while intoxicated was exactly the sort of thing Montbray was likely to do. Oliver, therefore, had no reason to doubt the circumstances either. And yet he did: it was too convenient a death.

"How are *you*, Oliver?" Charlotte asked, holding him at arm's length and examining him. "I didn't think you gave a fig for Montbray, but your eyes look—"

"I'm fine," he said quickly.

"Only think," Charlotte continued, her hands clasped in front of her chest, "after a year in black I can go back to a normal life and pretend Montbray never even existed." She started to laugh and clamped a hand over her mouth so as not to be overheard. "I'm going to have to go into very deep mourning indeed, Oliver, and retire from all company. Because I don't think I can be relied upon to hide my delight. It would never do for that to be discovered. Very bad *ton*."

Oliver was disconcerted to hear his sister actually giggle when her husband's blood was freshly mopped from the floor. But why shouldn't Charlotte laugh? Hadn't Oliver spent a decade purposefully killing Frenchmen who had done far less to merit death than Montbray had?

But that was no way to think. The war was over, and the dubious ethics of war had no place in Charlotte's drawing room. It wasn't for Oliver to decide who deserved to live and who deserved to die.

Nor was it for Jack Turner to decide, no matter what the man might believe. Oliver sighed. The man was unscrupulous and unlawful and, worst of all, Oliver found that he loved him anyway. Because try as he might, Oliver couldn't delude himself into thinking that what he felt for Jack was simple, uncomplicated desire. If only it were, then he could wash his hands, walk away, stop trying to tie his conscience into knots.

Miss Sutherland entered wearing a plain gray frock; there had been no time yet for her to have her clothes dyed. Her eyes were red, her face lined with weariness. Oliver was certain she had spent more time crying than she had sleeping in the last two days. Charlotte immediately wiped all traces of happiness from her expression, and Oliver recalled that the dead man had been Miss Sutherland's cousin. And even though ten days ago she had been grimly determined to see Montbray taken far away from his wife and child, for all Oliver knew, she had been childhood playmates with the man.

"William is asleep," she told Charlotte, her voice as weary and wrung out as the rest of her.

"You should do the same, you know," Charlotte responded. "Take one of the sleeping draughts the doctor left."

"No, I'll be fine." She sank onto the sofa beside Charlotte and the two women exchanged a glance that Oliver couldn't read.

The mood in the room hovered uncomfortably between relief and distress, between anxiety and calm, as if none of them knew what they ought to feel or say. Oliver left, gathering that his sister and her friend would speak honestly to one another once they were relieved of his company.

He descended the stairs to the street, not sure of anything, not even which way to turn. There was nowhere he wanted to go, nowhere he was wanted. His body seemed to want to take him to Sackville Street, which only went to show that love made a man delusional.

After meandering aimlessly for a quarter of an hour, he decided to seek solace at his club. If any place could provide the illusion of a sane and well-ordered world, it was White's. Even at this hour there were already a dozen men present, all dressed precisely the same as Oliver himself, all drinking either port or brandy, all reading one of the London papers or conversing in hushed tones. The more raucous young bucks were in the gaming rooms or still at home dressing for the evening. After a week spent insinuating his way into various households under false pretenses and chasing the threads of a mystery, it all seemed very pointless. This club might as well be a storehouse for useless gentlemen. Glancing around, Oliver realized he might be the youngest man in the room.

No, he was wrong there. Wraxhall was present, and had just caught sight of Oliver. With more good manners than interest in Wraxhall's company, Oliver gestured to the empty seat beside him. If anything, he would have preferred to pretend Wraxhall didn't exist. He felt that he had failed the man. Oliver had gone to Yorkshire intending to ensure that the Wraxhalls' affairs were set right without too many of

Turner's extralegal flourishes. But those blasted letters were still missing and Oliver had been too busy falling in love with Turner to think twice about the man's methods.

As Wraxhall approached, Oliver noticed circles under the other man's eyes. He looked almost ill. He must have been spending enough time here for his habits to become generally known, because no sooner had he sat down than a footman arrived with a glass of wine.

"There you are, Rivington. Haven't seen you in days. I'd wondered if you'd been unwell."

"No, only out of town." Oliver found that he was touched that Wraxhall had even noticed his absence.

"Why ever did you come back?" Wraxhall glanced up from his wine. "I'm dying to get out of London. Feel like I've been here forever. My wife's mother arrived yesterday and we're to travel together to Kent tomorrow."

It took Oliver a moment to sift through his jumbled thoughts and recollect that Wraxhall's mother-in-law was the very same Mrs. Durbin he and Jack hadn't been able to track down in Yorkshire. His first thought was that he ought to tell Jack that the woman was this very moment in London. He'd want to talk to her, both to find out what she knew about the letters and also in case she heard that someone had visited Pickworth asking questions about her daughter.

Oliver had promised himself that he would do what he could to help the Wraxhalls, and right now that meant telling Jack where he could find Mrs. Durbin. Avoiding Jack entirely would have been so much easier, so much wiser, but Oliver was never one to shirk duty. Every minute Oliver spent with him, the further he got tangled up with the man's shadowy way of thinking. He felt that he had lost his heart and his sense of righteousness all at once.

Aching and tired after so many hours in the mail coach, Jack returned to his rooms only to find Sarah lying in wait.

She was sitting in Jack's chair, hemming a length of silk by the light of a single candle. "You could have left a note, Jack."

It hadn't occurred to him to do anything of the sort. He had been coming and going as he pleased for years and Sarah knew it. "I'm sorry." He was too exhausted to argue the point. "I thought you'd know I had been in Yorkshire—"

"Of course I did." She waved her hand dismissively, the needle glinting in the candlelight. "But then Georgie came around this afternoon with some tale about how you ran off with a gentleman and how it's only a matter of time before you come to grief."

Jack dropped his valise to the floor and tried to decide how much to tell his sister. "I went to Yorkshire on a case, and from there to Alder Court. I'm touched that you and Georgie think my virtue needs protection."

"Alder Court." She narrowed her eyes, probably running through the stockpile of information she stored away about potential clients. "So Georgie was right? You're thick as thieves with Lord Rutland's son?" She shook her head disbelievingly. "I'm only amazed that he brought you there. And that you agreed to go. What can the two of you have been thinking?"

Since Sarah was sitting in his own chair, Jack sat in what he had come to think of as Oliver's chair. "Rivington wanted to see his father for a day or two and I could hardly refuse." Which was nonsense, now that he thought of it. Of course he could have refused. He could have taken the stagecoach home from Yorkshire. But at the time he hadn't wanted to deny Oliver even the slightest thing.

Sarah paused with the needle in midair, her eyes round with astonishment. "You can't mean to say that you actually were a guest at Alder Court? An invited guest?"

"I can't tell if you're impressed or horrified."

"Neither can I, to be perfectly frank." Sarah lay down her needle and abandoned her sewing entirely. "It's not safe for you to be carrying on like that with this gentleman of yours."

"Rivington isn't anything of mine." Oliver's name now felt out of place on his tongue, like a word from another language that he had no business attempting to speak. He caught his hand straying towards the breast pocket that held the silver card case, and he knew Sarah would have caught the movement.

"You know precisely what I mean. If the two of you are found out, you'll be the only one to pay the price."

"You mean that an earl's son isn't going to hang for buggery but plain Jack Turner could."

"Plain Jack Turner ought to be careful. That's all I mean."

He tipped his head against the back of his chair to avoid having to see the worry on his sister's face. "I was very careful, but it doesn't matter anyway. Rivington had a timely reminder that I'm no fit company for an upstanding gentleman."

He expected a cutting comment to the effect that Oliver had the right of it, that Jack was a bad lot. But instead Sarah's expression softened. "As bad as all that?"

Worse. Much worse. He met his sister's eyes for a fleeting moment and shrugged helplessly.

"I'm sure you're best rid of him, then," she said quietly, resuming her stitching. The gentleness of Sarah's voice was worse than any insult. She knew him too well. Jack should have known better than to try to hide heartbreak from a person who had known him his entire life.

He unpacked his valise and turned down his bed, but still Sarah didn't leave. She must have decided that he needed company, or maybe only wanted to keep an eye on him. In either case he wasn't about to stop her.

Only when they heard the downstairs clock strike nine did Sarah leave. A few minutes later Betsy poked her head in the door. "The fine gentleman is here again, Mr. Turner."

Oliver walked through the door with his jaw set, one hand in his pocket and the other holding his walking stick as if he'd need to defend himself against marauders at any moment. Gone were all traces of the boyishly handsome man who had coaxed Jack out of his sullenness. Gone was the man who had given himself over to pleasure and passion without the slightest hint of those bloody manners.

"Very lord of the manor this evening, aren't we, Mr. Rivington?" Jack asked, mainly to provoke the man, but also to be the first to revert to using titles. He would not have formality and station thrust upon him. For good measure, he propped his feet on the desk before him so his posture could communicate any insolence his mouth had failed to.

Once again, though, his hand drifted to the pocket that

held the silver card case. To return it, he told himself. But instead he only patted his coat, assuring himself that the case was where he had put it, and took his hand away.

Oliver shut the door behind him but didn't sit. "I want to know precisely what role you had in Montbray's death," he said so quietly his voice could not even be overheard by a person listening at the keyhole. Which was a show of consideration Jack found both endearing and completely ridiculous, because anyone who might be in the habit of listening at Jack's keyhole—Sarah, Betsy, Georgie—had heard a good deal worse over the years.

Jack forcibly reminded himself that consideration couldn't possibly have anything to do with it. Despite Jack's assurances that he had nothing to do with Montbray's death, Oliver had come here tonight demanding to know what role Jack had played, not whether he had played a role. Oliver was no better than his father: he thought Jack could be hired to perform any act, no matter how heinous.

"I've already answered that." He wasn't going to defend his bloody character. If Oliver wanted to despise him, then so be it, but Jack wasn't arguing the point.

"If it wasn't you, then who was it?" Oliver looked down at Jack with a haughtiness that held the full weight of his rank and breeding. His lip curled in the beginnings of a sneer. And yet, when Jack looked at him, he saw the fear and uncertainty that lay behind the aristocratic façade. Now that he had known Oliver as a person, he couldn't stop seeing the man behind the breeding.

"You seem awfully certain that Montbray didn't fall by accident." Jack hooked his hands behind his head.

Oliver barked out a bitter laugh that reminded Jack of Rutland. "I wish I did think the man died accidentally. But I should have thought Montbray had a good deal of practice in not falling down stairs while drunk."

The same thought had crossed Jack's mind. If it had also occurred to Oliver, then it might occur to the magistrate. That could pose a problem—not for Jack, but for whoever had done the deed. And the last thing Jack wanted was for anyone to be punished for Montbray's death. Jack tapped his fingers on his desk, considering the issue.

With a look that failed to meet Jack's eyes, Oliver said, "My sister was in Richmond." There was something very much like defensiveness in his voice.

Jack wasn't going to point out that Richmond was hardly the antipodes. But it was difficult to picture flighty, fashionable Lady Montbray ordering a carriage, contriving to get her husband to the top of a convenient flight of stairs, shoving him down, and then climbing back into the carriage and ordering the coachman to take her back to Richmond.

Difficult, but not impossible.

A lady who was both an earl's daughter and a viscount's wife wouldn't be tried for murder unless she held a dripping knife. Still, this wasn't the kind of suspicion anyone wanted hanging over them.

"I'll look into it," Jack said, entirely against his better judgment. "But if I find who did it, I'll want to shake his hand. I'm not turning anyone over to a magistrate."

Oliver sniffed. "Justice—"

"Bugger your justice." No, Jack would not get angry, would not show how much he cared about this. "Montbray locked your sister in her boudoir and threatened to take her child away if she didn't accede to his demands." He had done other things besides, but if Lady Montbray hadn't confided in her brother then it wasn't Jack's place to tell the tale. "And now he's dead. If that isn't justice, then I don't know what is."

Oliver waved his hand in a gesture that seemed to dismiss Jack's concept of justice along with Jack himself. "What you're describing is anarchy, not justice," he said, as if his opinions on the matter were worth more than Jack's own. "We have laws for a reason. There can't be one person who decides who deserves to live."

Jack tamped down a surge of irritation, as well as something fiercer than irritation. He was a fool to expect a gentleman to understand, but he wanted so badly for Oliver to know how much Jack's work mattered to him. "You have more faith in judges and juries than I do." He tipped his chair back onto two legs so that his posture was casual and wouldn't belie the seriousness of his words. "But that stands to reason, I suppose. The entire system is meant to prop up people like you—"

"People like me?" Oliver's cheeks reddened with indignation.

*Good,* Jack thought. *Get angry, then sod off before you insult me any further.* "Rich men. Gentlemen, specifically. The idea that you bloody nobs are so superior, so important—that's why everywhere we went together, people opened their doors to us. It was as if your presence was some sort of blessing. It's also why your brother-in-law couldn't have been brought to any kind of justice other than the kind you look down your nose at."

"Those are entirely different situations," Oliver protested, his nostrils flaring.

"They really aren't, though. The only thing that puzzles me is that you have such a high regard for the rule of law when you yourself break the law with pleasure." He dropped his voice so there could be no mistaking what law he was referring to. "And abandon," he added for the sheer sake of being offensive, and maybe also because it was the truth.

Oliver's face turned crimson and his jaw went even more rigid. His blue eyes turned icy and he flashed a look of pure fury at Jack, who instinctively took his feet off the desk to ready himself in case Oliver punched him as soundly as he had in the Pickworth graveyard.

At that moment, he felt that it would be well worth being on the receiving end of a punch or two if it meant that Oliver Rivington left for good. Here Jack was, volunteering to poke around in a death best left unresolved. There was no reason for Jack to interfere in that business except Oliver's peace of mind, and Oliver wasn't a client. He was just some aristocratic bastard Jack had had the bad luck to fall in love with.

A month ago, if an earl's son had come to Oliver, accused him of criminal acts, argued with him about the rule of law, and then expressed concern about a grand lady's good name possibly being tarnished by connection with a murder, Jack would have—

Well, Jack would not have let the earl's son into his office in the first place, would he? That was where he had gone wrong, clearly. But it was too late to wring his hands over that. However it had happened, Jack now had Oliver Rivington's needs and interests mixed up in his own, and he couldn't see his way out of it.

Oliver turned for the door without even offering Jack a handshake. "Oh, by the by," he said, half out the door and looking back over his shoulder. "Mrs. Durbin is spending tonight at her daughter's house, and then leaving for Kent."

Jack could care less about Mrs. Durbin or blackmail or anything else. He'd be damned if he was going to drag his tired, travel-stained, stupidly heartsick body to the Wraxhalls' house and finagle a way inside. He was in no mood for subterfuge.

Distracted, he caught himself reaching for the card case yet again. He took it out of his pocket, intending to immediately wrap it in paper and send it by messenger to Rutland House. Or maybe he'd hurl it out the window.

Instead he absently traced the initial and returned the case to his breast pocket.

# Chapter Fourteen

The brick wall in the lane behind Lady Montbray's house was still cold despite the warmth of the day. Jack leaned against it, letting its coolness seep into his body.

"How long are you going to keep this up?" asked a familiar voice. It was Georgie, plainly wearing last night's evening clothes, cravat rakishly askew.

Jack didn't answer, keeping his gaze fixed on the back entrance of the house. He had been watching the comings and goings here for most of the morning and a good part of yesterday as well.

Georgie idly kicked up small clouds of dust with the toe of an expensive-looking boot. "Your friend is inside, visiting his sister."

"He's not my friend," Jack replied automatically.

"I can call him the toff you're shagging, if you require that level of specificity, dear brother."

"If you're going to pester me, at least be quiet about it. I'd rather not draw too much attention. Don't you have somewhere else to be?"

"Don't *you* have somewhere else to be? Like attending to the business of paying clients, for example?"

Jack made a dismissive noise. He ought to have followed Oliver's suggestion and found a way to speak to Mrs. Durbin, but that matter seemed to be less pressing than standing around in Oliver's sister's mews.

"It's over and done with Rivington," Jack said. "So you can relax and stop pestering me about it."

"Oh, so that's why you've been outside his sister's house for hours? Makes perfect sense. Carry on, then."

Jack pressed his palms into the rough bricks at his back. "I want to know who offed Montbray."

Georgie was silent for a moment. "I thought the inquest found that his death was accidental."

That was true but irrelevant and they both knew it. Jack held up his hand to silence any argument Georgie was about to make, because at that moment the upstairs maid came out of the house. She was met in the lane by the groom, a man who had been in service at this house since before Jack had served as Montbray's valet. Yesterday had been the man's half day off, and Jack had taken him to the nearest public house to loosen his tongue.

The groom had told him that Montbray began "bothering," as he called it, the upstairs maid and one of the kitchen maids almost immediately upon his arrival in London. The second footman, who was willing to speak freely in exchange for a few coins, confirmed what the groom said, adding that Montbray and his wife had the sort of quarrel that ended with the footman being required to sweep up the remains of a smashed decanter, and the lady's maid summoned to pack her mistress's trunk.

As for the night of Montbray's death, neither of the servants Jack spoke with had noticed anything out of the ordinary—or if they had, they weren't telling Jack about it. Montbray had been, according to the footman, drunk as a wheelbarrow. He had gone out drunk, come home even worse, and then the next thing anyone knew he was dead at the bottom of the stairs. The only people in the house had been servants; only the nursery staff and lady's maid had traveled to Richmond with Lady Montbray and Miss Sutherland. But the footman had noted that he and the butler had spent a good portion of the evening trying to remove a copious quantity of sick from the library carpet, so there could have been a time when someone slipped inside and did away with the master.

Jack now watched the upstairs maid talk with the groom. He wasn't close enough to overhear their conversation, but based on the way he glanced shyly at the girl, and the way she brushed some dust off his coat, he thought they were likely stepping out together or soon would be. Both of them had every reason to wish Montbray dead, and they had both been present the night of his death. He didn't want either of them to hang for it.

"Think of everything in that house that you could steal," Georgie mused. "Watches, silver, all those little bits of nonsense made of ivory and whatnot. You could set yourself up for life, and they wouldn't even know they were missing anything."

"You could also get yourself hanged or transported," Jack felt obligated to point out, even though he knew Georgie was too brashly confident to worry about getting caught. Neither had Jack when he was younger.

"But that's not why you don't take anything from this lot." Georgie gestured to the house. "You leave them be because you're fond of them." His tone made it clear that the words were an accusation.

"Bollocks." He didn't steal anymore because he had other, more reliable, ways to earn a living.

"That's also why you're looking into this Montbray affair. You're up to your ears in nobs. It's only a matter of time before you forget where your interests end and theirs begin."

That really was the limit. "And where did Georgie Turner, revolutionary, spend last night?" he asked facetiously. "In the company of dockworkers and street sweepers?" He let his gaze linger on Georgie's finery—dinner coat, snowy linen, highly polished top boots. "Somehow I doubt that." Something else occurred to Jack. "How the hell did you know I was here, anyway?"

"Lucky guess. Take care of yourself, Jack. Don't forget that at the end of the day, they don't care whether you live or die." Georgie slipped out of the lane and out of Jack's sight.

Jack already knew that. What troubled him now was that he didn't seem to mind in the least. He pushed himself away from the wall and headed home, the sunlight blinding his eyes as he stepped out of the shadows.

For Oliver, the day dawned with the unwelcome realization that he had erred. Well, maybe erred was putting too strong a spin on the thing. Jack clearly ought not to take the law into his own hands, but Oliver need not have said so in quite so insulting a manner. He had behaved badly and now he would have to do something about it.

That wasn't quite true, strictly speaking. He supposed he could leave well enough alone, leave Jack to his own affairs and meanwhile carry on with his own life, such as it was.

At the moment all Oliver could think to do with his life was avoid Rutland House, where every post brought irate missives from his father, ordering him to return to Alder Court and cease associating with "that blackguard." Oliver had spent the morning driving aimlessly through Hyde Park, and now he was holed up in Charlotte's house while attempting to play spillikins with his nephew. Or, rather, play spillikins near his nephew, because Oliver seemed to be the only one with any interest in the game.

"Long, try for that one near your foot," Oliver advised.

"Stick," said young Lord Montbray, and reached clumsily for the stick he fancied at the bottom of the pile. "Mine," he said proudly, as the sticks toppled.

Oliver gathered up the sticks for another round of not-spillikins, because evidently that was how he was spending his day. Charlotte and Miss Sutherland were huddled over a book of fashion plates, determining what mourning clothes they required, and neither of them had any interest in coaxing Oliver out of his bad mood. Even William seemed to be barely tolerating Oliver's interference in his game of sticks.

One of the sticks slid under the sofa, William cried, and before Oliver could try to comfort him, Nurse materialized to whisk the child off to his nap. Oliver was left sitting alone on the floor, no real idea of where to go or what to do. He didn't really even have any idea of how he was going to get off the floor without hurting either himself or Charlotte's fragile-looking furniture.

"Charlotte," he said, thinking to have her ring for a footman. But she didn't answer, and when he looked over he saw that his sister had her arm around Miss Sutherland, which wouldn't have been so remarkable except that the companion was sobbing into Charlotte's gown. Charlotte was kissing her head and murmuring things Oliver couldn't hear.

Oliver felt a pang of envy at the closeness his sister shared with her friend. He had spent so many years alone, without anyone to confide in, anyone to turn to in moments of grief or turmoil, that he had almost forgotten why people sought companionship in the first place. The comfort and affection that existed between Charlotte and Miss Sutherland were things he would never have and he desperately craved them.

It was likely delusion to think that he could have those things with Jack, but he'd be damned if he wouldn't at least try. He dragged himself to his feet and slipped from the room without either of the ladies noticing he had left.

The first thing Jack saw when he turned onto Sackville Street was Oliver's curricle outside Sarah's shop, the ribbons being held by a groom.

"Fuck and damn," he muttered. What did the man want now?

But when he climbed the stairs he found his office empty. He bounded back down the stairs to demand an explanation from Betsy, only to hear the sound of a too-familiar laugh coming from Sarah's private parlor.

He headed directly back, past the bolts of silk and muslin in the showroom, past the workroom where Sarah's seamstresses looked up in mild consternation, and paused before the sitting room where she met with her preferred clients. He rapped smartly on the door.

Sarah opened the door, a stunned but not displeased expression on her face. On the table sat an arrangement of hothouse blooms that certainly hadn't been there earlier.

"Come in, Jack. Mr. Rivington was telling me that he needs to see you on some matter of business, but I didn't want to leave him upstairs alone."

Like hell she didn't. Oliver was sitting with one of Sarah's best china teacups in his long, elegant fingers, a stack of dreary-looking fabric samples wrapped up on the table before him. He must have mentioned that his sister was in need of a mourning wardrobe. And by the looks of things, Sarah had gone along with that plan merrily enough.

But when he saw Jack at the door he put down his cup and rose immediately to his feet. "Mr. Turner, I owe you an apology," he said promptly, his clear blue eyes looking genuinely remorseful.

Jack thought he could actually hear Sarah's jaw drop. For that matter, he had to consciously work to keep his own jaw decently closed.

Oliver *apologized?* Jack did not think he had ever received an apology from a gentleman. Not for wages that came weeks late, not for errands that had put him in the way of highwaymen or worse. Never.

"No harm, no foul," Jack managed.

Sarah must have had a client waiting, or perhaps she understood the need for privacy, because she slipped out of the room after assuring Oliver that she would herself conduct Lady Montbray's fittings should the lady so desire. Before leaving, she shot Jack a glance that was equal parts concern and curiosity.

"I'm very sorry," Oliver continued, his too-blue eyes looking penitential. "I didn't realize how wrongly I had spoken until after I had left you. I offended you and spoke poorly of the work you do, when the plain truth of the matter is that you were right." His mouth quirked up in the beginnings of an embarrassed little smile. "I mean, it's very high-hat of me to take issue with your practices when I myself break the law when I see fit. I apologize."

What was this, then? Jack found himself totally disarmed, in the sense that he didn't have a single damned defense left against this man. Helpless, he sat in the chair Sarah had vacated, and watched as Oliver sat as well. He knew perfectly well that Oliver was using his manners and his winning ways to cudgel Jack into amity, but Jack found he couldn't protest.

He tried to force a hard edge into his voice but was afraid he sounded dazed nonetheless. "What, you didn't realize buggery was a crime?"

Oliver's incipient smile exploded into the real thing. "Don't be daft." Then the smile was gone again. "It's only that I prefer to think that there's some order governing the world, some absolute rights and wrongs, and I like to think that order overlaps with the law at least to some extent."

"It does, somewhat." Barely. Sometimes. On a good day, and only if you squinted your eyes.

"In any event," Oliver went on, "I don't think it matters that we differ about whether Montbray's killer ought to be brought to justice."

Jack had to disagree with him on that point. It most certainly did matter. Oliver had an utterly misguided faith that anything approaching justice could be carried out in a world where one group of people—men like Oliver himself—had most of the money and influence.

"Why did you even care in the first place?" Jack absently picked up the stack of fabric samples. Black crepe, black bombazine, some dove gray muslin for later on. So fine, so thoroughly a part of the world that Oliver belonged to. Jack was hardly even fit to launder anything so costly.

Oliver was silent for a moment before he spoke, but he didn't once look away from Jack. "My father bought my commission when I was seventeen, and I stayed in the army until a few months ago. That life was all I knew. I had hoped that life in peacetime would have less . . . moral ambiguity. Less chaos."

Jack noticed how Oliver failed to mention exactly what chaos his life in the army had involved, but he could fill in the details well enough using his imagination and what he had read in the newspaper. Small wonder Oliver had returned to the country of his birth hoping to find a dreamland where virtue was rewarded and vice punished.

Jack got to his feet to open the cupboard where Sarah kept her secret stash of brandy and sloshed some into two glasses. Handing one to Oliver, he asked the question he needed the answer to. "Why did you come here today?"

Another long pause as Rivington swirled the brandy in his glass. "When you insult a man, you apologize."

Sodding honor. "What did you think I was going to do, slap you with my glove? Challenge you to a duel? Bugger off, Rivington."

"That's not it at all, blast it. I care for you, you stubborn jackass. I did wrong by you, and I want to make it right. And if it's amenable to you, I'd like to go back to being friends."

Maybe Jack found him easier to believe when his speech was laced through with profanities, all that expensive polish replaced by frustration and impatience. "Friends."

Oliver scrubbed his hand across the back of his neck. "Oh, so you've heard of it." He looked up with a smile that made Jack want to sink to his knees.

This was dangerous ground. The safe thing to do was to send the man on his way. Jack was stingy with his trust and affection as a matter of basic self-preservation. Most people were terrifically bad bets. Jack had learned that lesson early and he had learned it well. Like as not, your average bloke would stab you in the back and never have a moment's regret. With gentlemen the odds were even worse.

He would have liked to think that Rivington deserved the feelings that Jack had tried and failed to suppress, but the plain truth was that the man was too kind, too charming, too utterly indiscriminate with both those qualities for Jack to know exactly where he stood. All signs indicated that Oliver Rivington was looking for an antidote to the boredom that had afflicted him since his return to England, as well as to the loneliness that had probably been with him always.

And Jack didn't want that at all. If he wanted to minister to the needs of bored aristocrats he could have remained a valet. If he wanted the pleasures of the flesh he knew where to find them and how to proceed so that he didn't get caught up in anything other than physical release. With Oliver, he didn't think he could do that. God damn it, he already knew he couldn't.

"You're looking at me like you're trying to turn me to stone." A faint and irresistible blush spread over Oliver's cheeks.

"Upstairs," Jack growled. If the man wanted amusement then that's what he'd get. "Now."

# CHAPTER FIFTEEN

Somehow they managed to get the door to Jack's office closed behind them before they so much as touched one another.

Oliver found himself shoved against the door, the solid length of Jack's body pressing him flat, leaving him almost pinned in place. But his hands were free, so he used them to squeeze and shape the firm muscles of Jack's arms, the taut flesh of his arse. It had only been days since their last encounter, but evidently Oliver's fingers needed reassurance that this was truly happening again, because he couldn't stop exploring Jack's body.

Jack didn't seem to mind. His lips were hot and demanding, his kisses so relentless and thorough that Oliver didn't know if this was punishment or seduction. Both, most likely. He ground his pelvis against Oliver's in rhythm to his kisses, and the feel of that thick, hardening member rubbing against his own made Oliver go nearly boneless with desire.

When Jack finally stepped away, Oliver thought he might slump to the ground, but he found a strong arm wrapped around his hips, steering him through the rooms to the bedchamber beyond. Jack gently pushed Oliver to the bed and then crawled on top of him to begin tearing off both their clothes.

The sun streamed patchily through the sooty window, giving just enough light to let Oliver see the intent expression on Jack's face.

"Christ," Jack growled, and it sounded to Oliver nearly reverent. "You're beautiful."

Oliver tried to imagine how he looked to Jack—spread out beneath him, naked and wanton. Decadent. He felt a blush tingle its way down his body. "I'm yours." He meant it.

Jack's only answer was a choked-sounding noise. He straddled Oliver's torso so that the head of his cock was in reach of Oliver's mouth.

Oliver needed no further invitation. He flicked out his tongue, sweeping it over the broad head. Jack braced one hand on the headboard behind Oliver, his body taut with tension and desire. Oliver slid his lips along the shaft, grasping Jack's hips to guide his thrusts.

Why had Oliver never contemplated performing this act while lying down? He supposed he'd have to chalk that up to a total failure of imagination on his part. This arrangement accommodated his leg as well as whatever peculiar perverseness made him go wild at the sight of a strong man kneeling over him, thrusting his rigid cock into his willing mouth.

"I'm fucking your mouth, Rivington." Jack's voice was nearly a purr, and Oliver was just coherent enough to detect that faint tinge of coarseness that crept occasionally into Jack's accent. "And then, if you're very, very good, I'll fuck your arse."

This was filthy language of the sort a man might expect to hear during an anonymous coupling in a foul alleyway, not in his lover's bed. But the sound of those words fueled Oliver's desire. He moaned again, letting the sound vibrate against Jack's cock.

Remembering their last encounter, he thought he had a fairly good idea of what "very good" entailed. Making sure Jack was watching him, Oliver pulled away long enough to deliberately suck one of his fingers, and then traced it down the cleft of his lover's arse.

"Holy God," Jack said as Oliver eased that wet finger inside him, so very slowly. "God help me, Oliver. I can't hold back with you doing—oh *fuck*."

Oliver didn't know why there was this talk of holding back—that would seem to be entirely beside the point of the exercise. He only sucked harder, using his finger to find the spot he knew would send his lover over the edge. When Jack came—with a groan and a shudder that sounded like the climax was being forcibly torn out of him—Oliver greedily licked up every drop of spend.

"Fucking hell," Jack breathed, still kneeling over Oliver, his powerful chest heaving with each breath. He leaned down to kiss Oliver slowly but deeply, gradually lowering himself onto Oliver's body. They rested that way for a moment, hearts pounding against sweat-slick skin, Jack's face buried in Oliver's neck.

"Roll over," Jack ordered gruffly as he climbed off Oliver.

Oliver complied, and allowed Jack to tug his hips up, leaving him entirely exposed. He felt strong hands caress his hips, his lower back, his backside.

"Is that all right?" Jack asked, his voice low and hoarse. "For your leg, I mean?"

It hurt—it always hurt, but now it hurt in a good way because he knew this meant he was about to have Jack. "It's fine," he murmured. "You can't be hard again already, can you?"

"Oh, I will be." Jack laughed softly, the puff of air cooling the damp skin of Oliver's shoulder. "And when I am, you'll know about it."

Oliver felt Jack press a gentle kiss at the nape of his neck and then a line of deliriously soft and wet kisses leading all the way down to the small of his back. Jack's mouth lingered there before trailing soft kisses all the way down to his entrance. Oliver pressed his face into the pillow to muffle his cries of pleasure. Jack's hands firmly gripped his hips, and then—*oh Christ*—Jack's tongue was doing unspeakable things. Surely he ought to object—this was a degree of lewdness he hadn't even allowed himself to consider.

"Jack," he managed, but he couldn't form the words to complete the request. He couldn't even form the thoughts. His entire existence had collapsed into Jack's mouth and hands. Instead he let himself sink into the pleasure, filthy and lovely and *theirs*.

When Jack stopped, Oliver nearly sobbed with dismay.

"I'm right here." Jack smoothed a rough hand over Oliver's shoulder.

Oliver heard a bottle being uncorked and then felt slick fingers inside him, and then finally, oh God finally, Jack was there, the blunt head of his cock pressing into him. Oliver accepted the invasion, inch by inch, until he felt Jack's hips settle against him.

They stayed like that for a moment, Jack still except for his hands stroking Oliver's back and shoulders. Oliver shivered, savoring the feel of Jack inside him, thick and hard, too much and so right all at once.

"Please." Oliver turned his head to see Jack. The look on his face was fierce, intent. A lock of hair had fallen onto his forehead and his jaw was clenched with determination as he began to thrust.

"It's all right, love," Jack murmured, so softly Oliver thought he might have dreamt it up. And then he felt calloused fingers wipe wetness off his face. Had he been crying? This afternoon he was doomed to die of either shame or arousal, it would seem. He turned his face into the pillow to hide his tears and smother the sounds of whatever he was about to say. Because he was almost certainly about to say something mortifying in the extreme.

"No, don't do that," Jack said, his voice gruff. "I want to see you. I want to hear you." He carefully pulled out despite Oliver's sob of protest. Gently, he rolled Oliver over and positioned their bodies so they were face-to-face.

Oliver complied, wrapping his legs around Jack's hips. This arrangement was not ideal for his injured leg, but he was well and truly beyond giving a damn about that leg, or anything else really, besides Jack and pleasure.

"Touch yourself," Jack said once they were joined again. Oliver took his cock in hand and stroked it while Jack looked down at him.

Oliver didn't know where to fix his gaze—the dark expression on Jack's face, Jack's glistening chest and perfect arms, or the place where their bodies met. So he squeezed his eyes shut and focused on his mounting climax, the almost unbearable tension that was finally going to break.

"Yes," Jack urged. "Do it."

Oliver came, pleasure shaking his body in wave after wave, spilling hot and sticky over his hand and belly. Jack thrust a few more times and then groaned, collapsing on the bed, his head resting on Oliver's shoulder.

"I'm dead," Oliver said, his voice ragged. His whole body felt ragged, for that matter—well-used and ridden hard. "I don't know how the hell I'm going to walk. It's enough of a hassle as it is, to be honest."

Jack laughed, giving Oliver a rare chance to see how a smile transformed the man's face from stern to radiant. "Well, we'd better manage something, because your curricle and groom are still in the street."

Oliver groaned, and Jack got out of bed to wash up and throw Oliver a wet cloth. Later, Jack tied Oliver's cravat and smoothed his hair with a level of care that Oliver tried not to dwell on, and finally pulled him down for a quick kiss. "Tomorrow?" Jack asked, and the note of hopefulness in his voice nearly made Oliver go weak in the knees.

"Tomorrow," Oliver agreed.

Everywhere they went they drew attention. Rivington simply didn't look like the sort of fellow to take his pot luck at an inn off the Ratcliffe Highway. He ought to be dining with the Chancellor of the Exchequer or a Russian princess, not Jack.

But this tavern had the best eel pie in the kingdom and

Jack was determined to tempt Oliver's appetite, so here they were. It would take more than a curious innkeeper to deter him from seeing Oliver decently fed.

"I was thinking of letting a small house in the country this autumn." Oliver, gratifyingly, had finished his pie and was now popping grapes into his mouth. "Something very modest. A hunting lodge, perhaps."

In other words, not small at all. Four bedrooms at a minimum, servants all over the place. "Mmm-hmm," Jack murmured, reaching across the table to take a grape for himself, letting his hand brush Oliver's, so discreetly nobody could notice.

"Something small enough that I wouldn't need live-in servants." Now Oliver brushed Jack's hand.

All these secret touches were a sort of code, Jack thought. Like ships communicating by semaphore. Jesus, he must be soft in the head. These touches were no code, they were a message written in invisible ink, and if you held it over a lamp you'd reveal the words *Jack Turner is an idiot.*

"Would you visit me in a place like that?" Oliver hadn't even tried to keep the feeling out of his voice. His hope was right there, out in the open, and Jack wanted to look away.

"No." Jack snatched his hand back. Then, seeing a look of hurt wash over Oliver's face, he started to explain. "I need to work. Besides, how would you explain your sudden urge to take holidays with me? Servants or no, people would guess that we were up to no good, because there isn't a single reputable reason for someone like you to spend time with someone like me. It's easier to hide our . . . friendship in London."

"I see," Oliver said, looking like he didn't see at all. He had to be living in a fantasy land if he thought the two of them could jaunt off to the country without raising suspicion. The son of an earl going to a hunting lodge with his brother-in-law's former valet? The only question on anyone's mind would be whether Oliver and Jack were going to bed together or doing something even worse.

"We can see one another in London," Jack suggested, torn between wanting to flee the premises and wishing he could pull Oliver into his arms to show him that this wasn't a rebuff but an offer.

"We can see one another in London," Oliver repeated, but with a curl to his lip that made it clear exactly how paltry an offer he considered it. "We'll come up with pretexts for visits. We'll slip through alleyways to avoid being seen."

Yes, that was precisely what Jack had been suggesting. They would embrace all the behaviors of secrecy and shame. Until someone noticed, that was. And then they'd avoid one another forever. That was the way these things worked.

"You're so caught up in the differences between us," Oliver was now saying, leaning back in his seat and regarding Jack with narrowed eyes. "Like we're of two different species. I've gone about with men from all walks of life—"

"Oh have you?" Jack said, unable to repress a raised eyebrow and an affable leer. He watched in delight as a blush spread over Oliver's face.

"No, no, not like this," Oliver said quickly. "That's not what I'm talking about. I've never had anything like this." Neither had Jack, for that matter, but he wasn't going to say so. "What I mean is that I've eaten lunch and ridden in curricles and visited gaming halls with people who didn't go to

Eton. The mere fact of us spending time together isn't as fascinating to the general public as you imagine."

"Did you see the looks we got when we walked in here? The innkeeper's wife took one look at your coat with those shiny buttons, another look at your boots, and then a third look at me, and I don't know what conclusions she drew, only that they weren't favorable to either of us."

Oliver pressed his lips together, likely thinking of how he could charm his way into the innkeeper's wife's good graces. But then his expression changed, tight-lipped concern replaced with outright mirth. "God help me, Jack, but do you have a looking glass? I swear to you, if I put you next to half the gentlemen of my acquaintance there would be hardly any difference in your appearances except that you're better-looking and more disheveled. I don't know how you manage to tie your cravat in a way that's so . . . well, offensive to the very notion of cravats—"

"Years of practice," Jack said dryly.

"In any event, there's nothing about your manner or your speech that says you aren't a gentleman."

"Oh, I know that I'm a passable copy. But like with paste, when you compare it to a real diamond you can spot the difference straightaway."

Oliver held his hands up, palms out, as if to stop Jack from saying anything further. "I take it I'm the real diamond in that revolting metaphor?"

Jack refused to smile. "Precisely so."

"The way you talk about yourself, sometimes I think you're under the impression that you're still an urchin on the streets of St. Giles."

"I might as well be, for all I have any business consorting with the Honorable Captain Rivington."

Oliver laughed and changed the topic, evidently giving up the argument, at least for now.

Jack realized that he was fighting the wrong battle, though. The real danger wasn't exposure. No, the end would come not with the fear of discovery but rather when Oliver found some other way to quench his boredom and fill his time. He'd stand for Parliament or start breeding horses. Maybe he'd take an interest in astronomy or agriculture. He'd look back on this time with Jack as a strange and vaguely embarrassing interlude: *I spent a month getting fucked by my brother-in-law's valet and mucking about with blackmail. How odd. How very déclassé.*

He glanced across the table at Oliver, who was eating grapes and giving Jack smiles he'd one day regret. The man had no idea that he'd look back on this day with shame, and Jack didn't want to be anywhere nearby when Oliver came to that realization. Jack needed to scrape together whatever last shreds of dignity he had left and find a way to say good-bye before things got worse.

The next day, Oliver left his curricle behind and walked the short distance to Sackville Street, where Jack greeted him by throwing him onto the bed and slowly making him come unglued. He seemed to take a wicked pleasure in watching Oliver unravel before him. Afterwards, Oliver lay on his side, sated and spent and too exhausted to do much of anything besides watch Jack arrange his cards on the table. Jack wore only trousers, lamplight casting a warm glow on his bare chest and arms. His hair was in total disarray, sticking up at improbable angles that only grew more absurd as Jack absently scrubbed his hand across his scalp, deep in thought.

"Are you entirely sure you aren't doing something mystical with those cards?" Oliver asked after a few moments of watching Jack repeatedly shuffle and lay out the cards. "Perhaps you have a family talent for that sort of thing." He tried for a light tone, knowing that Jack never said much about his family.

Jack flashed him a quelling look. "The only thing my family has a gift for is crime, I assure you. If you're referring to my mother's . . . career, I'm afraid she had no unnatural abilities. She tricked men into paying her to prevent whatever disaster she foretold in her cards. One of her clients caught on to the scheme and killed her. Presumably a person who could actually see the future would have been able to avoid that outcome."

"Oh," Oliver said, regretting having introduced the topic.

"You sound disappointed." Jack deftly gathered his cards. "Would you prefer it if I claimed to be able to see the future, or the past, or have the cards reveal divine truths to me? Would that make it easier for you to accept what I do?"

"That's not what I said at all." Oliver wished he was wearing clothing. "Forget I said anything, in fact." He moved to the edge of the bed and lay a hand on Jack's shoulder. "I told you that topic doesn't matter to me. And I didn't realize about your mother—"

Jack waved his hand to dismiss that thought and shrugged away from Oliver's touch. Suddenly, Oliver was struck with a realization. "Your mother's killer was never punished," he said softly.

"Of course not. Nobody cares much about dead whores." Jack turned his attention back to his cards and for a moment Oliver thought that would be the end of the conversation, possibly the end of the evening. But then his hand stilled over one card. "Precious little was done to find out who the man even was."

"I'm sorry." Oliver would have asked if his mother's death had driven Jack to pursue justice on his own terms, but he knew he wouldn't get a decent response.

"Did you learn anything new about the Wraxhall matter?" he asked instead, trying to change the topic. He had noticed that the cards Jack examined pertained to a different case.

When Jack spoke the edge was gone from his voice, a sign that he was ready to let Oliver cajole him back to good humor. "The lady is not in London, which is why I haven't been able to get in touch with her."

The Season was drawing to a close and families were trickling out of London. "Yes, she invited me for a house party in Kent next week." When Jack looked at him oddly, Oliver quickly added, "What? I've gotten friendly with Wraxhall." And when Jack's eyebrows arched in disbelief, he protested, "I get quite a lot of invitations. Don't act so shocked that somebody wants my company."

Jack rose out of his chair and eased onto the bed. "It will never surprise me to hear that someone wants your company," he said in a tone that made Oliver shiver with anticipation. "But sometimes I forget that you're on terms of intimacy with bloody everyone. You're a regular man about town."

"Oh, shut up," Oliver said as Jack's body slid over his own. "Are you going to go?"

"To what?" Oliver was distracted by Jack's mouth on his neck.

"To Mrs. Wraxhall's house party," Jack laughed into Oliver's ear.

Oliver tried to focus on the conversation, and not on the desire that was pooling in his belly. "I hadn't decided. It's awkward—Montbray was no relation of mine so I don't need to go into mourning, but I still don't want to gad about. Do you want me to go?"

"I'd love to search that house," Jack said in between kisses.

"Why not ask Mrs. Wraxhall? She's paying you, after all."

Jack propped himself on an elbow, evidently too distracted by Oliver's obtuseness to continue with his ministrations. "Because if the letters are in her house, it's because either she or her husband—or far less likely, one of the servants—put them there. So if I inform her that I want to make a search, it's excellent odds that the letters will be removed elsewhere."

"Then come with me." He hesitated, knowing that Jack wouldn't like what he was about to suggest. "You could pose as my valet."

The temperature in the room seemed to drop a few degrees. Jack didn't pull away, but he went perfectly still. "I've already told you that I'll do no such thing. It's—"

"It's demeaning, I know. Especially given how things are between us." He gestured at the bed, at his own naked body, as if the point needed clarification. "But I wouldn't suggest it if I could think of something else. You wouldn't do any actual valeting, of course."

That suggestion was apparently ridiculous enough to amuse Jack out of his bad humor. "Oh, so the Earl of Rutland's son will arrive at this house party carrying his own valises while his valet trots along empty-handed? Likely story."

"Leave it to me." He could think of a dozen ways to render his valet superfluous—he'd have his luggage sent ahead, great quantities of clothing so nothing would need to be pressed or brushed until they returned to London.

Jack lay back on the pillow, staring at the ceiling as if it would provide an answer. "All right," he agreed.

Oliver climbed on top of him. "Fair warning. I will most definitely ring the bell and expect you to arrive in my chamber at odd hours of the night."

"Taskmaster." Jack smoothed his hands firmly down Oliver's back. "I could sob at the idea of having to leave London again, though."

"A little fresh country air won't hurt you."

"No, my love, that won't hurt me at all."

Oliver searched Jack's face for some indication that those words were anything more than a meaningless endearment. He knew by now that he loved this strange, brilliant, prickly man. The thought that Jack might feel the same way seemed an impossible blessing.

But when he looked at Jack's face he saw a raw vulnerability that reassured and terrified him at once.

# Chapter Sixteen

It was the easiest thing in the world, cozying up to a fellow servant at a country house, especially at a party as sparsely attended as this one. The poor bastards were bored senseless, especially the ones who were used to a busy London household. Wraxhall's valet, a young man who cheerily introduced himself as Fred Harley, greeted Jack's arrival as a drowning man might view a floating piece of timber, only more so.

They were in a room off the kitchens where Harley was merrily extolling the virtues of a particular formula for boot black. "It's the beeswax that makes it so fine. I can write down the receipt, if you'd like."

Jack hoped he'd never have occasion to polish a pair of boots or anything else for the rest of his life, but he thanked the man and accepted his offer. "You're young to be a gentleman's gentleman," he added. "But you keep Mr. Wraxhall in fine trim."

Harley beamed. "He's an easy gentleman to work for."

"We should all be so lucky," Jack said darkly. He had no compunctions about slandering Oliver's character, partly because it was Oliver's fault that Jack was standing in the still room at Branson Court in bloody Kent, but also because defaming his purported master would be the best way to get Harley to talk about his own employer. "I hate to speak ill of the man," Jack lied, "but I'll say that he's sowing plenty of wild oats right now." He pursed his lips in an approximation of moral outrage, consciously imitating Sarah. "Women," he said in a sinister tone, figuring that this could do Oliver's reputation no harm.

"Oh dear," Harley said, plainly hoping to hear salacious details. "Many of them?"

Jack only nodded his head grimly in the hope that the younger man would fill the silence with gossip of his own.

"Mr. Wraxhall has no such vices," Harley said, possibly disappointed. "And I've been with him since before his marriage."

Jack ran his fingers along a row of upside-down jam jars, all awaiting this summer's fruits. "He married some kind of heiress, didn't he?" He examined one of the jars, as if it were more interesting to him than gossip. "I suppose he had to. Heaven knows Mr. Rivington will need to find a wealthy wife when he finally settles down." Between that and the rumors of Oliver's insatiable appetite for female companionship that Harley would surely spread, Jack thought he could keep Oliver away from the clutches of matrimony for a good while. Although he preferred not to consider how much that mattered to him.

"I wouldn't say Mr. Wraxhall *had* to marry an heiress, exactly," Harley said, keeping his voice low enough to avoid being overheard by any other servants who passed by the open door to the still room. "He had what Mr. Smythe, the butler, called a small independence. Enough to live on."

"But not enough to live like this." Jack gestured to the house around them.

"No, but he never paid me late, even before his marriage. Besides, he scarcely touches the money she brought with her." Harley paused in the stirring of his bootblack, as if he suddenly realizing he had said too much.

Jack pretended he hadn't noticed anything. "My wages are always late, when I get paid at all," he lamented. "And when you think of all the times I've had to drag him home from bawdy houses, all the gin I've cleaned off his waistcoats . . ." He shook his head, letting his voice trail off ominously.

Harley looked both shocked and delighted, and since he had given Jack valuable information, he would be rewarded with stories to tell belowstairs. Jack regaled him with tales of Oliver's dissipation—flinging linens about, leaving loaded pistols where one would least expect them, disappearing for days at a time and then reappearing with a host of opera dancers who needed bed and board.

No, there would be no young ladies clamoring after Oliver when Jack was through.

God help him but this was an awkward business. If Mrs. Wraxhall had staged this house party in an effort to put herself on the map as a hostess, her plan had not been a success. Oliver didn't know how many invitations Mrs. Wraxhall had sent, but there were a bare half dozen guests at Branson Court.

One of the guests was Mrs. Wraxhall's mother, Mrs. Durbin, a shrewd lady who had few pretensions to gentility. Within a quarter of an hour of meeting Oliver, she informed him that her father had been a grocer and her grandfather a costermonger, as if daring him to snub her.

He didn't take the bait. After spending a few weeks in Jack Turner's company, Oliver knew when he was being baited.

"I dare say, now that you're here, the ladies will start trickling in," Mrs. Durbin said at the breakfast table on Oliver's first morning at Branson Court. She and Oliver were the only guests who had come down. "An earl's son. What a coup for Lydia," she said in a tone that made it clear she was not even slightly interested in earls' sons or social coups.

Oliver glanced up from the freshly ironed London paper a footman had brought him. "Ladies?" he asked, not quite following.

"Well, obviously. A bachelor from a good family? The vicar has three daughters, you know," Mrs. Durbin explained between bites of kippers.

"I'll take that under advisement," Oliver said, faintly startled by the lady's forthrightness.

"My son-in-law will let you hide in the library with him. He may even still be sober, at this hour."

How on earth could nervous, painfully correct Lydia Wraxhall be this woman's daughter? Oliver had to hand it to Mrs. Wraxhall. Another lady might have tried to keep such a mother hidden away in order to bury her own common roots. Either Mrs. Wraxhall cared less for society's opinion of her than Oliver had supposed, or she had guessed that meeting her mother would prevent people from imagining a far more vulgar parent lurking in the north. Or perhaps Mrs. Durbin had simply invited herself.

He didn't even seriously consider the possibility that Mrs. Wraxhall had invited her mother out of filial fondness. That was something else that time with Jack had taught him—always distrust sentimental motives.

"What *are* you doing here, Mr. Rivington?" she asked, startling Oliver with how similar her train of thought was to his own. "You don't seem to be on intimate terms with my daughter or her husband. I imagine you have a dozen better places to be." Oliver opened his mouth to say something vague and complimentary about his hostess, but Mrs. Durbin spoke first. "I received a letter that a man named Rivington was visiting Pickworth, near my own home."

A letter! Now, who in Pickworth would have informed Mrs. Durbin of their visit? Miss Barrow? It had to have been her, Oliver guessed, remembering that Mrs. Durbin had given Alice Barrow the use of that charming cottage. Jack had been certain that this put Miss Barrow in the old lady's pocket, and he must have been right.

"Yorkshire is lovely this time of year." Oliver didn't think for a minute that he had tricked the woman into believing that he had traveled north to enjoy its dubious climate.

"She's in some kind of trouble. Don't think I can't tell. I'm her mother." She gestured at him with a fork. "She looks like death warmed over—she's not yet twenty five but you'd never know it. He sits in his library drinking, she frets and paces. There ought to be a baby by now, but there isn't. I may be an old woman and you may be a gentleman, but let me tell you, my boy, if I find out that you're part of the reason my daughter is unhappy, you'll pay for it."

She delivered that message in a quiet voice, but Oliver had no doubt that at least one footman had overheard and would no doubt tell the tale to great success belowstairs. Oliver shuddered to think how amused Jack would be.

"I assure you I am not part of her trouble," Oliver tried to reassure the lady. "She invited me because I'm friendly with Wraxhall. This visit is totally unconnected with my business in Yorkshire." This was not far from the truth, in that Mrs. Wraxhall hadn't known Oliver was connected with her blackmail inquiry when she invited him.

Mrs. Durbin seemed to recall the presence of servants and waved her hand to dismiss them from the room. "She was always ambitious. She wanted a Season in London even though the assembly rooms in York were good enough for her cousins. Besides which, she had a good man ready to marry her, a man with a sight more money than her Mr. Wraxhall. But that wasn't good enough. And if that same ambition has gotten her into a mess with a scapegrace like you, then you'll be the one who pays the price."

Jack pushed open the door to Oliver's room without knocking. "What the devil do you mean by not informing me when you've received a direct threat?"

Oliver glanced up from his looking glass, razor in hand and shaving soap still on his chin. He had the nerve to look surprised at Jack's furor. "Do you mean Mrs. Durbin? She has to be sixty."

"I don't care how old she is." He walked over and took the razor out of Oliver's hands, crouching before him. "She threatened you. Do you not see how that might be relevant to me, both professionally and personally, Oliver? I'm here, looking for information that might shed some light on this matter, and you learn that the client's mother is in the practice of issuing threats, but you don't tell me?"

"And personally?" He turned away from Jack to arrange the objects on the shaving table, as if he suddenly needed the shaving soap to be at right angles to his comb.

"You dimwit," Jack said with a degree of fondness he should have been ashamed to own. "Here, hold still. You've missed a place." He gently scraped the razor across Oliver's jaw. "Now tell me what else you learned from the old lady." As Oliver related the details of his conversation with Mrs. Durbin, Jack felt like this tangle was starting to unknot itself. "So, according to her mother, Mrs. Wraxhall married for status. But according to his valet, Mr. Wraxhall did not marry out of a pressing need for funds."

"That brings us back to whether they had to marry for other reasons. Charlotte was quite sure the two of them were caught out on a balcony at some gathering in Brighton and married to avoid the scandal."

"They don't seem the sort for a grope and tickle behind a potted plant, do they?" Jack asked, tying Oliver's cravat with mathematical precision.

"Hardly." Oliver tilted his chin up to give Jack room to work. "But if Lydia Durbin wanted to marry a man with pretensions to gentility, she might well have lured Wraxhall out to a balcony."

Jack stood back to admire his handiwork. Now *that* was a well-tied cravat. "She'd have done better to lure someone with a family less inclined to disown him. An ambitious girl would do her research, I would have thought."

"Do you think they were in love?" Oliver looked impossibly perfect in his evening attire, his long-limbed gracefulness accentuated by the perfect tailoring of his clothes. Whatever fortune he had spent on that getup had been worth it, even if such a shameful expenditure ought to have Jack yearning for the guillotine. "Are you going to answer me or ogle me?" Oliver was blushing and Jack wanted to strip off those perfect clothes bit by bit to see how far the blush spread. But that would have to wait for later, because in a few minutes Oliver would have to go downstairs and be charming to this wretched crew over the dinner table.

Jack didn't know how to answer him, though. He wanted to disparage the idea of love, but that ship had sailed. He sighed. "A love story was the last thing I expected to find in this matter, but I do think Mr. Wraxhall may have been fond of his wife." Whether his feelings had altered was another matter. But Jack didn't want to speak of altered feelings, not tonight.

"Mrs. Durbin would have preferred that her daughter marry Hector Lewis," Oliver said. "She disapproves of her daughter's ambition. Sees it as a slap in the face."

"Which it is," Jack pointed out.

"But she still gave her daughter a handsome dowry. She could have refused, and I think she wishes she had."

Jack risked mussing Oliver's hair and cravat by pulling him in for a kiss. "I love that you feel bad for a person who threatened you with bodily harm." He needed to stop saying that word, but it kept leaking out of him like water out of an old tea kettle.

Oliver seemed to understand not to make too much of it, though. He only took Jack's face in his hands and kissed him back, slowly but thoroughly. Jack smoothed Oliver's hair back into something presentable, and watched him head out the door to mingle with his equals.

Oliver was left alone at the dinner table with his very inebriated host. Wraxhall looked wrung out, used up, a raggedy version of the man Oliver had met at White's a month or so ago. By the looks of things, all it would take would be another glass or two of brandy and Wraxhall would be insensible. Then Oliver would pack him off to bed, allowing Jack to make a thorough search of the library.

"You were better off in the army, Rivington," Wraxhall slurred, his eyes bleary. He was slumped in his chair, and as he spoke he didn't look away from the glass in his hand.

Oliver tamped down the surge of irritation he felt whenever someone presumed to tell him how lucky he had been to be a soldier. "Better off than what?" was all he asked, though. Better off than spending that decade warm and safe, far away from musket fire and typhus and pestilential infestations of body lice? Better off than watching his friends die or suffer or commit acts of sickening depravity simply because they could?

"Better than marrying." Wraxhall's voice was thick with drink and disuse. That was not the answer Oliver was expecting. "Maybe the marrying wasn't the problem," Wraxhall continued with the exaggerated seriousness of a man very much in his cups, "so much as the . . ." His voice trailed off and he took a long pull of brandy. "So much as the loving," he concluded, looking embarrassed.

"The loving?" Oliver asked, because he couldn't think of any other response to make. The loving? What did that even mean? And how drunk did a man have to be to say such a thing out loud in his own dining room?

"I loved her. Nobody believed it, including her, I suppose." He let out a huff of unamused laughter. "But I loved her."

Oliver didn't know which question to ask first: Did she love you in return? Do you love her still? He settled on, "What are you going to do?"

Wraxhall laughed again, bitter and brief. "About this?" He made a sweeping gesture that took in the house, his life, and there was no telling what else. "God knows." Another long swig of brandy. "I'm going to tell other men not to make the same mistake. Not that it'll do much good. Everyone told me, after all. My parents, my brother, my friends."

"What did they tell you?" Oliver was having a hard time following.

"Not to marry a woman on so short an acquaintance." He ticked the items off on his fingers. "Not to marry someone outside our social sphere." He said those last words so that Oliver thought he could hear the quotation marks. "And not to marry for love."

Oliver could imagine his father saying much the same thing. He had heard Charlotte repeat the sentiment, even though she surely knew only too well how badly marriage could work out even when marrying a social equal whose family one has known since the cradle and for whom one harbors no fond feelings whatsoever. Oliver didn't think he agreed with this wisdom, but he also knew that he'd never have to put that to the test. He would never marry for love, nor for any other reason.

But he would have liked to think that if he were the sort of man who could feel for a woman half of what he felt for Jack Turner, he would marry her in a heartbeat, angry families and social awkwardness be damned. Love was something one ought to cling to with both hands.

"An idealist, I see." Wraxhall turned his unfocused gaze onto Oliver and evidently guessed the turn of his thoughts. "You think my family is cynical. You think *I* am cynical."

Oliver's every instinct was to smooth things over, to steer this conversation away from a topic that was so obviously distressing before the man drunkenly said something he might regret. It would take nothing at all to introduce a safer topic—a remark about grain prices or Parliament and then they'd be back on level ground. But he felt that he had a duty to Jack to see if he could learn something useful about Mrs. Wraxhall and her letters. Wraxhall, after all, was talkative and too drunk to know what he shouldn't be talking about.

"I don't think you're cynical," Oliver said. "I think there's something you want to tell me."

For a moment, Oliver thought he had overplayed his hand. Wraxhall stared at him, something like wariness flitting across his face. But then he spoke. "I found something." Oliver nodded, trying to encourage the man without interrupting his thoughts. "Letters." The word was scarcely more than a breath.

"Oh?" Oliver took another sip of brandy, as if the matter was of no consequence to him. As if his heart wasn't pounding.

"Between my wife and another man." The word *wife* was the saddest syllable Oliver had ever heard, seemingly consisting of layers of sorrow and anger and disappointment held together by nothing but brandy. "They dated from before our marriage, but the fact that she kept them is . . . not promising."

"What was in these letters?"

He laughed mirthlessly. "Exactly what you'd expect. The letters she wrote were typical girlish nonsense. The ones from him, however." He shook his head, as if trying to shake the memory from his mind. "They were not the sort of thing any gentleman would put to paper. But this man was no gentleman. And it showed."

Oliver was silent for a moment, trying to make sense of this new information. Finally, he asked, "Why do you think she kept them?"

Wraxhall made a noise between a laugh and a snort. "Presumably to pore over them and . . . reminisce."

"Surely there could be another reason? After all, she didn't marry this man." Oliver couldn't very well say that he knew Lydia Durbin had thrown over Lewis in order to marry Wraxhall, but surely Wraxhall already knew that fact.

Wraxhall only shook his head. "Perhaps she did love him. My family thought she only wanted to marry me to social climb. I didn't think they were right, and I wouldn't have cared even if they were. But to think that all along she harbored a *tendre* for this revolting fellow . . ." His voice trailed off.

"I suppose you burnt these letters?" Oliver asked, trying not to betray his interest in the fate of the correspondence.

"That's just the problem, Rivington. I meant to, but I kept thinking I might show the letters to her and she'd have a decent explanation. What that would be, I can't even imagine. But that last night in London, I went to burn them and they were gone from my desk."

"What can it all mean?" Oliver asked, after telling Jack everything Wraxhall had said.

"It means we don't have to search the bloody library, and thank God for that." The library was two stories high and filled with a thousand places a sheaf of letters could be hidden away.

"You know what I meant. Who took the letters from Wraxhall?"

Oliver was wearing his perfect evening clothes and an adorably confused expression. Jack wanted to kiss him. For a minute, he thought he'd managed to ride out the urge, but the next thing he knew he had pulled Oliver in for a kiss. Oliver came willingly, almost meltingly. He always did.

"Here's what we know," Jack said, after a minute. They were on the chaise in Oliver's bedchamber, Jack reclining against Oliver's chest. "First, the letters were either explicit or pornographic or contained some other information that disturbed Wraxhall. Therefore, these letters were not something Lewis or his wife would want exposed. Second, it seems unlikely that she was in love with Lewis—she didn't marry him, after all, and if she was a social climber she ought to have done a better job of it than marry Wraxhall."

"If—wait—what?" More adorable confusion.

Jack was tempted to drag this out, but he'd much rather find the blasted letters and get back to London as quick as humanly possible. "No, my dear. Miss Lydia Durbin did not marry Wraxhall for status. She had a dowry big enough to buy a house at one of the best addresses in London and this house as well. If she wanted to buy herself a place in society she could have aimed higher than Wraxhall. There are plenty of gents who don't have a pot to piss in and whose families would have welcomed her and her money with open arms."

"Wraxhall's family seems to have dropped him outright. Nobody even presented Mrs. Wraxhall at court."

"Exactly. So Wraxhall fell in love with rich, rich Lydia Durbin when they were both in Brighton. And the lady either loved him in return or simply liked him better than she liked Hector Lewis. As I can't imagine anyone liking Lewis in the least bit, that doesn't much surprise me. The girl had probably gone along her entire life thinking she was to marry Lewis— their fathers were in business together, remember—but he turned out to be a nasty piece of work. So she set her cap at the next person she met who was a better match than Lewis."

Oliver had been absently stroking his hands up and down Jack's arms but he stopped abruptly. "How long have you known all that?"

"From when we saw Mrs. Lewis," Jack admitted.

"So, why did Mrs. Wraxhall keep the letters?"

Jack craned his head around, wanting to see what Oliver's face looked like when he figured it out.

"Oh, no," Oliver said slowly, his features collapsing in disappointment.

"Oh, definitely. She wanted to blackmail him."

Oliver sighed. "You were right all along."

"Often am," Jack said matter-of-factly.

"But why? You just said she has piles of money."

"The terms of the marriage settlement gave it all to Wraxhall. She only has pin money and I reckon she had an urgent need of funds." There were reasons a lady might need money, none of which he wanted to discuss in Oliver's arms. So he rose to his feet.

"Jack. Where are the letters now?" Oliver was still sprawled languidly on the chaise.

Jack needed to get out of this room before he started saying things that would later embarrass him. "Follow me and I'll show you." He dearly hoped he was right, because getting this wrong would make him look a right clod.

They crept down the dark corridors without even a candle. It was a tricky business, feeling your way around a strange house, but Jack had paced out the distance earlier in the evening. The house was quiet. Even the servants were likely in bed at this hour, and the only sound was the scuff of their boots against thick carpeting. But when they turned into the final corridor, Jack heard an abrupt and very out of place sound. A soft metallic click, the unmistakable sound of a pistol being cocked. He didn't need to turn to know who held the weapon.

"Rivington!" He threw himself on top of Oliver immediately before hearing the pistol's report.

Only after the two of them landed on the ground did Jack realize that he had been shot.

# CHAPTER SEVENTEEN

"It's only a scratch," Jack protested as Oliver dragged him through the darkened passageways. Behind them, he could hear doors opening and the raised voices of guests who had been startled awake by the shot.

"I don't give a damn what it is," Oliver growled as soon as they were safely back to his room, the door closed behind them. He sounded as fierce as Jack had ever heard him. "Either you let me tend to it or I'm summoning a surgeon, and that's final." With that, he proceeded to efficiently strip off Jack's blood-soaked clothes.

Jack could clearly see a little hole on one side of his arm. Likely there was a matching wound on the other side. The thought made him go a little faint.

"Damn," he heard Oliver say, and the next thing he knew he was being shoved into a chair. Oliver was pressing a piece of toweling to the wound in order to staunch the blood. The acrid aroma of smelling salts wafted into Jack's nostrils.

"Christ, Rivington. Do you travel with those?" he asked after his head was clear enough to speak.

"I put them in my case in the event you got sick in the carriage."

"Oh, very funny." But the salts had done away with his wooziness, and now Jack could study Oliver's face. He was ashen. "I'll be fine, you know." Jack put his uninjured hand on Oliver's arm.

They sat in silence for several minutes, Oliver's hand pressing the cloth hard onto Jack's wound. In the distance, there was the sound of voices and footsteps. Jack hoped the shooter had enough presence of mind to deliver the usual falsehoods about improperly cleaning one's weapon. "Did we leave a trail of blood leading back here?"

Oliver gaped at him. "That's what you're thinking of right now?"

"Never mind, I remember that the carpets are red."

"Are you going to tell me who did this? I assume you know."

"Yes. Obviously. But I don't want to talk about it now. Tomorrow." First he would get the letters back, then he'd talk to Mrs. Wraxhall, then he'd go to London and spend about a week in bed. He'd let Sarah fuss over him as much as she cared to.

"I'm afraid I'm being very tiresome," Oliver said with a rare edge to his voice, "but do we need to worry about being shot in our beds while we sleep?"

"No." An insufficient answer, but the best he could do right now.

Oliver gingerly lifted the cloth. The bleeding had slowed. "You'll heal better with a couple of stitches," he said, his voice strained, "but I'm not fool enough to ask whether you'll let me call for a surgeon. And the truth is that I've seen worse wounds heal without being sewn up."

The pistol had likely been one of those tiny weapons women carry in their reticules, and it hadn't been fired at close range. Jack closed his eyes and heard Oliver rummaging around in his valise. A few moments later he felt a glass pressed into his hand. He sipped tentatively. Brandy and the unmistakable bitterness of laudanum. "I don't need—"

"Oh, yes you do. In an hour or two when your nerves wear off, the pain will hit." Oliver began unwinding his cravat with one bloody hand. "Do you often have people shooting at you?"

Sometimes. "No."

"I don't like this at all."

Jack drained the glass of laudanum-laced brandy. "This is what I do."

"Well, stop, Jack. Stop. I was serious about buying a house somewhere. Come with me." He was wrapping the cravat around Jack's arm.

"No." Jack winced, more at the waste of an expensive cravat than at the pain.

Oliver knotted the makeshift bandage. "You cannot possibly prefer being shot at to being with me." His voice was withering. Scornful.

Jack remained silent.

"Oh, I see." Oliver brought over the washbasin and ewer and began to wash the blood off the uninjured parts of Jack's chest and arm. "You actually do prefer being shot. More fool me." There was more venom in Oliver's voice than Jack had thought possible.

"Oliver." He reached out again.

"Don't," Oliver said softly. But this time he didn't move away.

"I wasn't the target tonight."

"Pardon?" He glanced at Jack with the same confused expression that had seemed adorable less than an hour ago but now was heartbreaking.

"The shooter was aiming for you."

Oliver reared back and stared at Jack. After a moment he let out a puff of breath and raked his hands through his hair. He'd probably find blood there in the morning, Jack thought.

"You heard the pistol being cocked, you knew the shooter was aiming for me, and you threw yourself on top of me. You literally took a bullet for me."

That was about the size of it. "You make it seem more valiant than it was." He would take a dozen more bullets, along with some knives and cudgels, if that's what it took to keep Oliver safe. "I just didn't want you to get hurt." He rested his head against the back of the chair in order to look up at Oliver.

"Like I said, you took a bullet for me." Oliver took a deep, shaky breath. "Listen to me, Jack. I don't want you to be shot, and I especially don't want you to be shot for me."

"Well, it's not your choice, is it?"

"You stubborn, ignorant bastard." He was speaking through gritted teeth. "I love you. I don't want you to die for me. I don't want you to be hurt at all. I want you to be safe, with me. Why is that so hard to understand? What if you had died tonight? What the hell would I have done with myself once I had figured out that you did it for me?"

Jack forced himself to look directly at Oliver. "Then you would have known that you were loved in return."

Oliver's eyes flickered with frustration and gratification. "That's your only way of showing it, then? Dying for someone?"

Jack nodded, grateful not to have to explain.

"You bastard. I want you to stay alive so I can continue to love you." He bent down to kiss Jack softly, bracing his hands against the arms of Jack's chair.

That should have been enough. Maybe for a reasonable person it would be. He sighed and rubbed his uninjured hand along the back of his neck. "God, Oliver. I need you to stop asking me to give up my life." *I love you too much to keep saying no.*

"You need to spend the rest of the night here," Oliver insisted. "So I can keep an eye on your arm."

"My arm," Jack said slowly. "Right." He was leaning back in his chair, his uninjured arm hooked behind his head. He was shirtless and smirking and irresistible.

"Please," Oliver said with a roll of his eyes. "You've just been shot. You can't mean to . . ." He let his voice trail off, reluctant to specify exactly what he didn't think Jack ought to be doing so soon after being shot.

But Jack wasn't having any of that, evidently. "I can't mean to *what*, Oliver?" he rumbled, his smirk dangerously close to an actual smile now. Likely if he knew he'd replace it with something less winning, Oliver thought.

Really. By all rights the man ought to be asleep. Oliver sighed. "You can't mean to fuck me, Jack. There you go. Happy now? And you really *can't* mean to, so go to bed and I'll change your dressing in the morning."

Jack didn't move. "I don't mean to fuck you. Technically speaking, at least. I mean for you to fuck me."

That got Oliver's interest. Jack asking for anything was an astonishing novelty. "Do you now?" And then reason descended. "That's even more ludicrous. Go to bed."

"Is there some kind of pamphlet that lists what sexual practices are acceptable after being shot? Perhaps you could lend it to me so I don't make the same faux pas twice." Jack had put on a crisp accent that Oliver gathered was supposed to be a parody of Oliver's own.

Oliver raised an eyebrow. "Are you quite done?"

Apparently not. "The truth is that I've had a trying day." He gestured casually to his bandage. "And tomorrow is likely to be tedious. I need to speak to all these people and make them behave like good children."

That was his plan? "God forbid you summon a magistrate over something so trifling as attempted murder."

"We are not having this conversation again," Jack said firmly, his smile faltering only by the slightest degree. "The plain fact of the matter is that I would like to forget all about things like blackmail and pistols, and if you could assist in that matter I'd be much obliged."

Oliver wondered if the plummy accent and the unusual verbosity were Jack's way of hiding what he really wanted in a cloud of scornful sounding nonsense. The smirk had dropped from his face, replaced with a questioning, hopeful look.

As if Oliver could deny him anything.

"Get in bed, then." Oliver grasped the hand of Jack's uninjured arm and tugged him close. Cupping Jack's face in his other hand, he kissed him as gently as he dared.

Oliver sat on the edge of the bed and unfastened Jack's trousers, shoving them down. Bending his head, he licked the dab of moisture that had already beaded on the tip of the rigid erection he had exposed, then swirled his tongue around the head.

"I don't need that," Jack said, his voice hoarse. "You can go ahead and—"

"Oh, shut up and take what you have coming." If Jack wanted oblivion via a good hard fucking, then that's what he'd get, but it would be on Oliver's terms and at Oliver's pace. He heard Jack sigh with what sounded like capitulation, and then Oliver felt a hand on his head, sifting through his hair, caressing the outside of his ear.

The intimacy of those gestures felt stabbingly perfect, almost . . . imaginary. Impossible. He had never really dared to think that about sharing something like this with a man he loved and who professed to love him in return.

But the rest of this night felt pieced together out of moments from Oliver's worst dreams. Gunfire, the sound of his name being shouted in warning, the smell of gunpowder and blood. The ever-present threat of danger and death. He had seen enough gunshot wounds to know that Jack's arm would be fine as long as infection didn't set in, but what if that bullet had hit a few inches to the side, what if the pistol had been fired at slightly closer range?

Tomorrow would be no improvement: Jack would sweep violence and blackmail into the shadows, making himself as good as complicit. Even now, his lips wrapped around his lover, Oliver felt the threat of chaos closing in on him. He couldn't live like this. He knew he couldn't. He loved this man, but it would cost him his soul and maybe his sanity to face death and danger and chaos again and again. He could give Jack what he needed tonight, but he didn't know about tomorrow, or the day after that.

He pulled away and pushed Jack backwards onto the bed, then removed both their remaining clothing. "Oliver," Jack said, panting. He was lying on his back, his injured arm carefully resting at his side and his cock jutting eagerly up towards his belly. "Now." He sounded desperate, urgent.

"I've got you," Oliver said, wishing it were true.

There was oil in the chest of drawers near the bed. That morning Oliver had watched Jack toss the bottle in the drawer with a shrug and a raised eyebrow. That moment felt a month or a year ago, as distant as life before his injury, even before Badajoz.

"You don't need to bother with that," Jack said as Oliver began probing him with one slick finger.

Predictable bastard, resisting anything that looked like caring. "Oh, I'll bother all right," Oliver retorted, watching Jack's face contort with pleasure as his finger reached the spot he had been seeking. He added another finger, never taking his eyes from Jack's face. This was precious, seeing Jack like this—spread out before him, his eyes glassy with need and his breath ragged. He usually kept such a tight rein on his control, but now he had cast it off like a knight might have cast off his armor. He was strong and fierce beneath those layers of carefully crafted protection, but he was Oliver's for the taking.

A third finger, a moan of pleasure from both of them, and then Oliver slicked oil along his length and carefully pressed into his lover.

It had been a long time since he had done this. As a rule, this particular act was not his favorite way to seek physical release. But, God above, watching Jack's face as he accepted the intrusion, the mingled pleasure and tension, it was perfect.

He thrust the rest of the way in, Jack's legs closing around his back. With a groan, he began thrusting, keeping an eye on Jack's face to make sure he wasn't being too rough, giving too much. There was no possibility that Jack would ask Oliver to stop even if he were in pain, so Oliver let part of his pleasure be the thought that he was keeping Jack safe.

He took a moment to adjust his angle, tilting his hips up as much as his bad leg would allow, and Jack shivered in response. *There.* Now he began thrusting in earnest, a thrill coursing through his body as he watched Jack dissolve into incoherence.

"I love you," Oliver said, because he couldn't not. Jack murmured something in response, something that sounded like affirmation.

He kept his pace slower than Jack might have preferred, but there was more than one way to get this job done. Right now, Oliver was choosing the excruciatingly gentle way to drive Jack's troubles from his mind.

"Damn it, Oliver. Please." Jack's fingers dragged along Oliver's back, then lower, until reaching Oliver's entrance.

"Please what?" Oliver managed to say as a finger began to probe him.

Jack swore. "Fuck me harder."

And so he did. Briefly. Each time he slowed down, Jack cursed and begged. Oliver tried to save up the sound of those words coming out of Jack's mouth, to store them in his heart for some bleak future time, like a squirrel burying morsels to sustain him through the winter.

Oliver bent his head to kiss Jack and was surprised to find tears on Jack's face. "Are you all right?"

"Goddamn you," Jack groaned.

Oliver gave him what he needed then, pounding into him relentlessly, unremittingly. He growled in satisfaction when he saw pleasure wash over Jack's face and then felt the hot and sticky spill on both their bellies. Oliver's own climax followed, pouring into his lover's body.

He stayed there for a moment, propped up on his arms, staring down at the face of the man he loved. Oliver carefully pulled himself out and collapsed onto Jack's chest, burying his head in Jack's neck. "I wish we could stay like this," Oliver said, knowing it was pathetic, plaintive.

Jack was silent for a moment. "So do I."

Neither of them had to say that they couldn't.

# CHAPTER EIGHTEEN

Jack dressed before dawn in one of Oliver's spare shirts and his own blood-spattered breeches. He wanted to be dressed before talking to Oliver, knowing that he would need to avail himself of every advantage today.

"You brought twenty-four shirts for a week in the country," he said when he saw Oliver's eyes open. Jack owned eight shirts and considered at least four of them to be embarrassing luxuries.

Absurdly blue eyes gazed at him, equally absurd golden hair haloed on the pillow. What in the name of all that was holy was a specimen like this doing with a bastard like Jack Turner? It bloody well defied explanation. And then Oliver smiled—a flash of improbably even teeth—and it only got worse.

"I brought enough clothing so you wouldn't have to be bothered with trying to get stains out of them or pressing cravats." Oliver's voice was still thick with sleep. "That was our arrangement. You wouldn't have to do any valeting."

That also explained the twelve waistcoats and seven identical pairs of breeches. Jack didn't know whether to be touched by the consideration or horrified by the extravagance.

Oliver sat up in bed and Jack had to avert his eyes before he got distracted by the sight. "How does your arm feel?"

Horrible. "Fine. I already took some more of your medicine and changed the dressing." And a sodding nuisance it had been, trying to wrap one of Oliver's four dozen cravats around his arm single-handed. But anything was better than submitting to Oliver's ministrations. There was only so much tenderheartedness Jack could take and that quota had been exceeded tenfold last night. "All told, I think I prefer knife wounds."

Oliver seemed to notice what Jack was doing. "Why are you packing my things, though?"

"You can leave whenever you like. After I speak with the Wraxhalls, there won't be any need to maintain the pretense that I'm your valet."

Oliver reached for one of the clean shirts and threw it over his head. When his golden head emerged from the folds of snowy linen he was no longer sleepy, languorous Oliver. His expression was carefully neutral, betraying nothing more than a dozen generations of money and privilege. "Are you going to explain who shot at us last night? Or are you going to pack me off and let me read about it in the papers? Not that anything will be in the papers, of course, because when Jack Turner is involved the proceedings are always *sub rosa*."

Jack had no idea what that meant and didn't care. "That's right, they are." He watched Oliver slide into his breeches and boots with more grace than anyone ought to have at this hour. "But I'll tell you." It was only right for a man to know who had shot at him, after all.

Oliver noticed the tray carrying tea and toast. "You already rang for my breakfast?"

He had, and the housemaid had been very distressed to learn of the indisposition that would force Mr. Rivington to leave the party early. "Yes," was all he said.

"Thank you."

And now, Jack knew how Oliver thanked his valet for his morning tea.

"It was Mrs. Durbin who tried to shoot you," Jack said abruptly, wanting to shake Oliver out of his cool composure.

Oliver nearly spat out his tea. "She's an old lady!"

"She's vicious." There was no way he could say those words that didn't sound like praise.

"But why?"

"She thinks you're leading her daughter down the garden path. I . . . may have spread rumors about your insatiable appetite for women and your empty pockets. She knew about your trip to Yorkshire and put two and two together to get seventeen."

Oliver had paused with his teacup halfway to his mouth, staring off at nothing in particular. "I've never thought of myself as the type of man to be shot in a crime of passion."

"That's because you aren't. I, however, am." He gestured to his arm.

"Point taken," Oliver conceded. "And the letters?"

"Wraxhall said they disappeared from his home in London the night he saw you at your club. You told me his mother-in-law was paying them a visit that night. I think she saw immediately that her daughter's marriage was in shambles. Being an enterprising woman, she must have gone straight

to Wraxhall's desk to look for incriminating evidence." Jack
could have kicked himself for not having searched that desk
before making his escape through the window. "She found
the letters and thought Wraxhall had intercepted her daughter's efforts to blackmail Lewis."

"Why would she think that, of all things? Wouldn't she, like
Wraxhall, assume that her daughter had a *tendre* for Lewis?"

That bothered Jack, too. "Perhaps she knew something of
Lewis. In any event, when she saw you creeping through the
corridors last night, she thought you were paying a visit to her
daughter, possibly to demand money. So, she shot you."

"Good God. I'm quite a blackguard."

Jack grinned. "That's about the lay of the land. I'll talk to
Mrs. Durbin and make sure she sees the error of her ways.
Maybe ask her to marry me. It's not every woman who con-
templates shooting an aristocrat. I've had the urge myself.
Surely that's enough to build a life on."

Oliver did not look amused, however. He glanced from
Jack to the packed valise and sighed with what looked like
resignation.

Mrs. Durbin was already dressed, standing by the window
of her bedchamber as if she had been expecting Jack. She was
stout and wore unrelieved black despite having been widowed
over a year ago. Her hair was covered by a monstrous white
cap, her face lined with age. She looked so thoroughly in-
nocuous that he understood why Oliver hadn't believed her
to be capable of violence. But her small gray eyes were sharp,
her jaw firm.

"The letters, please," he said by way of greeting. "If you'd prefer to throw them into the fire yourself I won't object. But they need to be burnt and I'm not leaving this room until it's done."

"Who the devil are you to tell me what to do with them?" She didn't deny knowing what letters he referred to, which only increased his opinion of her.

He had to give the woman credit. She had seen that her daughter was about to do something terrible and simply did what it took to prevent that from happening. Her reasoning was faulty and her methods were flawed—pistols were decidedly excessive—but he admired how she simply was not going to let her daughter cross the line from good to evil. Jack had to admire a parent who thought along those lines, when his own manifestly had not.

"I'm the man you shot last night." He gestured at the sling Oliver had fashioned out of one of Oliver's cravats. "Your daughter hired me to find her letters."

If Mrs. Durbin was surprised, she didn't show it. "Silly girl. I'd like to know why the fool didn't come to me for money if she needed it so desperately and didn't want to go to her husband. Why blackmail? I wouldn't have thought her capable of it."

"Maybe she was afraid you would rub her nose in her disaster of a marriage, and remind her that you were right to warn her against it."

"And wasn't I? Right, that is? Only look at them." She shook her head in derision. "Pride," Mrs. Durbin said acidly. "In addition to blackmail." But she retrieved a packet of letters from the inside of a scuffed and disreputable-looking ankle boot—a much better hiding place than a jewel box, he was pleased to note.

Wordlessly, she passed the letters to Jack. He quickly thumbed through the sheaf, taking note of Lewis's coarse language, descriptions of— "Good God, have you read these letters?"

The old lady actually blushed. "Only the most cursory glance." She sounded defensive, as well she ought to, Jack thought.

"At the time you were ready to marry your daughter to this man, had you any notion he was so . . ." Lewd? Obscene? Casually pornographic? It would be one thing if the girl had liked getting that sort of letter, but she had repeatedly asked that he confine his correspondence to more genteel topics.

"Of course not!" Mrs. Durbin sniffed. "He seemed such an upstanding lad."

Jack wondered if any son of Mr. Durbin's business partner would be considered upstanding. Both families would have gained a lot by that marriage.

The last letter was dated immediately before she had left for Brighton. No wonder she had thrown herself at Wraxhall instead. Now that was not a man who would burden a lady with unwanted amateur pornography. Again, Jack remembered the scullery maid's two pairs of boots.

Instead of throwing the letters into the fire, he tucked them into his coat pocket and went in search of the lady of the house. He found her closeted in her dressing room. She was perched nervously on a divan, wearing a wrapper, curling papers still in her hair. Toast and an egg sat untouched on a tray before her.

"Mr. Turner." Mrs. Wraxhall's voice hovered between confusion and hope. She could not have expected to see Jack here in Kent, but he could tell that she was desperate enough to overlook that irregularity and many more if only she had her letters returned to her. "I wasn't expecting you."

"Let's pass over all that," he suggested. "And I'll pass over the matter of how you lied about receiving a blackmail note. That fib made things a good deal more complicated." He took the letters out of his pocket and handed them to her.

"Thank God," she said, her voice grave. She did not look pleased, only relieved, as she flipped through the packet. "You have no idea how much this means. Mary said you'd be able to manage it, and you did."

"Those are nasty letters, Mrs. Wraxhall." He thought he knew what was going on here, but he wanted to hear it from her.

"Awful," she agreed, flicking a wary glance in his direction.

"Your husband found them—although I don't know what he was doing in your jewel box." Snooping, most likely. "He thought you kept them out of sentiment."

"Oh no." Her face went even paler. "That explains why he can scarcely look at me."

"Your mother then found the letters in your husband's desk. She thought you planned to use the letters to blackmail Lewis. I confess that I was under the same impression until I read them."

Her fingers wrapped tightly around the packet. "That's not far off the mark."

"But it's not money you sought from Lewis."

Now she was holding the letters with both hands, as if she were afraid Jack would take them back. "No, not money."

"Is the current Mrs. Lewis a friend of yours?"

"No. I never met her. I don't care if she's the greatest villain in the world. She still doesn't deserve to be . . . mistreated."

"Did Hector Lewis mistreat you?"

"Only slightly," she said cryptically, but her jaw was set the way Oliver's got when he talked about Badajoz. Or rather, when he didn't. "Enough to convince me he'd be a terrible husband, no matter what my parents thought."

"So, you made your escape. You arranged for Wraxhall to have to marry you, is that right?"

"It was an underhanded trick I served Francis, and I knew it. But I couldn't think of another way to get out of the match with Lewis without putting my parents into a stew. Which is cowardly, but there you have it. I wrote to Lewis, informing him that if I heard the faintest whisper of his mistreating his wife, I would have the letters published. I sent another letter to his wife, saying much the same thing and assuring her of my aid should she need it. She never wrote back."

"Why?" She had gone to a great deal of trouble to help a stranger.

"I felt guilty. I made my escape, but I didn't think of anyone's safety but my own."

As simple as that. The woman had been beside herself for months, had become physically ill from worry for this stranger. She had paid Jack a sizable sum of money to find letters that would ensure the safety of a woman she had never met.

"If you'll pardon me for speaking freely," he said, adopting as deferential a tone as he could summon, "there's nothing at all cowardly about anything you've done."

Thinking of what she had said, he saw a pattern emerge as surely as if he had his cards spread out before him. Everywhere he looked there were women trying to help one another in dubious ways when there didn't seem to be any other solution. Mrs. Durbin had stolen the letters to prevent her daughter from doing something wicked. Mrs. Wraxhall had committed blackmail and possibly extortion and spent a fortune hiring Jack, all to secure a stranger's safety.

He was still thinking about this pattern when he arrived at Oliver's room, only to find it empty, no trace of Oliver or his belongings. A housemaid was taking the linens off the bed.

"Where is he?" he demanded. Jack had wanted Oliver to go back to London, had practically insisted he do so, but didn't think the man would leave without a word.

"You don't know?" the housemaid asked, too pert by half.

Jack remembered that he was supposed to be the man's valet. "No," he said from between ground teeth. His arm hurt and he needed to know Oliver was safe.

"Don't fuss yourself. He left you a note. And money, by the looks of things."

It was a single sheet of paper folded over a couple of banknotes. *Turner, I've been called away. Please use enclosed to travel safely to London. R.*

What the bloody hell?

"He got a letter bearing the Rutland seal," the maid chirped. "Mr. Smythe told me so," she added, supposing correctly that Jack would trust the butler's ability to recognize the Rutland seal.

Jack knew he had no business feeling anything about

Oliver's departure, not when he had always known it was inevitable. Hell, he preferred it when he didn't feel much of anything at all. Still, his vision darkened with rage and loss and sorrow, and they felt like emotions belonging to someone else entirely.

# CHAPTER NINETEEN

Oliver could have ignored the letter. He had been ignoring his father's letters for weeks and lived to tell the tale. But this latest missive had arrived so providentially, and sometimes providence was hard to ignore, especially when served up on a silver salver. He had been pacing the room, his peace of mind shredded by the knowledge that at that very moment Jack was orchestrating the concealment of more than one crime. And Oliver, because he knew of these goings on, was now complicit as well. He had almost let himself believe that he and Jack weren't so different after all, that Jack's penchant for self-made justice wasn't such an insurmountable obstacle. But now that Jack's actions had bled over into Oliver's conscience, he felt much less sure.

So when the letter arrived, demanding Oliver's presence in London, he grabbed the valise Jack had already packed and walked out the door. He was halfway to London before he identified the unfamiliar feeling chewing at the edges of his consciousness as shame. He had left Jack with nothing more than a terse letter and a random assortment of banknotes.

And this, not twenty-four hours after the man had taken a bullet for him.

Oliver knew he had behaved inexcusably. Turner would never look at him again, and rightly so.

Oliver found his father waiting for him at Rutland House, standing before the hearth in the stale and decaying parlor that had once been his mother's domain.

"I was surprised to hear you were in London, sir." Oliver attempted a show of cordiality.

Lord Rutland was having none of it. "You answered none of my letters. What did you expect me to do? Sit idly by while my son keeps company with . . ." He let his voice trail off while glancing around the room, as if there was no way he could complete his sentence in the late Lady Rutland's drawing room. "What do you know about that man?" Lounging at his feet were a pair of aged hounds, which Oliver recognized as heralds of a long visit. If his father had only planned to stay for a few days, he might have left his dogs at home.

"Which man?" Oliver asked, as if there could ever have been any doubt.

"Don't play the fool, Oliver. I'm talking about Turner."

"He's a . . ." Oliver had no idea what to say. A month ago, he would have said "criminal" or "scoundrel," which were true enough. Instead he said, "He's a friend," which was by now as good as a lie.

"Ha!" his father spat, with more emphasis than Oliver had thought him capable of. "I offered him money to stay away from you, you know."

Oliver's fingers clenched around the back of the nearest chair, squeezing hard enough to hurt his own hand. "Did he accept? Because if he did, you made a bad bargain. I'm afraid he definitely hasn't been staying away from me, Father. Far from it."

If the earl understood Oliver's meaning he did not betray it. "Listen, my boy, you have no idea what you're dealing with. His mother was a whore, among other things. His father—or the man who was married to his mother, at least—was a common street criminal who raised your Mr. Turner to bring in money by whatever means necessary, including stealing from his employers and most likely whoring himself."

Oliver felt his ears start to ring, as if he were standing too near an organ at church. His father's words were barely distinguishable above the hum. The room around him seemed to lose coherency, the old-fashioned chairs and faded draperies blending into one another in an alarming way. He knew he really ought to sit but he'd be damned if he displayed any kind of weakness in front of his father.

All Oliver could remember was Jack sinking to his knees before him, Jack's body beneath his own. He had sensed at the time that those actions somehow cost Jack something they didn't cost Oliver, but he hadn't known why. Now, he thought he understood, and felt another pang at having thrown away that man's friendship and companionship.

And then, like a blow to the back of the head, he remembered the money he had left behind at Branson Court, and what that must have looked like to Jack.

"He is depraved, Oliver. A criminal through and through," his father said in his most stentorian tones, forcing Oliver's attention back to the present.

Hearing his own darkest fears spoken aloud by his father

caused Oliver's world to pivot on its axis. He felt his thoughts reshape themselves as if for no other reason than to disagree with his father, and the new shape they took felt like a revelation.

"Likely so." Oliver straightened his back and donned his best manners as if they were a newly tailored coat. "He acts without any regard for whether something is a crime." He thought of what criminal behavior Jack had engaged in since Oliver had met him. Besides trespassing in his client's house, his only other crimes had been those he committed with Oliver. "Thank God for it," he said, and he meant it. If those acts were crimes, Oliver suddenly felt less confident that it mattered whether anything was a crime. "He does what he knows to be right. He helps people, sir. And you know that, because he helped Charlotte when nobody else did." It wasn't that nobody else could, Oliver realized, but that nobody else wanted to risk their neck.

Lord Rutland regarded Oliver for a long moment, his eyes hard and cold. "I think you've gone stark mad. You're not the same man since you've returned to England. You hear tales of men who survive battle only to be not quite right in the head afterward, and I worry that you're one of them."

Oliver knew his father said this to wound him. He knew the words were picked out less because they were true and more because they would cut to the bone. But they hurt because they touched Oliver's own lurking suspicion.

"No," he said in the same voice he would use to order tea. "I'm not mad, but it's quite true that I'm not the same man I was before . . ." Before what? Before his injury. Before Badajoz.

Before Jack.

Everything Oliver had experienced during the war had turned his world upside down, and he had come home trying to set it right side up again, only to fall in with a man who set the entire operation even more radically askew. And now, in this moldering old room, he felt that he had his feet firmly planted for the first time in years.

But he wasn't going to say any of that to his father. "I'm capable of making my own decisions. I understand that you disapprove of my acquaintance with Mr. Turner, and I regret if it reflects poorly on you, but I've made up my mind." He gave his father his most correct bow before heading out the front door.

Jack threw his belongings into his valise and headed out on foot towards the nearest coaching inn. Or, at least, in the direction that he hoped would bring him to the nearest coaching inn. Truth be told, on the way to Branson Court, he had been paying closer attention to Oliver's hands on the ribbons than he had to his surroundings. He had a laundry list of depravities he wanted those hands to commit, and not a single idea how to get to the inn.

Blast and hell and fuck. He shouldn't feel half so ripped apart by Rivington's departure. Some inane part of him felt betrayed, as if he didn't know perfectly well what betrayal actually looked like. A highborn man leaving twenty pounds—twenty pounds, for the love of God—on a nightstand and then buggering off was no betrayal. It was boringly predictable and nothing more.

This was not heartbreak, nor was it grief. Oliver hadn't owed him anything. Not friendship, not trust, certainly not twenty pounds, so really Jack ought to count himself ahead of the game.

He had known it would end badly, dallying with such a dazzlingly perfect piece of goods as Oliver Rivington, a man who by all rights he should never even have met. Oliver deserved to be surrounded by cleanliness and virtue, ladies and gentlemen who drank wine and wore silk and pretended the rest of the world was either invisible or irrelevant. Jack felt ashamed, but also sickly thrilled that he had dragged Oliver into that sordid and shabby underworld of whorehouse kitchens and stolen letters.

He kicked a rock to see if it made him feel any better.

It did not.

For years, Jack hadn't needed anybody, hadn't wanted anybody. He trusted Sarah and Georgie, at least most of the time, but had always known it would be ruinous to trust anyone else. That principle had been implicit in everything he had learned from his father, mixed in with how to nick a pocket watch and how to cheat at cards.

But Jack had trusted Oliver. Call it love, call it want, call it whatever you please, but the plain fact of the matter was that Jack Turner had abandoned what had always been a core tenet of his life.

Which was why he was not only miserable but also lost and stranded in a strange place.

To make matters worse, the countryside he was walking through was appalling, almost jeering at him with its completely unnecessary cheerfulness. Birds sang, fluffy little sheep dotted wildflower-strewn hillsides, all of it so god-damned charming and picturesque. Oliver would love it. Jack hated it all, not only for his usual reason of hating the countryside's failure to be London, but for the more pressing reason that on a day like today there ought to be nothing around him but fire and rocks, an outrageous hellscape mirroring his state of mind.

He stopped to take his coat off, not even sure why he had put the blasted thing on in the first place. He had nobody to impress right now. His job was done, Oliver was gone, and Sarah would never hear about any of today's sartorial transgressions. He could wear a nightcap and ball gown. He could wear pantaloons and dancing slippers and nothing else. And who would care? Bloody nobody, that's who.

Just for the sake of the thing, he took his waistcoat off too. "There!" he said, trying to sound satisfied. Nobody was around to hear him but the sodding sheep.

He turned down the lane that led, with any luck, to the inn, but something made him balk. Now, why in hell did he feel like he ought to be heading back to Branson Court? There was nothing left for him to do there. Mrs. Wraxhall had her letters, Jack had his money, everyone was satisfied.

Except for how they weren't. Mr. Wraxhall was under the impression that his wife harbored pornographic longings for a former lover. Mrs. Durbin thought her daughter had been about to commit an act of hardened criminality. And he had left Mrs. Wraxhall alone to sort it all out, which was especially poor payment for her having gone out of her way to protect a perfect stranger.

And the Wraxhalls—a decent pair of people who were

generous to their servants—were going to go back to London to be social outcasts once again.

That last bit really shouldn't have bothered him in the least. What did Jack care for social standing? Today, of all days—he remembered the money on the nightstand—he ought to have no respect for class. And yet it did bother him. More to the point, he felt that Oliver would think he ought to do more. Oliver, whose opinion ought to be the farthest thing from Jack's mind.

Jack found that he wanted the Wraxhalls to be happy. Because maybe, just maybe, if there could be a happy ending for such an unlikely pair as the Wraxhalls, there could be one for someone as tarnished and wrong and twisted as he was— maybe Sarah, maybe even Georgie. And if getting a voucher to bloody Almack's was what Mrs. Wraxhall needed for a happy ending, then he'd make damned sure that she got one. Jack, for the first time he could remember, felt something like faith that happy endings could be achieved.

For lack of any better idea of what to do with himself, Oliver went to Charlotte, intending to beg use of her spare room for a few nights while he sought lodgings. It was past time for him to leave Rutland House and his father's arrival had provided a timely motivation.

Charlotte's house, however, was in a genteel sort of chaos as servants draped furniture in holland covers and packed silver away into the safe. Miss Sutherland absently directed him to a one of the few rooms not yet packed up, and Oliver was left to spend a restless, regretful night. In the morning he found Charlotte in the drawing room, amidst tissue paper and half-filled crates.

"Are you leaving for the country already?" he asked.

"As soon as we can," she answered, hardly looking up from the letter she was writing, "London is a dead bore when you can't go to parties." Really, when she talked like that, and when one considered the state of her marriage, her widow's weeds seemed preposterous. He hoped she put off mourning altogether once she left Town. "At least in Hampshire I can ride."

"I'll come in August and we'll ride out together. Is William big enough to be put before me on the saddle?"

Before Charlotte could answer, a footman entered carrying a calling card. Oliver recognized it on sight, its edges soft and bent from careless handling. He knew without reading the boldly printed name that it was Jack's card.

That was the last thing Oliver needed, the prospect of coming face-to-face in his sister's drawing room with the man who until yesterday had been his lover, the man he had abandoned and insulted. Good God, it would be anyone's guess which of them would be the most mortified by the predicament.

Then Jack was being shown into the room, Miss Sutherland on his heels. Jack's arm was in a sling, his face weary. He ought to be in bed, but he must have traveled through the night to reach London.

The two ladies exchanged a glance. Miss Sutherland nodded, an almost imperceptible movement, and Charlotte returned the gesture. Only then did Oliver stop to wonder why, precisely, Jack had come to Charlotte's house. He suddenly felt that he might be sick.

Miss Sutherland soundlessly shut the door behind her.

"Jack," Oliver said, remembering his manners and rising to his feet.

Only when Jack responded with a raised eyebrow and a chilly, "Mr. Rivington," did Oliver realize he had betrayed too much by addressing Jack so informally.

But nobody was paying any attention to Oliver.

Charlotte patted the seat next to her on the settee, gesturing for her companion to sit there. "Perhaps we ought to have tea." Her tone of voice suggested that tea could conceivably be a viable solution to the problem that brought Jack to call on them.

"I'm here about Montbray," Jack said, and if anyone in the room was surprised they didn't show it. "Ought I to come back another time?" he asked. "Or is there somewhere more private—"

"No, it's quite all right." It was Miss Sutherland who spoke. "I can't see what difference it makes." She reached for the teacup Charlotte had filled for her, but when she discovered that her hands were shaking, she abandoned the effort.

"This needs to be gotten out in the open," Jack said. "And then we can see what needs to be done." He was even more unkempt than usual and dirty too, meaning he had likely come directly here upon arriving in London. Oliver tried to focus on Jack's ragged appearance, the sound of his voice, anything other than the meaning of the words he was saying.

Miss Sutherland breathed out a sound that was neither a sob nor a laugh, but somewhere in between. "He was my cousin."

"And you killed him," Jack said calmly and so very gently.

Oliver realized that Jack had spoken the words so Miss Sutherland didn't have to. How long had he known? "You pushed him down the stairs, I think?"

"He was my cousin," Miss Sutherland repeated. Around her shoulders she pulled a shawl that was the exact color of dust. Charlotte reached out and took her hand.

Oliver didn't know whether she said this by way of clarifying how painful it had been to push him down the stairs, or in order to explain how she came to understand why he needed to be pushed in the first place. But it hardly mattered.

"Surely, you acted in self-defense," Oliver suggested, dearly hoping it was true.

Miss Sutherland kept her gaze on Jack, who was leaning forward in his chair in the manner of a vicar counseling a troubled parishioner. "I came back from Richmond hoping to persuade him to leave, for good this time," she said. "I slipped inside without anyone knowing, thinking that he'd be less likely to shout and bluster if he weren't expecting me. He was very drunk when he came home. When he found me here, well, it became abundantly clear that I had made a mistake."

"He threatened you, then?" Oliver asked.

Miss Sutherland hesitated, and when she spoke it wasn't in answer to Oliver's question. "I have three brothers, you know. I know how to trip a man. So, when he got to the top of the stairs, that's what I did." She choked out another strangled-sounding laugh.

Oliver's gaze flicked over to Jack and caught there, like a burr on a rabbit. Jack was watching him back, likely waiting for some sign of outrage or revulsion.

Miss Sutherland opened her mouth and closed it again.

She darted a glance at Charlotte, who then looked askance at Jack. Every single person in this room was likely wondering if Oliver was about to play the role of righteous, law-abiding English gentleman.

Oliver was wondering the same thing.

Instead, he looked carefully at his sister's companion. He didn't see evil or lawlessness. He saw a woman who had done a damned hard thing to save her friend's life. She didn't need the gallows. She needed understanding. And Oliver might be the only person in the room who could give it to her.

"I suppose it doesn't matter terribly whether you were technically acting in self-defense," Oliver said, hearing his voice echo uncomfortably in his ears. "You acted in defense of someone—if not yourself, then certainly my sister and nephew, and for that I have to thank you. And while I'm no expert, I believe the law requires more, ah, immediacy in the threat, but morality can perhaps abide by a more generous standard." His mouth went dry. "I might have done the same thing in that situation."

No, no, that was not enough. Such a statement omitted so much that it was nearly a lie. "To be quite fair, I suppose I did do the same thing once. In Badajoz." He kept his eyes on his teacup and spoke quickly to get the confession out before he thought better of it, but he wanted Miss Sutherland to know that she wasn't alone. "You know what happened in the battle. We won, but not before there were thousands of British dead, bodies piled as high as this ceiling." This conversation was truly unsuitable for a lady's drawing room and it was only going to get worse. "Afterward, some of our soldiers unleashed hell on the local people in retaliation. For three days, even after Wellington ordered them to stop. Three days of pillaging and raping, not to put too fine a point on it. Some men killed officers who tried to stop them. It was the closest thing to a mutiny I've ever seen. One of my own men was amongst the worst. I shot him in between his bouts of depravity."

Nobody said anything, God damn it, so he kept talking. "Of course, the rules of war aren't well defined but it was a dashed nasty business. Since then, I've felt that if you're lucky enough to live in a place and time with rules and laws and people able to enforce them, the least you can do is abide by them. But there weren't any laws to protect Charlotte. Instead, she had you, Miss Sutherland, and I'm glad for it."

Well, Oliver had done it. He had confessed the worst sin of his life in front of Charlotte and Jack, the two people he cared the most for. And now they might well despise him. He felt Jack's eyes boring into him. With what? Disgust for Oliver's hypocrisy?

Oliver made a feeble excuse and limped blindly from the room.

Jack followed Oliver out, not even bothering to take his leave. That was one of the advantages to being outside good society. You can behave as boorishly as you like and nobody expects anything different.

He caught up with Oliver before they reached the end of the block. "Walk with me this way, will you?" He indicated a quiet side street, gray with shadows.

If Oliver was dismayed to see Jack here, he didn't betray

it. But then he wouldn't, would he? Always so calm, so un-ruffled, so very much the picture of a gentleman. Jack knew he ought to be put off and hated that he wasn't.

Oliver had looked like he belonged in Lady Montbray's drawing room, the gold of his hair and the blue of his eyes matching the room's furnishings, as if he had been ordered as part of a suite of furniture. Jack should have been revolted that the thought even crossed his mind.

Instead he was touched, he was smitten, he was foolishly adoring. He loved this man, loved him despite being abandoned in the wilds of the English countryside. He loved that Oliver had exposed something ugly about himself in order to help that Sutherland woman. He loved that he now understood why Oliver was so opposed to taking the law into one's own hands—he was haunted by the memory of having done so himself.

In short, he loved Oliver. The good, the bad, the confusing, and the misguided.

And none of it mattered. Now was the time for a proper good-bye.

"That was decent of you to say all that to Miss Sutherland," Jack said as soon as he was certain they wouldn't be overheard. He had come today because he suspected Lady Montbray would be a terrible confidante for a woman who had taken another person's life. Miss Sutherland would need a better confessor, and Jack had come to fill that role. He hadn't dreamt that Oliver would take it upon himself. But Oliver's confession had done what's Jack's understanding never could—Oliver was a proper gentleman, and if he approved of Miss Sutherland's actions, then that would likely ease the lady's mind.

Oliver shrugged. "And it's decent of you to say so after I left you in Kent yesterday. I'm sorry about that. I behaved badly. Your arm . . ." His voice trailed off miserably.

Jack ought to be angry about that, but he wasn't. Today his brain was working counter to all reasonable expectations. "No worries," he heard himself saying.

"I'm sorry about the money, too. I didn't mean for . . . oh, the devil take it. I only wanted you to get back to London safely. I didn't mean to imply . . ."

"It's all right," Jack said, his voice gruff. "So, that was what your father had to tell you so urgently," he guessed.

Oliver nodded. For a moment, their silence was only broken by the sound of their footsteps and the clack of Oliver's walking stick. "There has to be a way forward, a way for this"—he gestured vaguely between the two of them—"to work."

"I don't think so," Jack said gently.

"Why the devil not?" Oliver stopped and turned to face Jack. "If it's more of that gammon about how a gentleman can't be seen consorting with a . . . whatever you think you are, then I don't have to be a gentleman anymore."

"Like hell you don't." Christ, just look at him. Even in the shadows, he fairly radiated birth and breeding.

"This city is filled with gently born people who have fallen on hard times." Oliver took a step closer to Jack. "I can be one of them," he said, his voice low.

Jack retreated a step. "There are no sons of earls who keep company with former servants." He wouldn't point out that Oliver, with his matched horses and fine curricle, his expert tailoring and glossy boots, would be even more conspicuous in low company. It was bred in the bone, whatever it was that made Oliver the golden, perfect specimen of English aristocracy.

"It's high time there is, then." Oliver edged forward, and when Jack stepped back he found he had been maneuvered into a doorway. "I could give my money away."

"It has nothing to do with money." Jack could almost laugh at the idea that this was a problem money could solve. "It's not about who your father is, either. It's about what your life is. White's and balls and the queen's bloody drawing room," he said. "Tea parties and soirees and—"

"I get the idea." When Oliver spoke Jack could feel the breath on his forehead.

"I don't think you do. You're welcome everywhere you go." He lowered his voice even further. "Your good name is enough to make a woman feel that she's been absolved of a capital offense."

Oliver shook his head, as if to dismiss Jack's words. "My father is going to disown me, so any good name I have will be quite shot through anyway."

"Ha! I should bloody well like to see you try to lose your good name." Then, he realized what Oliver was saying. "Your father is threatening to disown you because he doesn't want you around me." He ought to have realized this is what would happen. "He thinks I'm a corrupting influence. He's quite right, you know."

Oliver's mouth quirked up in a rueful smile. "What rot. You can't possibly think you've corrupted me."

"You're missing the point. No matter what you do, I'll be

the sordid part of your life." Jack loved Oliver too much to be a blot on the man's perfection. "I'll be a dirty secret."

"It wouldn't be like that," Oliver protested, touching Jack's cheek with his gloved hand.

"It would to me." Jack resisted the urge to press his face into Oliver's palm.

"What are we supposed to do, then?"

Jack sighed. "We part ways. We look back on this as a pleasant interlude." Neither of them would do anything of the sort, but it sounded better than, *We regret the entirety of the last month.* "That's all we can do."

Neither of them moved, though, and Jack wasn't surprised when Oliver bent down and swept his lips over Jack's own. The doorway was dark and secluded, the street empty of passersby. It was a good-bye kiss, Jack told himself. Nothing wrong with that. A kiss wouldn't make this parting hurt any more, because that was bloody impossible at this point.

He felt Oliver's thumb caressing his cheekbone as their mouths came together. The knowledge that this was their last kiss ruined Jack's ability to enjoy it. When Oliver's tongue met his own, Jack's felt a bolt of mingled sorrow and lust. *Kisses shouldn't be this sad*, he thought.

When he finally pulled away, the sun had passed behind a cloud and the street was nearly dark. Jack watched Oliver leave until the taller man was out of sight.

---

# CHAPTER TWENTY

Oliver found Charlotte in her boudoir, supervising her lady's maid in packing up gowns and baubles. She looked up in surprise when Oliver entered, and quickly dismissed her maid.

"Thank you for saying all that to Anne." She came forward to take his hands. "She's been in a frightful state since the . . . event. She's sleeping now, which is a good sign."

"You don't think less of me for it?"

She hugged him close, a gesture he found surprisingly maternal in his fashionable sister. "Oh, Oliver," she said without letting him go. "You always were harder on yourself than anyone else could ever be."

"I have a problem. A riddle of sorts," he said after she had loosened her hold on him. "What would I have to do to be considered no longer a gentleman?"

"Engage in trade," she said promptly.

"Be serious, Charlotte. You can't imagine someone would hire me as a clerk, or what have you. What else?"

"What on earth is going through your mind right now?" She settled into a low chair, ignoring the gowns that were strewn across it. Oliver followed her example, sitting on a divan that seemed to hold half his sister's autumn wardrobe, not a stitch of black in sight.

"I'm glad you're putting off mourning when you get to the country."

"Don't try to distract me."

"Fine. I find that I need to dissipate myself and destroy my character." He tried to read his sister's face for any signs of disapproval.

She only looked curious. "But why?"

"Perhaps I'm tired of it," he suggested, smoothing a fold of aubergine velvet that had landed on his lap.

"Of what? Decent behavior? Having friends? Being received in places that are neither gaming hells nor whorehouses?"

He thought about that. "Yes, that's about the size of it. It's all well and good to be the sort of fellow every lady is glad to have at her table and every man is glad to talk with at the club. But I can't be that man anymore. "

"Whyever not?"

"I'm cultivating a broader range of acquaintances," he said. "And not everyone wants to associate with a gentleman."

She narrowed her eyes, looking dreadfully like their father. "I feel certain that I ought to call in a specialist of some sort." She steepled her fingers under her chin. "And yet," she said musingly, "am I right that there was a—what did you call it—a broader range of acquaintance in my drawing room this morning?"

Sometimes he forgot that Charlotte had gotten their father's brains along with his eyes. "Turner is a friend. I would like to have an enduring friendship with him." He couldn't tell her the whole truth, but he hoped that little bit would get the point across. "He said he doesn't want to be the most sordid thing in my life."

"I see. And you took those words as a challenge to immerse yourself in other forms of sordidness?"

When she put it that way, it didn't seem half such a good idea. "More or less." He remembered Jack's words: *I should bloody well like to see you try to lose your good name.* Well, he was going to lose it, all right. Then a thought occurred to him. "Charlotte, you'll still receive me even if I sink below reproach, won't you?"

She gave him a look that plainly told him to stop being a nodcock.

"Sweet, stupid Oliver. A confessed murderess is this very minute reading fairy stories to my son. I will always receive you." She reached out and squeezed his hand. "If your friendship with Mr. Turner brings you happiness, then it brings me happiness as well. Let me see, then. You need to do the sort of thing that would earn the cut direct and get you barred from your club."

By the time the sun set, they had formed a plan.

"It would only be for one evening," Jack pleaded.

"That would be one evening too many," Sarah shot back. She was draping a dress form in blue satin. "And why do you care what happens to this Wraxhall woman anyway?"

"She tried to do right by someone and it all went straight to hell. We can do this one little thing to help her."

"Little thing, indeed," she said, holding a pin in her mouth. "If any of them were to recognize me, I'd be finished."

"They won't recognize you. All they'll see are the beads and the shawls. It's all they ever see." And that was because the costume was blindingly garish, which was the point of it in the first place.

She let out a sigh. "Let me think about it."

"We don't have time. It's the end of the season and all the bloody gentry are leaving London. This soiree—or musical evening, or whatever the nobs call it—is tomorrow night and there won't be another one like it until next year." At least not one he could get Sarah into.

"You truly do care about this. I never thought I'd see you assist a lady in becoming fashionable, of all things. Not that I object on those grounds—a little less contempt for the gentry might do you good. It's only that you've always hated the *ton*, and now you want me to stick my neck out to foist this woman upon them?"

"Maybe it's the dishonesty of the plan that appeals to me." He handed her a pin.

"I think it's more than that." She busied herself in adjusting the fall of satin, keeping her face hidden from Jack. "I think that once you started to hold one of them in esteem, you couldn't hate the rest of them."

She was right. He couldn't love Oliver yet despise his friends and family. "It's the thin end of the wedge," he said softly. "Next thing I know, I'll be doing the Duke of Devonshire's bidding. Might as well go back to being a servant."

"Don't be a ninny. You're too pigheaded for anything of the sort. All I meant was that the gentry exist, and you might as well be at peace with that. It's exhausting to carry around all that hatred. Besides, I like Mr. Rivington. He has excellent taste in fabric. And he obviously is fond of you. You'd be a perfect fool to whistle that down the wind." She looked like she wanted to say more, but instead snapped her attention back to the dress form. "What do I get out of it?"

"Mrs. Wraxhall will buy her wardrobe from you."

Sarah's hand stilled in between folds of silk. "How can you know that?"

"Molly Wilkins is her lady's maid." And Jack would owe Molly a favor that she'd surely cash in some ghastly manner.

"Fine," Sarah agreed. "Help Betsy bring down Mama's old trunk, and we'll see what fits me."

Jack took the stairs up to the attic two at a time.

Achieving a suitable level of disgrace was exhausting work. Oliver had spent the past six nights at Madame Louise's, and not sitting peacefully in the kitchen this time either. Two of the women upstairs had been happy enough to let him pay for the privilege of sitting with them in a private bedchamber, where they played *vingt-et-un* for farthing stakes.

He then had to drag his weary body to a string of gaming hells—really, the quantity of cards and endless flights of stairs involved in ruining oneself simply beggared belief.

After all that, he had to get up in the morning and search for suitable lodgings. He had a lengthy list of requirements. The neighborhood couldn't be fashionable but it couldn't be seedy, either; it could be no more than one flight of stairs up from the street; it had to be small enough so that Oliver could manage with a single maid coming in daily. He wrote a letter of character for his valet, paid the man his salary for the rest of the quarter, and bought a pair of boots that he could remove himself, if things came to that.

He did not go to Sackville Street, not even once, despite the fact that he thought Jack might not turn him away. Oliver wanted to wait until his plan was completed, and then present his ruination to Jack as a *fait accompli*, no possibility of reversing the process.

So far his behaviors had only caused a few raised eyebrows, perhaps a slight dwindling of invitations. Gambling and whoring were not nearly bad enough to make him an outcast, which was what he needed to accomplish before going to Jack. Tomorrow he would cheat at cards, and at his club, no less. Or, rather, he would attempt to cheat. This, Charlotte assured him, would blacken his reputation to the precise degree he required.

To this end, he had enlisted the help of a person he suspected might be an expert.

"You want me to teach you to cheat at cards?" Georgie Turner said incredulously. Oliver had found him in one of the larger gaming hells, a notorious courtesan perched on his lap.

"Yes, and in a fairly obvious way," Oliver explained. "I want to get caught."

Georgie idly lit his cheroot. "You'll get booted from your club, you know."

"I'm counting on it."

"Does my brother know about this?"

"Certainly not."

Georgie raised a finely arched eyebrow. "And I'm not to

tell him, I suppose." He puffed out a cloud of smoke. "Well, I've always longed to play Cupid. I'm dying of curiosity, but I think it would be beneath my dignity to beg for details." And then, without dislodging the woman from his lap, he proceeded to show Oliver the rudiments of card sharping.

Georgie interspersed his lessons with bits of commentary. "You know you'll never get another voucher to Almack's. No, no, dear fellow, you can't fold the edge down quite so much. They can see you doing it as far as Cheapside. Rein your degenerate impulses in a bit, if only to spare my sensibilities. Now, if this succeeds, even your sister won't invite you to her best parties—yes, that's precisely the way I meant for you to palm that card. People you've known all your life will pretend not to know you."

"That's rather the point. I don't care about any of that," Oliver assured him.

"You think you don't, but when people start looking at you like you're a rancid piece of meat, you'll change your tune fast enough." Georgie and the man across the table from him were now exchanging heavy-lidded glances that both Oliver and the courtesan found very interesting.

"Perhaps you're right," Oliver said. "I don't suppose I'll know until it's too late to go back." He had spent nearly thirty years being beloved and welcomed everywhere he went, and he didn't relish the prospect of being snubbed. But that still seemed preferable to a future without Jack.

"Tell me one thing. Exactly how cross will my brother be with me when he finds out what I've done?"

Oliver smiled. "I'm hoping he'll only be slightly irritated."

"Good God. A slight irritation in Jack Turner is a flight

of ecstasy in any other man. He's more than slightly irritated on the best of days. I wish you luck in your fall from grace."

By dawn, Oliver was ready to meet his fate.

Jack had opened and shut the silver card case so many times over the last week that he thought the clasp ought to snap off. But it didn't, which probably went to show that the Rivingtons knew how to spend their money. He could sell this trinket and use the proceeds to feed a family of five in the rookeries for God knew how long.

Not that he would. He was too much of a besotted idiot for that. He'd keep his case as a bloody keepsake, a reminder of precisely how daft he was capable of being. He remembered what Oliver had told him the day they'd met, about how he had once known a man who clung to his father's watch long after he ought to have sold it. So this was what it felt like to be a thoroughgoing idiot.

But here he was, opening and closing the case, watching the way the light from his candle glinted off the engraved *R*, running his hands along it as if it were some kind of rosary. Sarah had noticed him performing this ritual and remarked on the object's fine craftsmanship, from which Jack inferred that she was giving her blessing upon an affair with its original owner. As if her pointed remarks about missing "that nice Rivington man" weren't blessing enough.

Blessings were quite beside the point now, however. Oliver had returned to his life of honor and respectability, and rightly so. Jack might have hoped that every knock on his door was Oliver coming to wheedle his way back into Jack's life, he may have felt his heart race whenever he saw a curricle and matched grays being driven especially well. But he knew it was for the best that Oliver kept away.

As for Jack, he had too much pride to seek out a man who would eventually be embarrassed by his company. Truly, he told himself for the hundredth time this evening, it was all for the best that Oliver had made a clean break of it.

There was no wood in the fireplace at this time of year, but Jack tossed all the cards that had to do with the Wraxhalls onto the empty grate. Crouching down, he used his candle to light them on fire. He waited until they were ashes, and then stared at the case some more.

"You might have warned me," said a voice from the doorway. Jack turned to see Georgie, dressed in evening clothes. "I've come from Lady Bedford's musical evening last night, you know."

Alarmed, Jack got to his feet. "Did Sarah recognize you?"

"I dare say she didn't see me. Once I realized it was her under all those shawls, I did my damnedest to disappear into the shadows."

"Do you think it worked?"

"Like a charm. As soon as she began with that blasted glass ball and those accursed cards, she had them all eating out of her hand. She started with the usual rubbish—*I see a sea voyage in your future.* Offensively trite, the lot of it. And then she comes out with, *I see a W, a dark lady who brings good fortune.*"

Jack had managed things so Lady Bedford's personal maid, an enterprising young woman who had jumped at the chance to have Jack Turner in her debt, suggested to her mistress that it might be amusingly novel to have a fortune-teller as one of the entertainments at her musical evening.

"By the time the party broke up," Georgie continued, "two ladies were contemplating inviting both Lydia Wraxhall and Winifred Darby to various house parties. W females will be very fashionable this autumn. Don't you look like you've gotten the plum from the pie? No, don't explain why, I dare say I don't have the stomach for finer feelings tonight." Georgie turned to leave, but paused in the doorway. "Oh, before I leave, your friend is in a bad way. The pretty one."

Jack's mind reeled for a moment. "Rivington?" he asked.

"Do you have any other pretty friends? Or, really, any other friends at all?"

Ignoring that, Jack reached for his coat. "What's the matter with him?" He thought of ruffians lurking in dark alleys; he thought of the thousand ways a man could come to grief driving that godforsaken curricle.

"Gambling and women," Georgie said, barely able to suppress a laugh.

Oh for the love of— "Must be some other fellow." Jack dropped his coat over the chair and sat down again. "Rivington's road to hell would hardly be paved with those particular vices."

"No, I swear. It's Rivington, all right."

"Where is he, then?"

"What is it, eleven o'clock?" Georgie checked an undoubtedly stolen pocket watch. "He's likely still at Beale's." That was one of the nastier sorts of gambling hells. "That is, unless he's already left for his club, where he'll be caught cheating at cards."

"What?" Jack asked, shrugging into his coat and heading for the door. Thinking better of it, he returned to his desk for his pistol and another knife.

"Riding to the rescue?" Georgie's voice was mocking but not terribly unkind, all things considered. "You've let your head get turned by a pretty face, and now you're moved to heroics. I never thought I'd see the—"

"Sod off." Jack pat down his pockets to make sure everything was where he wanted it. "You wouldn't have told me unless you intended for me to run after him." As if it hadn't been obvious for days that Jack was clamoring for an excuse to accidentally encounter Rivington. "Anyway, I thought you wanted me to stay away from gentlemen?" Jack was already heading down the stairs.

"Oh, he's no gentleman, my dear brother. Gentlemen never cheat at cards."

Jack felt his heart give a thud with something that could have passed for hope.

"Georgie, what the devil have you done?"

How many more snifters of brandy could that potted plant take before it withered up and died? Oliver had, on the sly, been dumping nearly all his brandy into that poor plant for days now. But it looked perfectly well. Perhaps brandy was beneficial for house plants. It was terrible for sleight of hand, though, and since Georgie Turner had gone to such trouble to show Oliver how to throw every game of cards he played, Oliver figured the least he could do was to manage the thing soberly.

"Bad luck, Rivington," said the man to his right. "You ought to quit now before you're in too deep." The man spoke in the slow cadence one uses when speaking to a stubborn child or a roaring drunk.

The idea, Georgie had drummed into his head, was to lose miserably. Once Oliver was generally understood to be close to ruin, nobody would be surprised that he would turn to dishonesty to right his ship. He had one more hand to lose here, and then he'd go to his club, where he would clumsily cheat. After that, he'd be thoroughly discredited and ruined. And he would have Jack, if Jack would agree to have him.

"Can't quit yet. I'm due for a win, you see," Oliver slurred. "That's how it works. Maths." He tapped his forehead knowingly.

Another hand, another bit of trickery to engineer a loss. This was a shocking amount of money to waste in such a way, but he supposed he would have spent more on an engagement ball, if he had been the marrying sort. And it was for a good cause—the only cause that mattered at the moment. He could spend the rest of his days dressed like a ragamuffin and taking common hackneys, if only he were with Jack.

During the next round, even the dealer threw scornful glances at Oliver. Perfect. Let the whole room whisper about his dire straits, his impending ruin.

Suddenly, Oliver felt a hand on his shoulder. At first he feared that his sleight of hand had been detected, and he braced himself to be thrown bodily onto the street.

But then the hand squeezed his shoulder, and it was a touch he would have recognized anywhere.

"He folds." Jack addressed the dealer, using his free hand

to divest Oliver of his cards and throw them facedown on the table. "Out, Rivington."

Oliver, his heart pounding in his chest, made his excuses to the other gentlemen—a term he had to use loosely indeed in this company—and followed Jack down the stairs, into the street. Perhaps the few sips of brandy he had swallowed before pouring the rest into the plant had gone to his head, because he felt almost unsteady on his feet. He could feel his blood buzzing in his ears.

"Did Georgie teach you to fuzz the cards like that?" Jack demanded once they were far enough away from the gaming hell to avoid being overheard.

Of all the things to ask, that's what Jack wanted to know? "I see I was wrong to trust Georgie to keep my plans secret." Jack steered him into the shadows, and Oliver could not have gone more willingly. "Is that why you came? To save me from the dishonor of cheating at cards?"

Jack snorted. "No, I came to stop you before you landed in debtors' prison."

Oliver's back was flush with the stone wall now. "Very noble of you."

He watched in satisfaction as Jack decided whether that was supposed to be an insult. "Fuck you."

"Is that the plan?" Oliver widened his eyes innocently.

"I ought to be asking *you* precisely what the plan is, because I bloody well haven't the faintest idea. Did you set out to bankrupt yourself?"

"Of course not. I set out to create the appearance of having bankrupted myself." He looped his arms around Jack's neck and drew him close so they were both hidden deep in the shadows. "By the way," he said into Jack's ear. "I'm not the only one who's been playing at card tricks this week, am I?"

Jack straightened, pulling away from Oliver. "How did you—I don't know what you're—"

"It was kind of you." He had overheard a conversation earlier at his club about the mysterious fortune-teller at Lady Bedford's musical evening, and it hadn't taken much to guess who was responsible and what his purpose had been. "And Sarah, I presume." Oliver kept his voice firm, his arms still around Jack's shoulders.

"It wasn't anything of the—"

"It was. And you were kind to come help me tonight."

"Hmmph. It was only a matter of time before you got your arms broken by someone who realized you were cheating at cards, or whatever the hell it was you were doing in there."

"Likely so," Oliver replied lightly, reeling him in closer again. "I'm glad you came before that. I was getting bored by all the dissipation. So tedious, really," he drawled. Acting on a moment's inspiration, he brushed his hand across the pocket where he remembered Jack had kept the card case. There it was, the unmistakable rectangular shape of a calling-card case.

"Don't make too much of it," Jack said, his voice a little rough.

"I don't think I am," Oliver whispered.

Finally, finally, he felt Jack's hands settle on his hips. "You didn't need to make such a thorough disgrace of yourself, you know."

"I obviously did," Oliver protested. "You needed it spelled out, so what else could I do? No matter how often I told you that I want you more than decency or honor or rules, it still wouldn't get through your thick skull. So I decided to show you."

"Rubbish. You're never going to be anything other than good and honorable." Jack's voice was harsh.

Oliver felt those words like a slap. If, after all this, Jack still couldn't be made to understand that Oliver wanted him, on any terms at all, then he was at a dead loss. "Jack," he said, bending his head so he spoke into Jack's badly tied cravat, "you're killing me."

"You didn't let me finish." Jack's voice was in a deep, growly register that Oliver felt reverberate against his own chest. "You're never going to be anything other than good and honorable. And *mine*."

Oliver felt warm lips brush over his own, a kiss that was a promise of future kisses. "Do you mean it?"

"When Georgie told me you'd been gambling and drinking I didn't know what to think. I thought you must have lost your mind."

"So you came to rescue me?" Oliver asked, pleased.

"You're mine," Jack repeated, dusting kisses along Oliver's jaw. "I've tried being without you, and it's not any good, Oliver."

"It really isn't," Oliver agreed. "Let's not do that again."

"Never again. Come home with me, Oliver."

# CHAPTER TWENTY-ONE

From across the worn oak table of a Panton Street chop-house, Oliver watched Jack study the notices advertising houses to let. So far, the man had vetoed every one of Oliver's suggestions, calling them too shabby, too remote, too vulgar, too small. Jack, Oliver was delighted to discover, was a bit of a snob.

"You can't expect my clients to come to Hans Town," Jack said, his fork halfway to his mouth.

And that was how Oliver learned that Jack meant to live with him. He suppressed the urge to crow, and instead helped himself to a bite of mutton from Jack's plate.

"Sharing a house with an acquaintance is a reasonable economy that might be made by a gentleman who's had a run of bad luck at cards," Jack continued. There was something studied about his tone that made Oliver wonder if he had said been repeating that sentence to himself. Was he trying to convince himself or Oliver? Was he giving Oliver an excuse to live with him for reasons other than intimacy?

"Certainly." Under the table, Oliver hooked his foot

around Jack's leg. "Even more so if he sometimes assists that acquaintance in matters of business," he suggested.

Oliver could feel Jack's body go tense. "Is that what you have in mind?" Jack asked.

"Only if you wouldn't mind. I enjoyed working with you. I'm afraid that my spree of bad behavior will mean that I'll be of less use. My name will open fewer doors," he felt compelled to add. "Especially since my father has made it known that he disinherited me."

That news had arrived via Lord Rutland's solicitor. Oliver hadn't been surprised—his antics had practically been calculated with disinheritance as the goal—and he didn't want any of his father's money anyway. Maybe one day he would pay a visit to Alder Court and try to put things right between them, but for now he was content to think about the future he was building with Jack.

Jack was silent for a minute, his body too still for his silence to be a sign of relaxation. "So, is this to be a business arrangement?"

"No! Of course not. I want to share my meals and my bed and my life with the man I love. Christ, Jack. Don't say such filthy things."

Jack put down his fork and regarded Oliver very seriously. "I'd be glad to have your help with my work if you'd like that. What made people want to talk to you was never your breeding." He said "breeding" like someone would say "syphilis" or "bedbugs." Oliver held his napkin to his mouth to hide a smile. "It's your bloody charm," Jack grumbled.

"This is the place," Jack said two days later, as they inspected a narrow little house near the British Museum. "The bedchamber and office can both be on the ground floor, so you won't have to climb more stairs than absolutely necessary."

"I can manage stairs perfectly fine," Oliver lied. The week he had spent hauling himself up and down the stairs of whorehouses and gambling halls had been an unpleasant reminder of how bad his knee could get. Oliver knew that the time might come when even a single flight of stairs would prove impossible, even on a good day. And he was glad that Jack seemed to understand that too.

"Yes, you're sickeningly hale and hearty." Jack was opening and closing the windows, likely assessing the ease with which they could be broken into or jumped out of. "And only getting more so by the minute. I think you've put on half a stone in the last few weeks." This was a gross exaggeration, but Oliver tolerated it, knowing Jack took some perverse pleasure in making sure Oliver remembered to eat. "And it's all muscle." That much was true, Oliver fancied. "At this rate you'll be a regular Viking by Christmas."

Oliver barked out a laugh. "How exceedingly vulgar. I'll be nothing as brutish as a Viking, my dear. I'll be like the angel Gabriel in one of those pictures chaps are always painting on ceilings. All golden hair and glistening muscle."

"Well, unless you also plan on sprouting a pair of wings, I don't know how you'll get upstairs, so we'll put the bedchamber on the ground floor."

"I seem to remember that you're capable of carrying me," Oliver murmured, running a finger down Jack's arm. A few nights ago Jack had thrown a limping Oliver over his shoulder and carried him up the stairs to his Sackville Street rooms.

"I'm too old for feats of strength," Jack argued. "I'll be forty soon."

"When?" Oliver was genuinely curious.

Jack waved the question away. "Four years from now. Maybe five. Who's counting?"

Oliver would remember to ask Sarah about Jack's birthday.

"Anyway, I have every intention of being in this house when I'm forty, and also when I'm fifty, and until I draw my last breath, because I'm never moving again. So, we'd better get a house with a bedchamber on the ground floor, and that's final."

And that was how Oliver learned that Jack planned on the two of them living together for the rest of their lives.

Oliver watched Jack throw a careful look over his shoulder, confirming that they were still alone. He blushed, half expecting something filthy, but instead Jack leaned in and pressed a soft kiss to Oliver's burning cheeks. "I love you," Jack said, his voice gruff.

"I love you too," Oliver whispered.

They signed the lease that very day.

Jack hadn't been surprised to discover that all Oliver's worldly goods fit inside three valises with room to spare, and the bulk of it was finery that wouldn't even fit the man much longer. He didn't have so much as a bed quilt or umbrella stand to his name. Their new house came furnished with the bare necessities but few of the conveniences that Jack felt were required in a gentleman's home.

Because this *was* to be a gentleman's home, and Jack

would hear no rubbish from Oliver about how he would be happy in the gutter. Bollocks on the gutter. Jack had spent too many years there to wish it on his worst enemy.

Instead, they would meet somewhere in the middle. Oliver's run of debauchery had brought him down a few rungs on the social ladder, and Jack would fake and sham his way up a few rungs.

"I say, was that umbrella stand there earlier today?" Oliver asked when he arrived home.

"No." Jack didn't look up from the letter he was writing.

Oliver glanced around the sitting room. "This carpet is new as well."

Jack looked at the carpet, as if only now registering its presence. "So it is," he agreed, in a tone that indicated that helpful elves had perhaps delivered it.

"And those candlesticks," Oliver said wonderingly. "They're new."

So was the clock on the chimney piece, the footstool by Oliver's chair, and a ceramic figurine that bore an outrageous resemblance to Oliver. This last item had been a gift from Georgie, who had all along insisted that Jack's lover resembled a Dresden shepherdess. The other items, Jack had bought himself.

"You have to let me pay for some of these things, Jack."

"No, I really don't." There weren't many things in the world that Jack considered worth his money, but buying fine things for Oliver was oddly satisfying.

They were scrupulously dividing rent and housekeeping down the middle. Jack suspected that Oliver only agreed to that plan out of sensitivity for Jack's pride.

"I keep telling you, even after last month's losses, I have plenty of money safely invested in the five percents. I won't spend a quarter of my income living like this."

"Good. Save it away." Jack would have bet that Oliver would come to within the last shilling of his income. The man was forever tossing extra coins to crossing sweepers and flower girls. Jack himself was developing expensive habits—witness his recent purchase of lavender-scented soap for the laundry woman to use on Oliver's shirts, and the new pair of boots he bought for the little maid who brought up the coal.

Nobody had been more surprised than Jack to discover that when he was happy, he wanted to make others happy. What a soggy lot of rubbish, but there you had it.

"When you smile I want to do awful things to you," Oliver said, leering wolfishly.

"A lucky coincidence, because when I'm smiling it's because I'm thinking of you doing filthy things to me." Jack grinned back at him.

Oliver walked around the side of the desk and sat on the arm of Jack's chair. Jack tugged his lover down onto his lap and kissed him soundly.

"Have I mentioned how glad I am you came into my office that day?" Jack asked, a moment later.

"Once or twice, but feel free to tell me more," Oliver murmured.

And so Jack did, at length.

And coming February 2017,

Georgie Turner's story!

Pre-order now!

## ABOUT THE AUTHOR

**CAT SEBASTIAN** lives in a swampy part of the South with her husband, three kids, and two dogs. Before her kids were born, she practiced law and taught high school and college writing. When she isn't reading or writing, she's doing crossword puzzles, bird-watching, and wondering where she put her coffee cup.

Give in to your Impulses . . .
Continue reading for excerpts from
our newest Avon Impulse books.
Available now wherever ebooks are sold.

# THIS EARL IS ON FIRE
## The Season's Original Series
*by Vivienne Lorret*

# TORCH
## The Wildwood Series
*by Karen Erickson*

# HERO OF MINE
## The Men in Uniform Series
*by Codi Gary*

An Excerpt from

# THIS EARL IS ON FIRE
## The Season's Original Series

*By Vivienne Lorret*

Vivienne Lorret's Season's Original series continues with an earl whose friends are determined to turn him into a respectable member of society . . . and the one woman who could finally tame him.

Liam Cavanaugh grinned at the corrugated lines marking his cousin's lifted brows. It wasn't often that Northcliff Bromley, the Duke of Vale and renowned genius, showed astonishment.

Bending his dark head, Vale peered closer at the marble heads within the crates. "Remarkable. Even seeing them side by side, I hardly notice a difference. The *fellows* will be fascinated when you present this to the Royal Society at month's end."

"It was pure luck that I had the original as well." Liam shrugged as if he'd merely stumbled upon the differences between a genuine article and an imposter.

Vale turned, and his obsidian eyes sharpened on Liam. "No need to play the simpleton with me. You forget that I know your secret."

Liam cast a hasty glance around the sconce-lit, cluttered ballroom of Wolford House, ensuring they were alone. Fortunately, the vast space was empty aside from the two of them and a dozen or more large crates filled with artifacts. "By definition, a secret is that of which we do not speak. So lower your voice, if you please."

No one needed to know that he actually studied each piece of his collection in detail—enough that he'd learned how to spot a forgery in an instant.

"Afraid the servants will tell the *ton* your collection isn't merely a frivolous venture? Or that your housekeeper's complaints of dusty urns and statues crowding each room would suddenly fall silent?" Vale flashed a smile that bracketed his mouth with deep creases.

Liam pretended to consider his answer, pursing his lips. "It would be cruel of me to render Mrs. Brasher mute when she finds such enjoyment in haranguing me."

"She may have a point," Vale said, skirting in between two crates when a wayward nail snagged his coat, issuing a sharp *rip* of rending fabric. He stopped to examine the hole and shook his head. "Your collection has grown by leaps and bounds in the past few months. So much so that you were forced to purchase another property to house it all."

"The curse of immense wealth and boredom, I'm afraid."

His cousin's quick glower revealed that he was not amused by Liam's insouciant guise. Then, as if to punish him for it, he issued the foulest epithet known to man. "You should marry."

Not wanting to reveal the discomfort slowly clawing up his spine, Liam chuckled. "As a cure for boredom?"

Vale said nothing. He merely crossed his arms over his chest and waited.

It was a standoff now. They were nearly equal in regard to observation skills, but apparently Vale thought he had the upper hand.

Liam knew differently. He crossed his arms as well and smirked.

If anyone were to peer into the room at this moment, they might wonder if they were staring at matching wax figures. The two of them looked enough alike in build and coloring to be brothers, but with subtle differences. Vale's features were blunter, while Liam's were angular. And Vale's dark eyes were full of intellect, while Liam's green eyes tended to reveal the streak of mischief within.

"Marriage would do you good," Vale said.

Liam disagreed. "You're starting to sound like Thayne, always hinting of ways to improve my social standing."

The Marquess of Thayne was determined to reform Liam into the *ton*'s favorite pet—the Season's *Original*. In fact, Thayne had been so confident in success that he'd wagered on the outcome. *What a fool.*

"I never hint," Vale said.

Liam offered his cousin a nod. "True. You are a forthright, scientific gentleman, and I appreciate that about you. Therefore, I will give you the courtesy of answering in kind: No. I should *not* marry. I like my life just as it is." He lifted his hands in a gesture to encompass his collection within this room. "Besides, I could never respect a woman who would have me."

Vale scoffed. "Respect?"

"Very well. I could never *trust* a woman who desired to marry me. Not with my reputation. Such a woman would either be mad or conniving, and I want neither for a wife."

He'd nearly succumbed once, falling for the worst of all deceptions. After that narrow escape, he'd vowed never to be tricked again.

"Come now. There are many who care nothing for your reputation."

That statement only served to cement his belief. If his despoiled reputation were the only thing keeping him far afield of the *ton*'s conniving matchmakers, then he would make the most of it. And the perfect place to add the crème de la crème to his list of scandalous exploits would be at Lady Forester's masquerade tonight.

After all, he had a carefully crafted reputation of unrepentant debauchery to uphold.

Liam squared his shoulders and walked with his cousin to the door. "If the Fates have it in mind to see me married before I turn sixty, then they will have to knock me over the head and drag me to the altar."

An Excerpt from

# TORCH
## The Wildwood Series
*By Karen Erickson*

USA Today bestselling author Karen
Erickson continues her Wildwood series
with a hot firefighter who knows that
enemies make the best lovers . . .

Wren Gallagher wasn't the type to drown her sorrows in alcohol, but tonight seemed as good a time as any to start.

"Another Malibu and pineapple, Russ," she said to the bartender, who gave her a look before nodding reluctantly.

"That's your third drink," Russ said gruffly as he plunked the fresh glass in front of her.

She grabbed it and took a long sip from the skinny red straw. It was her third drink because the first two weren't potent enough. She didn't even feel that drunk. But how could she tell Russ that when he was the one mixing her drinks? "And they're equally delicious," she replied with a sweet smile.

He scowled at her, his bushy eyebrows threaded with gray hairs seeming to hang low over his eyes. "You all right, Wren?"

"I'm fine." She smiled but it felt incredibly false, so she let it fade before taking another sip of her drink.

Sighing, she pushed the wimpy straw out of the way and brought the glass to her lips, chugging the drink in a few long swallows. Polishing it off like a pro, she wiped her damp lips with the back of her hand as she set the glass down on the bar.

A low whistle sounded behind her and she went still, her breath trapped in her lungs.

"Trying to get drunk, Dove?"

That too-amused, too-arrogant voice was disappointingly familiar. Her shoulders slumping, she glanced to her right to watch as Tate Warren settled his too-perfect butt onto the barstool next to hers, a giant smile curving his too-sexy mouth as he looked her up and down. Her body heated everywhere his eyes landed and she frowned.

*Ugh.* She hated him. His new favorite thing was to call her every other bird name besides her own. It drove her crazy and he knew it. It didn't help that they ran into each other all the time. The town was too small, and their circle of mutual friends—and family members—even smaller.

Tate worked at Cal Fire with her brothers Weston and Holden. He was good friends with West and her oldest brother, Lane, so they all spent a lot of time together when they could. But fire season was in full swing and Tate had been at the station the last time they all got together.

She hadn't missed him either. Not one bit.

At least, that's what she told herself.

"What are you doing here?" Her tone was snottier than she intended and he noticed. His brows rose, surprise etching his very fine, very handsome features.

He was seriously too good-looking for words. Like Abercrombie & Fitch type good looking. With that pretty, pretty face and shock of dark hair and the finely muscled body and *oh shit*, that smile. Although, he wasn't flashing it at her right now like he usually did. Nope, not at all.

"I'm assuming you're looking to get drunk alone tonight?

I don't want to get in your way." He started to stand and she reached out, resting her hand on his forearm to stop him.

And *oh wow*, his skin was hot. And firm. As in, the boy's got muscles. Erm, the man. Tate could never be mistaken for a boy. He was all man. One hundred percent, delicious, sexy man . . .

"Don't go," she said, her eyes meeting his. His brows went up until they looked like they could reach his hairline and she snatched her hand away, her fingers still tingling where she touched him.

Whoo boy, that wasn't good. Could she blame it on the alcohol?

Tate settled his big body back on the barstool, ordering a Heineken when Russ asked what he wanted. "You all right, bird?" His voice was low and full of concern and her heart ached to say something. Admit her faults, her fears, and hope for some sympathy.

But she couldn't do that. Couldn't make a fool of herself in front of Tate. She'd never hear the end of it.

So she'd let the bird remark go. At least he hadn't called her Cuckoo or Woodpecker. "Having a bad day," she offered with a weak smile, lifting her ice-filled glass in a toasting gesture. At that precise moment, Russ delivered Tate's beer, and he raised it as well, clinking the green bottle against her glass.

"Me too," Tate murmured before he took a drink, his gaze never leaving hers.

Wren stared at him in a daze. How come she never noticed how green his eyes were before? They matched the beer bottle, which proved he didn't have the best taste in beer, but she'd forgive him for that.

But, yes. They were pretty eyes. Kind eyes. Amused eyes. Laughing eyes. Sexy eyes.

She tore her gaze away from his, mentally beating herself up. He chuckled under his breath and she wanted to beat him up too. Just before she ripped off his clothes and had her way with him . . .

Oh, jeez. Clearly she was drunker than she thought.

An Excerpt from

# HERO OF MINE
## The Men in Uniform Series
### *By Codi Gary*

The men of Codi Gary's Men in Uniform
series work hard and play hard ... but
when it comes to protecting the women
they love, nothing stands in their way.

Tyler Best didn't believe in fate.

Fate was an excuse people who'd experienced really bad shit or really astounding luck used in order to explain how their lives tended to twist and turn. Fate was a fantasy.

Tyler was a realist. He didn't rely on some imaginary force to direct him. He'd taken chances and gotten knocked on his ass a few times, but he kept going because that's what life was. You didn't give up when it got hard.

Even in the face of devastating loss.

Tyler stared at the picture of Rex, his military dog, and the ache in his heart was raw, even eight months later. Rex had been his for three years before getting killed in combat. While Tyler was overseas, away from his family and friends, the dog had been his best friend, bringing him great comfort. When he'd lost Rex, he'd almost quit working with dogs. It had been difficult to be around them.

Yet, here he was, waiting to be led back to the "last day" dogs at the Paws and Causes Shelter. It was his first time here, as it was relatively new. Most of the time he visited Front Street Animal Shelter or the one off of Bradshaw, but new rescues and shelters were being added to the program every day.

Ever since he'd become the head trainer for the Alpha Dog Training Program, a nonprofit created to help strengthen the connection between military personnel and their community, he'd become the last hope for a lot of dogs. If they passed their temperament test, they'd join the program. Not all of them did, and on those days it was hard to remember all the lives the program saved. It was hard to walk away from a dog's big soulful eyes when Tyler knew the only outcome was a needle filled with pink liquid death, but he couldn't save them all.

Just like he couldn't save Rex.

"Sergeant Best?" a woman called from behind the reception desk.

Tyler stood up and slipped his phone back into his pocket. "Yes, ma'am."

"You can go on through. Our tech, Dani, is waiting in the back to show you around. Just straight back; you'll see the double doors."

"Thank you." Tyler opened the door, assaulted by high-pitched barks of excitement and fear. As he passed by the kennels, he looked through, studying the dogs of all shapes and sizes. He wasn't sure why he was so melancholy today, but it had been coming on strong.

He pushed through the double doors and immediately realized the man and woman inside were arguing. Loudly.

"No, he has more time. I talked to Dr. Lynch, and he promised to give him until the end of the day in case his owners claim him." This was shouted by the woman with her back to him, her blonde ponytail swinging with every hand gesture.

"Don't be naïve. You've been here long enough to know

that he won't be claimed." This was said by the thin, balding man in the lab coat, who was pushing sixty and had the cold, cynical look of someone who'd been doing his job too long. Tyler had seen it on the faces of veterans who had found a way to steel themselves against the horrors that haunted them. But once you shut that part off, it was hard to find it again. "Even if they come looking, they'll just tell you to put him down anyway. If they had the money to pay for his care, then they could afford a proper fence. All you're doing is putting off the inevitable and wasting valuable pain meds."

He tried to sidestep the blonde, who was a good head shorter, but she planted herself right in his path. When she spoke, her voice was a low, deadly whisper. "If you make one more move toward that cage, I will body check you so hard you'll forget your own name."

Tyler's eyebrows shot up, and he crossed his arms, hoping like hell the guy tested her. He really wanted to see her Hulk out.